THE AT

"*The Atlantis Enigma* is right up there in the forefront of provocative and contentious debate. . . . A marvelous and informative read." —*Irish Independent*

"Well-written. Thought-provoking." —*East Anglian Daily Times*

"Excellently argued and hugely readable." —*South Wales Argus*

"Eye-opening." —*Southern Daily Echo*

"Brennan carefully wades through various theories and investigates everything from similarities between different myths throughout the world from darkest pre-history to the marks of devastation on planets in our solar system." —*Lancaster Evening Post*

"Brennan's easy style allows the reader to explore . . . and his conclusion is both shocking and revealing. Fascinating stuff." —*Bolton Evening News*

Other books by Herbie Brennan

*To find out more about the author and his books
visit Herbie Brennan's Bookshelf on the World Wide Web:*
http://homepage.eircom.net/~herbie

THE SECRET HISTORY OF

ANCIENT EGYPT

Electricity, Sonics, and the
Disappearance of an
Advanced Civilisation

HERBIE BRENNAN

BERKLEY BOOKS, NEW YORK

THE SECRET HISTORY OF ANCIENT EGYPT

A Berkley Book / published by arrangement with
Piatkus Books

PRINTING HISTORY
Published in the UK in 2000 by Judy Piatkus (Publishers) Limited
Berkley edition / August 2001

Visit our website at
www.penguinputnam.com

ISBN: 0-425-18101-4

BERKLEY®
Berkley Books are published by The Berkley Publishing Group,
a division of Penguin Putnam Inc.,
375 Hudson Street, New York, New York 10014.
BERKLEY and the "B" design
are trademarks belonging to Penguin Putnam Inc.

PRINTED IN THE UNITED STATES OF AMERICA

10 9 8 7 6 5 4 3 2 1

CONTENTS

> *"Any sufficiently advanced technology is
> indistinguishable from magic."*
>
> ARTHUR C. CLARKE

INTRODUCTION

SOMETHING is awry with our picture of early civilisation. In particular, something is awry with the way we think of Ancient Egypt.

The Egyptian civilisation appears to have sprung up out of nowhere on the banks of the Nile. There is precious little evidence of a gradual climb from any earlier Neolithic culture—yet Egyptologists assure us this must have been what happened.

In terms of technical sophistication, Egypt peaked in the Old Kingdom, very shortly after those same Egyptologists say the state was founded. Then it began a long, slow decline over several thousand years.

This is a picture that makes little sense, but the acknowledged experts ignore the problems instead of trying to explain them.

There have, of course, been challenges to orthodox ideas of Egypt in recent years. Robert Bauval's *Orion Mystery* claimed that the pyramids at Giza were built to reflect the position of stars in the constellation of Orion. Geologists have suggested that the Sphinx is far older than previously supposed. Several authors—myself included—have put forward the theory that what we now call Ancient Egypt was actually the resurrection of a far older culture that perished towards the end of the Pleistocene.

This idea goes a long way towards explaining the known anomalies. If there really *was* a prehistoric Egypt, then the Egypt we know did not spring up suddenly, fully formed. It drew on the techniques, technologies and traditions of an earlier culture. The engineering peaks of the Old Kingdom are then exactly what you would expect, and the long, slow decline becomes predictable as well. Inherited knowledge does not necessarily include inherited understanding, so the further you get from the source, the more mistakes you are likely to make.

All the same, the idea of a prehistoric Egypt presents its own difficulties. Where is the evidence for its existence? How do you make room for it within the accepted Darwinian picture of human evolution? What caused it to disappear? How was it resurrected?

These are some of the questions the present book sets out to answer. But the investigation goes a great deal further . . . and takes us into fascinating territory.

Until now, few have been prepared to speculate on the nature of that earlier culture and the techniques carried forward into Old Kingdom times. I suspect the reason for this is that the evidence points to something quite fantastic. My own research suggests that Egypt developed—then more or less lost—a hi-tech scientific civilisation in the most literal sense of the term. This has been missed by orthodox investigators for a very specific reason.

The basis of Ancient Egyptian technology was so different from our own that it has gone largely unrecognised and its accomplishments—like the building of the Great Pyramid—have been either labelled mysteries or explained away. It is rather as if archaeologists from a distant future with no knowledge of lasers or electricity discovered a compact disc. They might be forgiven for deciding it was an ornament or ritual object, since the idea that it might be used for data storage would be incredible to them.

Our own industrial revolution developed from steam, then passed on to an alternating current electrical power base. On this base is built virtually all our familiar technology, from the light bulb to the computer.

But, while there is some indication that steam power was known and used (albeit in a small way) in Ancient Egypt, this did not lead to the development of an alternating current electrical technology as happened in our own time. Instead, the Egyptians—and, one suspects, several other early cultures—applied their scientific insights to develop other, highly effective forms of energy. This book explores the evidence for their use of highly sophisticated technology based on these other forms of energy. It also looks at the implications of all this for our beliefs about the true origins of Egyptian civilisation.

CHAPTER 1

THE PYRAMID
MYSTERY

ACCORDING to conventional Egyptology, there wasn't a great deal of human activity in the Nile Valley during Palaeolithic times (2,500,000–10,000 BP). The climate was wet, so there was no need for anybody to stay close to the river. Small bands of hunter-gatherers roamed the region in search of food. A few of them even ventured into the Great Sand Sea, an inhospitable area that eventually became the Sahara Desert.

But North Africa improved considerably as the weather got warmer. The ground dried out, and some time after 5000 BC people began raising crops.

Although generations of archaeologists have swarmed over the valley, the evidence for this important cultural transition is still rather confusing. There doesn't *seem* to have been a widespread introduction of farming as happened elsewhere. Horticultural techniques were simply adopted by small local groups. Since their crops were native to the Near East, it has been assumed that they got the idea of growing food from there. In time, this small-scale farming moved south throughout Egypt. And in due course, the local groupings evolved into small, but distinct Neolithic cultures. Excavations at sites like Marimda Bani Salama, southwest of the Delta, show that inhabitants lived in huts, buried their dead and were capable of making sun-dried pottery.

In Upper Egypt (i.e. further south) there are signs of more sophistication. Cemetery sites between Asyut and Luxor have yielded glazed beads, some worked copper and the inevitable pottery, but without any indication or evidence of central authority or, indeed, anything much more advanced than a tribal culture. Rock drawings throughout the area suggest that nomadic peoples were commonplace alongside the few small settled communities.

As time went by, a culture known as the Gerzean sprang up and spread throughout the country—although with substantial gaps. The pottery made by these people was rather better than earlier finds and often decorated. There was some stonework, and even evidence of trade—lapis lazuli was imported from as far afield as Afghanistan. But the level of sophistication was only relative. Knives, for example, were still being made from flint.

Then, somewhere around 3100 BC, Egypt suddenly got civilised.

THE FOUNDING OF THE FIRST DYNASTY

Egyptologists, whose job it is to make sense of archaeological finds, assume that the spread of a unifying culture sparked some sort of political unification as well. But it's an assumption that lacks hard evidence. They also assume that local states may have formed at Kawm al-Ahmar, Naqadah, Abydos, Buto and Sais, although there's not much hard evidence for that either.

What the evidence does show is that civilisation sprang

up *fully formed* in the Nile Valley. This picture is so clear that a few academics have suggested the culture might have developed somewhere else and arrived as the result of an immigration. But, since they can't show where the immigrants came from, the idea is not taken seriously by the majority of Egyptologists who insist that their (hypothetical) local states somehow coalesced into two (hypothetical) kingdoms, Upper and Lower Egypt.

Until quite recently, they also believed that these kingdoms were unified by King Menes around 3100 BC. Today they're not so sure. Widespread finds of the Horus falcon on pottery and other objects have led them to speculate about the evolution of a single state a century or so earlier—or at least the development of a single royal line, which amounts to much the same thing.

Not much is known about the early line of Horus-kings, except that the last of them was probably called Narmer—his name has been found at various sites. For example, relief scenes on a palette (engraved stone tablet) from Kawm al-Ahmar show him wearing the twin crowns of Egypt and defeating northern enemies. While these may just be stereotypes of royal power rather than records of actual events, they certainly suggest that Egypt achieved unification before Menes.

Narmer's successor is named in the written record as Aha, the pharaoh now credited with the foundation of the First Dynasty around 2925 BC. But if you were taught that Menes founded the First Dynasty, this may not be wrong. Egyptologists believe it's entirely possible that they were one and the same person. Some of them think Menes was actually Narmer himself. Or possibly a different king named Scorpion.

Whether known as Menes, Narmer, Scorpion or Aha, this early pharaoh left behind an impressive tomb at Abydos. Other substantial structures quickly followed. Within 300 years, the Egyptians were building pyramids.

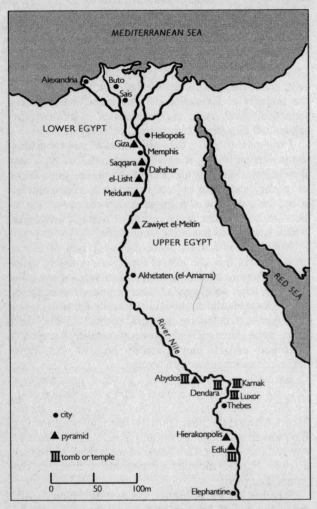

Map of Egypt showing the location of the pyramids and temples

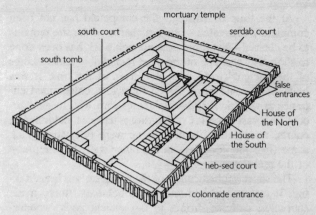

The compound at Saqqara showing the Step Pyramid, temples and other buildings

It's those pyramids that make you wonder if the Egyptologists have got it wrong.

THE MIRACLE OF THE STEP PYRAMID

The earliest pyramid we know about, according to conventional dating, is the Step Pyramid at Saqqara. To build it, the Egyptians first cleared a 15 hectare (37 acre) site on the Saqqara plateau, an area equivalent at the time to a large town. This they surrounded with a 10.5 m (34 ft) high limestone wall, some 1,645 m (5,397 ft) long.

The wall was a miracle in itself. It featured a multitude of bastions (projections) and ornamental (non-functioning) doorways into which were *hand-carved* a total of 1,680 recessed panels, each one more than 9 m (30 ft) high. Within the enclosure it formed, they began a veritable orgy of building.

At the time of writing,[1] the compound has not been completely excavated—about a quarter of the site remains to be cleared—but more than enough work has been done to show this was one of the most remarkable undertakings of the ancient world. Had you lived at the time it was built, you would have passed through a colonnaded entrance at the southern end of the eastern wall to gain access to a vast complex of pavilions, terraces, colonnades, courts, temples and tombs. Some were fully functional, some (like the doorways in the outer wall) false replicas of the real thing.

The sheer sophistication of the complex was breathtaking. It featured ribbed and fluted columns, finely made stairways, delicate shrines to the ancient gods, wonderfully wrought life-size statues. It contained Egypt's first portico, first hypostyle (pillared) hall, first torus-moulding (a large convex bun-shaped moulding forming the lowest part of a column), and first cavetto cornice (an ornamental moulding just below the ceiling). Those colonnades were the first ever seen in Egypt. So were the amazing statues.

But they all pale into insignificance beside the other great first—Egypt's first pyramid. This massive structure occupied a central position in the enclosure, covering a base area of 121 × 109 m (403 × 360 ft) and towering to a height of 60 m (197 ft). Some 330,400 cu m (11,668,000 cu ft) of stone and clay went into its construction, as did engineering skills so advanced that it still stands to this day.

What appears on the surface is remarkable enough, but excavations have shown that the Egyptians went on to construct more than 5.7 km (3½ miles) of subterranean passages, shafts, stairways, galleries and chambers cut into the bedrock of the plateau. Directly below the pyramid is a 7 m (23 ft) square central shaft that sinks to a depth of 28 m (92 ft). The shaft accesses what Egyptologists believe to be a granite burial vault and joins a warren of interconnected shafts and tunnels. Three parallel central corridors connect no fewer than 400 underground rooms. A seemingly endless carved stone stairway reaches upwards to a massive gallery (apparently used to store food) which in turn gives access to an ascending passage nearly 1.8 m (6 ft) high and 1.2 m (4 ft) wide, connecting the complex, via another staircase, to the courtyard of the pyramid temple.

To the south and east are the most remarkable of the underground rooms. Egyptologists see them as royal apartments designed to house the pharaoh's soul after his death. Certainly they are chambers fit for a king. In one, six panels of exquisite blue tiles are set with raised limestone bands to create a stunning simulation of reed matting. In another, three of the panels are topped with an arch supported by lotus pillars simulated in stone. Between two of them is a doorway, the frame of which is inscribed with the name Netjerkhet. Three false doors to the south feature stelae (inscribed pillars) depicting this pharaoh visiting the shrines of the gods. The same name appears again and again on decorations in several areas of the complex. To the north of the pyramid, in what is known as a *serdab* (a special chamber found in many Old Kingdom sites), Netjerkhet's life-size statue gazed with quartz crystal eyes through peepholes to the sky.

Egyptologists equate Netjerkhet with Djoser, a pharaoh they believe to have ruled from 2630 to 2611 BC. According to them, this entire astonishing feat of engineering is therefore supposed to have been carried out only nine generations after the people of Egypt emerged from the Stone Age.

For anyone other than an Egyptologist, this is extremely difficult to believe.

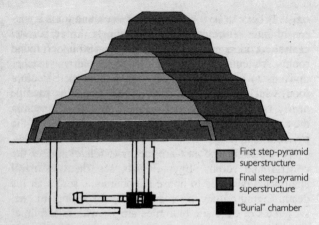

First step-pyramid
superstructure

Final step-pyramid
superstructure

"Burial" chamber

Cross-section of the Step Pyramid showing the shafts and "burial" chamber

A STONE AGE PYRAMID?

There are a number of problems with the dating of this pyramid.

First, *Djoser* is a title rather than a name. It means "Holy One." Next, the Egyptologists" identification of Netjerkhet with Djoser does not rely on contemporary records. It is based on the opinion of visitors to Saqqara at the time of the New Kingdom, more than 1,100 years after Djoser died. This is roughly equivalent to a modern historian seeking information on Edward the Confessor by chatting with tourists in Westminster Abbey.

The question of whether Netjerkhet really *was* Djoser becomes acute when you realise that Djoser ruled Egypt for only nineteen years. There's clear evidence that the Step Pyramid was built in six stages. This means that each stage had to be completed in just over three years, assuming Djoser began the building work immediately after he came to the throne. Add to this the planning time, the construction of the other major buildings, the excavation of the vast underground complex and you wonder how he could possibly have managed it.

To put the work into some sort of context, Saladin's son, Malek Abd al-Aziz Othman ben Yusuf, decided in AD 1196 to demolish the pyramid of Menkaure to provide himself with building materials. Although demolition is a far faster process than construction and ben Yusuf had huge reserves of manpower at his disposal, he abandoned the project after eight months, having done little more than scar the pyramid's northern face.

The Menkaure pyramid is a lot smaller than the Step Pyramid—235,138 cu m (8,302,000 cu ft) as compared with 330,400 cu m (11,665,000 cu ft)—and the builders at Saqqara had the whole subsidiary complex, above and below ground, to complete as well. Since this was (supposedly) the first time such a massive engineering work had ever been undertaken, since Egyptologists claim the wheel (and hence the pulley) was unknown, and since the only available tools were made from soft copper, not hardened steel, nineteen years hardly seems anything like enough time.

But if Netjerkhet wasn't Djoser, who was he?

Archaeologists investigating the complex discovered close on 40,000 plates, cups and vases of various materials stored in the underground galleries. Many bear inscriptions that indicate they were not made for Djoser, as you would expect if this really was his tomb, but date from a much earlier period. The quality of the workmanship suggests they may have been royal property—an idea borne out by the fact that many of the vases were inscribed with the names of pre-dynastic rulers like Narmer, Djer, Djet, Den and Khasekhemwy.

Egyptologists defend their position by claiming that Djoser looted an ancient tomb and purloined the grave goods for his own use. If so, he must have stolen a body as well, because the mummified remains of a woman found beneath the pyramid have also been (carbon) dated to a much earlier period.

It begins to look as if Netjerkhet may not have been Djoser at all, but a much earlier king. If so, the latest date the Saqqara complex could have been built was the latter part of Egypt's Stone Age—a possibility that borders on the incredible.

But the Saqqara Pyramid is not the only incredible discovery in Ancient Egypt.

BURYING THE EVIDENCE . . .

A pharaoh named Sekhemkhet (identified by Egyptologists as Djoser's successor Djoserty) tried to build another step pyramid at Saqqara, southwest of the one we've been examining. But it never got higher than its enclosure wall and is known today, rather disparagingly, as the "Buried Pyramid."

Someone else seems to have been building at much the same time. There is another major, but unfinished, step pyramid complex about 6 km (4 miles) north of Saqqara on a ridge above the flood plain. Who was responsible for this one is anybody's guess. The Horus-name Khaba was found inscribed on stone vases in a nearby mastaba (an early type of Egyptian tomb), but there was nothing in the pyramid itself—and, besides, Egyptologists have no idea who Khaba was.

There's also something of a mystery beneath the Buried Pyramid. Archaeologist Zakaria Goneim discovered subterranean passages and broke through three huge blocks to find what he took to be a burial chamber. Since Egyptologists firmly believe all pyramids are tombs and Old Kingdom pyramids are pharaonic tombs, this was an exciting moment. The fact that the passage was plugged suggested a burial had taken place. And the fact that the plugs were intact suggested it had been left untouched by grave-robbers.

Excitement mounted further when Goneim reached an alabaster sarcophagus in the centre of the room. The desiccated remains of an ancient funerary wreath were still visible on the top, but, most important of all, the sliding door of the sarcophagus—which had been cut from a single block of stone—was still tightly sealed with mortar. Clearly, this tomb was in its original condition.

Goneim opened the sarcophagus with great difficulty. It was empty.

There was no sign of a mummy in what we might conveniently call Khaba's Pyramid either, but this was a different situation altogether. Khaba's Pyramid was clearly abandoned before any burial could take place. The Buried Pyramid was also unfinished, but the crypt beneath was complete. If Sekhemkhet's body was ever laid to rest in the sarcophagus, it disappeared as mysteriously as a conjuror's assistant.

Neither Goneim nor his fellow archaeologists now believe that Sekhemkhet *was* buried in this tomb, although Goneim remains convinced there was no disturbance of the site after its original sealing. Even the "funerary wreath" turned out not to be a funerary wreath at all. Chemical analysis showed that the desiccated material was actually tree bark.

But if the "burial chamber" was not used for burial and the "sarcophagus" contained no body, it's difficult to understand why the ancient masons sealed it up so carefully. It's tempting to wonder if the alabaster casket really was a sarcophagus or whether it was designed to serve some other purpose—whether, indeed, the whole sealed area was designed to serve some other purpose.

NOT ALL PYRAMIDS ARE TOMBS

The conceit, propagated by many Egyptologists, that *all* Egyptian pyramids were tombs can only be maintained by ignoring evidence to the contrary.

There are seven small step pyramids scattered around Egypt. One is on the island of Elephantine, another near Ombos, a third near Edfu, a fourth near Abydos and a fifth near Hierakonpolis. The remaining two are located respectively at Zawiyet el-Meitin in Middle Egypt and Seila, overlooking the Fayum from a desert spur. None of them contains anything remotely resembling a burial chamber, let alone a sarcophagus or mummified body.

A subterranean room beneath one of the earliest true (i.e. smooth-sided) pyramids, constructed at Meidum, is routinely described as the "burial chamber," despite the fact that neither remains, nor a sarcophagus, were ever found in it. The construction is attributed to the Pharaoh Sneferu, but once again on scant evidence. There is mention of Sneferu in texts found at the site (although these do not name him as the builder) and an old name for Meidum is "Sneferu Endures."

Meidum started out as a step pyramid, but was transformed—in two stages, many years apart—into the true form. Egyptologists tell us Sneferu built it, abandoned it, then returned to it for reasons unknown. What he did not do was have his name inscribed on the identifying stelae. The omission is inexplicable, since we know from the Pyramid Texts and various papyrus sources that the Ancient Egyptians believed a monument lacked "power" without its name.

Two further pyramids are attributed to Sneferu—the Bent Pyramid and the Red Pyramid, both located at Dahshur. Yet there is little indication that he was actually buried at either, although fragments of human remains *were* found inside the Red Pyramid. Despite the limited evidence, Egyptologists continue to use the term "burial chamber" for almost any structure with no other obvious purpose—including chambers at Saqqara and Dahshur that are too small to hold a human body.

There's no doubt that burials *have* taken place in pyramids. We've already noted the carbon dating of remains found beneath Netjerkhet's pyramid and the fragments found in the Red Pyramid. But, as several writers have pointed out, these don't actually prove that the pyramids were originally constructed as tombs—any more than the graves in Westminster Abbey show it was ever anything other than a church.

But if the Egyptians *didn't* build pyramids as tombs, what did they build them for? This point assumes real importance when we come to investigate the most impressive pyramids of all—the astonishing complex on the plateau at Giza.

CHAPTER 2

ᚲTHE GREAT PYRAMID

THE Great Pyramid of Giza is the largest of all Egyptian pyramids. The tallest structure in the world until the building of the Eiffel Tower, it was a feat of engineering unmatched in scale until the construction of Boulder Dam at Colorado. It has become known as the foremost of the Seven Wonders of the Ancient World. And Egyptologists insist it was built as a tomb for the Pharaoh Khufu.

Khufu was the second king of the Old Kingdom's Fourth Dynasty, conventionally dated as beginning in 2575 BC. Although written sources are scarce, Egyptologists have reconstructed a sketchy version of his life. He was the son and successor of King Sneferu (the one believed to have built the first true pyramid at Meidum) and his queen Hetepheres. He was married four times, including a union—scandalous to modern ears—with his own sister Nefert-kau. Two of his sons, Djedefre and Khafre, succeeded him in turn.

According to the most widely accepted academic estimate, Khufu ruled between 2551 and 2528 BC—a period of twenty-three years.

The Great Pyramid contains approximately 2,300,000 blocks of stone and weighs an estimated 5,750,000 tonnes. But this is only part of the story. The overall complex attributed to Khufu includes the Great Pyramid itself, a causeway which had foundations rising to 40 m (131 ft) in parts, two associated temples, several mastabas, six boat pits and four lesser pyramids.[2]

The combined mass of these various structures has been estimated at 2,700,000 cu m (95,310,000 cu ft). To build it within the twenty-three years attributed to Khufu's reign, his workmen would have had to quarry, dress and set 321.6 cu m (11,358 cu ft) of stone each day, around the clock, without fail, accident or interruption, from the moment he took the throne to the moment he died.

It is equivalent to quarrying, dressing, transporting and laying an average pyramid block every *two minutes*.

Although such a rate seems unlikely, Egyptologists insist on it. But most Egyptologists are historians, not engineers. One engineer, Christopher Dunn, reports that his fellow author Richard Noone commissioned a study from the Indiana Limestone Institute of America to determine how long it would take to quarry and ship enough limestone to duplicate the Great Pyramid.[3]

The findings were surprising. At its current output, using the most modern technology (including high explosives, power tools and diesel transport), the entire limestone industry of Indiana would need eighty-one years to fill the order.

After that, you still have to build the pyramid.

DUBIOUS DAUBINGS?

There are no incised hieroglyphics on or in the Great Pyramid, no carvings or decorations. There were no papyrus scrolls, no clay tablets, no writing of any sort found in its interior chambers. The causeway *did* have fine reliefs cut into its walls, but these were of animal figures rather than texts—and precious few have survived. No mummy was ever discovered in this "tomb," nor were any other human remains, ancient wood or the like, thus ruling out the possibility of carbon dating.

The *only* hard evidence linking Khufu with this pyramid was unearthed in the nineteenth century by a British Guards Officer, Colonel (and later General) Richard Howard-Vyse.

Howard-Vyse was not an appealing individual. He has been described as a humourless martinet who was such a trial to his family that they invested £10,000—a fortune at the time—in sending him to Egypt, purely for the pleasure of his absence. As a self-styled "fashionable amusement-seeker," he took the trip in 1836 and in November that year first laid eyes on the pyramids at Giza.

The Great Pyramid was under archaeological investigation (of a sort) at the time. A merchant seaman from Italy, Captain G. B. Caviglia, had been so taken by its mystery that he abandoned his ship and settled in Egypt to look into it. His motives were rather different from those of modern Egyptologists—he had a profound interest in magic and once told the then Lord Lindsay in Britain that he had pushed his studies "to the very verge of what is forbidden for man to know," an experience he claimed almost killed him. He believed the Great Pyramid contained occult secrets.

Howard-Vyse met up with Caviglia who, while clearly his social inferior, still managed to impress him with hermetic tales. Thoroughly intrigued, Howard-Vyse decided to collaborate in the investigation. He threw part of his considerable fortune into the effort, even to the extent of employing 700 men to help.

Despite the investment, Howard-Vyse remained a fashionable amusement-seeker and took a boat trip along the Nile that absented him from Giza for a considerable time. When he returned, he found to his horror that Caviglia had used the massive workforce, not to investigate the Great Pyramid but to hunt for mummies and "little green idols" in the nearby burial pits.

An explosive falling-out occurred, during which Caviglia claimed, with some justification, that the Colonel had brought nothing to the project but money. The Colonel responded by demanding the money back and received it at breakfast next day, disdainfully rolled up in an old sock. It was the end of a promising partnership and the end of Egyptian work altogether for Caviglia, who retired to Paris in a bad temper. For the first time, Howard-Vyse took personal charge of the operation.

Today we have become accustomed to television pictures of cautious archaeologists gently sweeping away sand with paintbrushes in their determination that no ancient monument should suffer the slightest damage. This civilised approach was far from typical of the nineteenth century. Howard-Vyse moved teams of workmen into the Queen's Chamber (one of the three chambers and a series of passages within the Great Pyramid [see page 111]) and instructed them to dig up the floor with pickaxes.

When this produced nothing more exciting than an old basket, he turned his attention to what is called Davison's Chamber. This is not, strictly speaking, a chamber at all but rather a space over the King's Chamber that Egyptologists believe was left by the original engineers to relieve the pressure of the massive stonework above. Howard-Vyse found a crack in the ceiling of Davison's Chamber and, having run a long reed into it, concluded there must be another chamber above it. After his workmen completely failed in their attempt to chisel through, he decided to use gunpowder.

The explosion blasted an entrance into a second low-ceilinged chamber, the surfaces of which were completely covered by powdered insect shells. Not content with this discovery, Howard-Vyse began to wonder if there might be further chambers above and ordered the blasting work to continue. Although overseen by an Arab who seems to have subsisted on a diet of hashish and alcohol, this actually did reveal three more smallish chambers above the first. Daubed with red paint on the wall of one of them were cartouches. (A cartouche is the stylised presentation of a pharaoh's name, surrounded by an oval.) Only kings' names were ever written in this way in Ancient Egypt.

Since the daubs were very crudely done and upside down, they were clearly not meant as decoration. Most experts, then and now, take them to be quarry marks. None the less, Howard-Vyse rightly believed they might provide powerful evidence for the origins of the pyramid and sent copies of them off to the British Museum. Most could not be interpreted at all, but one was identified as the cartouche of a King Suphis, or possibly Shofo or perhaps Khufu.

To this day, there are scholars who view these finds with profound suspicion. The marks were not immediately apparent when workmen first entered the chamber, but were discovered some time later. Then, too, there was the crude nature of the hieroglyphs, which seemed to have been painted by someone not altogether familiar with Egyptian writing. It has been suggested that the odious Howard-Vyse, determined to make his name, secretly entered the newly opened chamber at dead of night, made the marks himself, and left them to be found in the morning.

Whatever the truth of this, the majority of Egyptologists have seized on the daubs as proof positive that the Great Pyramid was designed as the tomb of a pharaoh named Khufu and all but completed in the seventeenth year of his reign.[4]

Until these discoveries, scholars had been forced to rely almost entirely on the work of the Greek historian Herodotus for information on the pyramid. Now they readily identify Khufu as the pharaoh named by Heredotus as its builder.

ACCORDING TO HERODOTUS . . .

Herodotus, often called the "father of history," visited Egypt some time in the fifth century BC. He saw the pyramids and was naturally curious. His interest led him to make inquiries of the Egyptian priesthood who were traditional keepers of their country's historical record. They told him that the Great Pyramid had been built by a particularly wicked pharaoh whom Herodotus—writing in Greek—named as "Cheops."

According to Herodotus, Cheops brought his people to every kind of evil, most of it associated with his construction works. Desperate for labour, he closed the country's temples, forbade sacrifices and ordered all the people to work for him. In the *Account of Egypt* that forms Book Two of his *History*, Herodotus wrote:

> Some were appointed to draw stones from the stonequarries in the Arabian mountains to the Nile, and others he ordered to receive the stones after they had been carried over the river in boats, and to draw them to those which are called the Libyan mountains; and they worked by a hundred thousand men at a time, for each three months continually.[5]

Herodotus records that these vast work teams first constructed the causeway of dressed stone, carved with figures in fine relief, some 5 furlongs long and 10 fathoms wide. Today we can only estimate what he meant by these figures since not all of the causeway has survived. A furlong was originally the measure of a ploughed furrow, now standardised as roughly 200 m (660 ft). This would make the construction something more than 0.8 km (½ mile) long. Fathoms, most often used in depth measurement, originated as the distance from the middle fingertip of one hand to the middle fingertip of the other hand of a large man holding his arms fully extended. (The root of the word actually means "outstretched arms.") This too has now been standardised at 2 m (6 ft), making the width of the causeway 20 m (60 ft). Herodotus mentions that at its highest the causeway rose to 8 fathoms or 14.6 m (48 ft), which is, as we have seen, a conservative figure.

His description of the pyramid itself contains the sort of errors you would expect from a casual visitor untrained as an engineer. For example, he refers to the base as 244 m (800 ft) square when the actual length is a little over 233 m (765 ft). But he adds one important and intriguing detail. He recorded that there were underground chambers beneath the structure which Cheops intended as vaults for his own use. They were built "on a sort of island," surrounded by water introduced from the Nile by a canal. As we have seen, the Ancient Egyptians were perfectly capable of building substantial subterranean channels and chambers but, if Herodotus was right about these vaults, they have not yet been found.

Even without the subterranean aspect, such monumental construction work must have put considerable strain on the royal exchequer, but Herodotus was told that Pharaoh had devised a novel way of raising the money:

> Cheops moreover came, they said, to such a pitch of wickedness, that being in want of money he caused his own daughter to sit in the stews, and ordered her to obtain from those who came a certain amount of money (how much it was they did not tell me); and

she not only obtained the sum appointed by her father, but also she formed a design for herself privately to leave behind her a memorial, and she requested each man who came in to her to give her one stone upon her building: and of these stones, they told me, the pyramid was built which stands in front of the great pyramid in the middle of the three, each side being 150 feet in length.[6]

Although Herodotus was occasionally naive in dealing with his sources, it's difficult to imagine that he recorded this little story without his tongue in his cheek. But he was clearly quite serious when he suggested that the causeway alone took ten years to complete, while the Great Pyramid took a further twenty. He also mentions that the Egyptians told him that Cheops reigned for fifty years.

Although thirty years is a better time-scale for construction than the modern estimate of twenty-three, and fifty years is better still, neither figure will actually do. If we have to cut, dress, transport and lay a stone block every two minutes to finish the job in twenty-three years, the same miracle would have to be accomplished every 11.4 minutes, day and night, over a fifty-year period— still a ludicrous suggestion when we recall the modern estimate of eighty-one years just to quarry and deliver the stone.

Such a pace could not be achieved today using modern machinery. Furthermore, engineering principles dictate the way you can build a pyramid. Coming at it from two sides, for example, would require incredible accuracy to ensure that they met exactly, and this would slow the process down. Quarrying is admittedly a less exacting task that allows more manpower. But the quarries at Aswan and other local sites can only accommodate limited manpower both because of their overall size and the space available on the quarry face. The idea so frequently advanced in academic circles that multitudinous manpower reduces any job to manageable proportions ignores the fact there is an optimum number of people who can handle a piece of stone. Exceed it and they simply get in each other's way.

WHO WAS CHEOPS?

Along with Agatharchides of Cnidus, who wrote at the end of the second century BC, Herodotus is one of the only two original external sources we have on Ancient Egypt and its pyramids—and the most useful.[7] But even Herodotus has his limits. The pyramids were ancient when he visited them. He had no first-hand knowledge of who built them. He simply reported the tradition of the time—a notoriously unreliable approach to history. Even then he named the pyramid builder only as Cheops—the name "Khufu" appears nowhere in his *History*. Despite the insistence of modern Egyptology, we are entitled to ask if Cheops really was Khufu.

On the face of Herodotus' account, it actually seems quite unlikely. First, there is the obvious discrepancy in the length of reigns attributed to the two men. Khufu occupied the throne for twenty-three years, Cheops for fifty. This is no small difference. Then there was the question of reputation. Whatever the truth of the claim that Cheops prostituted his own daughter, it is clear that he was believed to have been a monstrous pharaoh. The same unfortunate moral character is nowhere attributed to Khufu.

But if Cheops was not Khufu, who was he? Herodotus records that he succeeded Rhampsinitos, a king for whom I can find no direct identification. (Modern Egyptologists assume him to be Sneferu, but this is backwards logic based on the idea that Cheops was Khufu.) According to

Herodotus, Rhampsinitos himself succeeded an Egyptian king named Proteus.

Proteus is, of course, a well-known name . . . but only in the realm of Greek mythology. There he features as the prophetic "old man of the sea" and shepherd of seals. He did have a connection with Egypt in that one of his two dwellings was reputed to have been on the island of Pharos, near the mouth of the Nile.[8] It may be that the Proteus myth is a distorted memory of an actual Egyptian king; or that the Proteus mentioned by Herodotus simply shared the name of the mythic figure. But neither possibility helps us establish the date of his reign.

Herodotus mentions that Proteus was visited by Helen of Troy, the "face that launched a thousand ships" to start the Trojan War. Unfortunately, scholars still consider the Trojan War to be legendary, so the mention takes us little further. Troy itself certainly existed. Latest archaeological research suggests the first settlement may have been established around 3000 BC, but since it did not finally fade into oblivion until AD 324, this produces no firm dating either.

Regrettably, the best we can deduce from Herodotus is that the Great Pyramid was built at an unspecified date by a pharaoh whose immediate successor is unknown and whose lineage appears to have been mythological.

OLDER THAN THE GREAT FLOOD?

While it is certainly possible that the Great Pyramid was constructed on the orders of a pharaoh named Khufu, it seems equally possible—and from the same academic source (Samuel Birch of the British Museum)—that he was actually called Suphis or Shofo. It is also possible that Khufu, Suphis and Shofo were alternative names for the same man, but this is by no means certain—they may have been three entirely different individuals. Then again, all three may be fictional creations of a British amateur in search of his own reputation in the history books.

Even if we accept (as an arbitrary decision) that Khufu was, so to speak, the main man, we cannot say for certain whether he was the same Khufu as the one modern Egyptologists believe ruled from 2551 to 2528 BC. He may have been an earlier king with the same name. Nor can we be sure that this Khufu, whenever he may have lived, was the same pharaoh Herodotus named as Cheops.

Even if he *was* Cheops, there is nothing in Herodotus that points clearly to the time he lived. The plain—and profoundly disturbing—fact is that we have no conclusive evidence at all for the age of the Great Pyramid and very little for several of the (supposedly) earlier pyramid structures we have been examining.

Moving outside the conventional interpretation of Egyptian history does little to clarify things. In Coptic legend, for example, it is a pharaoh named Surid who is credited with building the Great Pyramid. Surid, whose capital was at Amsus, lived "three centuries before the Flood"—perhaps the ultimate in imprecise dating. Prophetic dreams warned him about a forthcoming age of chaos from which only those who joined the "Lord of the Boat" would escape.

Curiously enough, the theme of this tale is echoed in a popular Arab legend that the pyramid was built on the orders of Thoth who wished to preserve ancient science from the forthcoming Flood.

Thoth was the Egyptian god of writing and magic and is seen as mythic by modern scholars—as, of course, is the Flood itself. There has been some attempt to equate Surid with Suphis and Amsus with the known Egyptian city of Memphis, apparently because they sound vaguely similar, but most Egyptologists dismiss both stories as no more than legends.

CHAPTER 3

OLDER EGYPT

IT must be clear by now that the historical edifice proposed by orthodox Egyptology rests on extremely insecure foundations. Much of what is taught in our schools and universities as established fact is actually a pastiche of guesswork and opinion based on personal interpretations of precious little evidence. Worse still, evidence that contradicts the orthodox consensus is often dismissed and sometimes ridiculed.

The most public example of this in recent years is the controversial redating of the Great Sphinx at Giza. For many years now, conventional Egyptologists have insisted that the Sphinx was created around 2500 BC by the Pharaoh Khafre in his own image. They claim the face of the Sphinx is that of Khafre himself.

We know what Khafre looked like. When his valley temple was excavated, it was found to contain statues of him in Nubian diorite, a particularly hard stone that resists the ravages of time extremely well. Although the same cannot be said for the Sphinx itself, which is carved from a bedrock knoll, Egyptologists saw the resemblance immediately. John Anthony West disagreed.

John Anthony West is a tour guide, author, amateur Egyptologist and a firm believer in Atlantis (the latter credential hardly likely to endear him to the archaeological establishment). Since West was convinced that the huge monument had been built by survivors of Atlantis, he had a specific interest in showing that the face could not be that of Khafre. To this end he called on the services of Frank Domingo, a forensic scientist from the New York Police Department.

In 1993, Domingo, an expert on photofit identification, compared the diorite face of Khafre with that of the Sphinx and concluded that they were two different people.

Whether or not this is an accurate assessment remains a matter of opinion. Dr. Mark Lehner, a pillar of the Egyptological establishment, spent five years (between 1979 and 1983) mapping the Sphinx. The resultant drawings were then digitised and a wireframe model generated on computer. This was transformed into a 3-D "solid" by plotting some 2.5 million surface points. Since the aim was to determine what the Sphinx originally looked like, the missing nose—prised off by vandals sometime between the twelfth and fifteenth centuries AD—was replaced by overlaying the face from an alabaster bust of Khafre in the Boston Museum of Fine Art. Dr. Lehner found the features "closely matched those of the Sphinx."

But West was far from finished. His next move was to call in Boston Professor of Geology Robert Schoch to examine weathering patterns on the Sphinx. Conventional Egyptologists believe the weathering was due to sand abrasion. Schoch concluded it was due to rain. Yet there had been no rain worth mentioning at Giza since the end of the Nabian Pluvial, 500 years before the Sphinx was supposed to have been built. Based on this and the degree of weathering, Schoch dated the core body of the monument to between 7000 and 5000 BC. Geologists who examined his findings concurred. Orthodox Egyptologists did not.

Following an all-too-familiar pattern, they mounted a dismissive attack. Carol Redmount of the University of California claimed that Schoch's dating was simply impossible. Peter Lacovara, assistant curator at the Egyptian Department of the Museum of Fine Arts in Boston, said it was ridiculous. Egyptologist Dr. K. Lal Gauri decided weathering evidence was irrelevant. Dr. Lehner voiced the opinion that Professor Schoch was practising pseudoscience. Dr. Zahi Hawass, Director of Antiquities of the Giza Plateau and Saqqara, dismissed his work as "American hallucinations."

All the same, there is other evidence which suggests that the state of Egypt itself may be a great deal older than orthodox Egyptologists currently allow.

THE MYSTERY OF THE HIEROGLYPHS

The Palette of Narmer is a heart-shaped engraved stone tablet discovered at Hierakonpolis in Upper Egypt, and now one of the most important archaeological treasures in the Cairo Museum. Many Egyptologists refer to it as the first page of Egyptian history.

One side of the palette shows the huge central figure of King Narmer holding the hair of a kneeling victim with his left hand. His right hand is raised high and holds a mace. The gesture is unmistakable. If this is the first page of Egyptian history, the book is a story of war and conflict. Watched by two horned faces, a round-headed, dwarf-like figure and a Horus-falcon, Narmer is clearly about to bash his prisoner's head in. Below the tableau, two further figures are shown in flight, one glancing back in terror at the scene.

Egyptologists are unanimous in their interpretation of the picture. It represents the violent unification of Upper and Lower Egypt, two primitive kingdoms—or possibly collections of kingdoms—that up to then had staunchly resisted the refining influence of centralisation. The date is around 3100 BC—or just possibly a century or so earlier. The country is emerging from the Stone Age to establish a dynamic civilisation. But there is hieroglyphic writing on Narmer's mace head.

The development of writing is generally acknowledged to be one of the most fundamental characteristics of civilisation. No one knows where Egyptian hieroglyphics originated. They did not develop from any other script and, like so many aspects of Egyptian culture, seem to have sprung up fully formed. Even the very earliest readable examples show hieroglyphic to be an actual phonetic script and not simple picture signs.

The symbols displayed on the mace translate as the number 1,422,000. The implications of these figures are far-reaching. As the British anthropologist Richard Rudgley points out, they show "beyond any shadow of a doubt that major intellectual developments occurred before the supposed advent of civilisation."[9]

You might be tempted to put it another way. The appearance of numerically sophisticated hieroglyphs on the Palette of Narmer could show this king represented a civilisation that *predated* the one he's supposed to have founded.

THE MYSTERY OF EGYPTIAN SCIENCE

The boundaries of most countries are organic. Tribal peoples move into an unpopulated area and spread as conditions allow. Eventually they stabilise, defining the borders of their territory with reference to natural obstruc-

tions such as rivers, mountain ranges, desert wastelands
and the like.

Cities arise in much the same way. A country's population will establish communities based on local factors
like convenient water supply, ease of defence, accessibil-
ity to trade and so on. Well-sited encampments grow into
towns and eventually cities. Examine any map and the
pattern is evident. The internal structure of most countries
follows no rational layout. But Ancient Egypt was an exception.

One of the terms used by the Egyptians to denote their
country was *To-Mera*, which translates as "the land of the
mr." The term *mr* is frequently rendered as "pyramid,"
interpreting the phrase as "the country of the pyramid."
But however appropriate this might seem, it's not entirely
accurate. A better translation might be "the country created to a geometric plan." "Pyramid" is a secondary meaning of *mr* and a derived one at that. In its prime meaning,
the term describes a very special right-angled triangle with
remaining angles of 36 and 54 degrees. The Egyptians
used the triangle to generate trigonometric functions.

This startling discovery was made by an Italian Professor of Ancient History, Livio Catullo Stecchini, who
specialises in the history of measurement and quantitative
science. His speciality, which involves a great deal of
mathematical calculation, is opaque to most Egyptologists—indeed to most academics generally—which may
be why so many of them have ignored his findings.

This is a pity, since his findings have not stopped at
Egyptian trigonometry. He has also discovered that
Egypt's buildings and cities were laid out according to a
deliberate—and elaborate—geometric plan.

The plan is far from obvious. It remains hidden without
an understanding of Egyptian units of measurement,
something that requires mathematical ability and application. While Stecchini was still a student at Harvard in

the 1960s he noticed that when his professors came to evaluate his papers, they passed quickly over any pages with formulae. One of them advised him bluntly to "cut down on all those numbers."

Fortunately he ignored the advice and has continued to investigate the numbers of Ancient Egypt—and several other ancient civilisations—with enormous diligence ever since. What he has discovered has profound implications for our understanding of the roots of Egyptian civilisation. He summed up his most dramatic discovery in these words:

> The Egyptians were proud that their country had some unique geographic features which could be expressed in rigorous geometric terms and had a shape which related to the order of the cosmos as they saw it. They believed that when the gods created the cosmos, they began by building Egypt and, having created it perfect, modelled the rest around it.[10]

Stecchini's use of the term *gods* is deceptive. According to both the Egyptian priest historian Manetho (writing between 305 and 282 BC) and the Turin Papyrus (compiled between 1279 and 1213 BC), the original founders of Egypt were considered deities. But their cultural descendants, the pharaohs, were also believed to be deities, suggesting that the founders may have been as human as anybody else, despite their exalted reputations. The belief that they created Egypt "perfect" is, however, no myth. From what we know of Egypt in historical times, the entire country shows signs of having been pre-planned.

It was the Egyptians who invented the column as an architectural element. Its appearance in the temple complex surrounding the Step Pyramid at Saqqara was a world debut. But its structure and decoration were not simply based on aesthetic considerations. Stecchini discovered the Egyptians used it as a stylised, but scientifically accurate, map of their country. Its proportions incorporated the relative sizes of Upper and Lower Egypt in the shaft and capital respectively. Much more surprisingly, the column also reflected the Earth's curvature and the problems of accurately projecting a flat map upon it.

In a sense, this is the reverse of the problems that faced more modern map-makers when they tackled the problem of representing the surface features of a more or less spherical planet on a flat map. The most popular solution, almost universally in use today, involved the use of a technique known as Mercator Projection. Stecchini's discovery suggests the Ancient Egyptians developed a different system entirely, creating a pillar which had a mathematical relationship to the curvature of the globe as a whole—or at least that part of it represented by Egypt—thus allowing an accurate representation of geographical features to be portrayed.

Pillars were not the only representations of Egyptian geographical structure. From the Fourth Dynasty onwards, every statue of the pharaoh's throne shows a distinctive design Egyptologists have called the "Unity of Egypt." Several drawings have also been discovered that suggest the design itself is substantially older and may even have been prehistoric. At the centre of the design is a hieroglyph that means "to unite." According to Stecchini, the entire design is a map of Egypt indicating the geodetic lines (the shortest line between two points on a curved or flat surface) and key geographical points.

Although conventional Egyptologists deny it (as indicating scientific knowledge far too advanced), Stecchini found proof that the Egyptians used degrees of latitude in their geographical measurements. Their standard unit was 6 minutes or $\frac{1}{10}$ of a degree. Unless this was one of the most astounding coincidences of the ancient world, it means they were capable of recognising and accurately analysing the curvature of the Earth (since you cannot accurately calculate degrees of latitude without doing so). They developed a geographic cubit and used it to measure the total length of their country (1,800,000 geographical cubits) with astonishing accuracy. From this unit they subsequently derived the more familiar royal cubit of approximately 46 cm (18 inches).

Such units were never arbitrary. They had real meaning in relation to the dimensions of the country or the planet as a whole. For example, a convenient unit for measuring large distances was the *atur* (equivalent, as Stecchini discovered, to 15,000 geographic cubits). This measurement allowed them to calculate the arc of meridian—a measurement of longitude—more conveniently and accurately than we do today.

With the advent of dynastic Egypt, the original geodetic system (used to determine the exact position of geographical points and the shape and size of the Earth) was modified to link the geography of Egypt more closely with the geography of the heavens. Many readers will be familiar with the work of Robert Bauval, a Belgian engineer, born in Egypt, who co-authored *The Orion Mystery* (Heinemann, London, 1994) and was featured in the subsequent television documentary of the same name. Bauval made the intriguing discovery that the pyramid complex at Giza appears to have been designed to mirror the position of the stars in Orion's Belt. Although the alignment seems partial in this case, it was no isolated example.[11] It is quite clear that the Egyptians saw their country as a mirror of the heavens as a whole and strove to make the reflection more complete. Stecchini was able to show that in about 1348 BC the Pharaoh Akhenaten (known as a heretic because he briefly introduced monotheism into Egypt) located his new capital city at Tel el-Amarna on strictly geodetic principles, despite the patent unsuitability of the location from a practical point of view. More ancient cities—notably those with strong religious significance—were apparently sited in accordance with the same principles.

Stecchini is a dense writer, even where his text remains free of calculations. But, though ignored by conventional Egyptologists, his fundamental findings can be expressed easily enough: from the very beginning of their history, the Ancient Egyptians possessed advanced geographical understanding—including a knowledge of longitude, latitude and the shape and dimensions of the planet—which enabled them to site their most important cities and monuments in strict accordance with the principles of what they believed to be a sacred science.

It was a well-developed science. The very earliest hieroglyphic texts examined by Stecchini show the Egyptians knew the Earth was round and had accurately calculated its circumference. They had developed techniques for mapping both the hemisphere of the heavens and the hemisphere of the planets.

Their knowledge of their own country was nothing short of astounding. Stecchini points out that measurements reported by Herodotus, long dismissed (without checking) by scholars as "impossible," turned out, when he examined them, to be wholly accurate. The Egyptians had measured and plotted the location of every major geographical feature from the equator to the Mediterranean.

The sophistication of their approach is seen in the fact that they used three different figures for the Tropic of Cancer. They recorded a precise calculation of 23 degrees 51 minutes, but had a simplified figure of 24 degrees for everyday use. Amazingly, they also developed an abstract figure of 24 degrees 6 minutes which enabled them to make accurate observations of the sun's shadow at the summer solstice.

Having accurately determined the dimensions of their country and the landmarks within it, the Egyptians developed a whole new system of geography using geometric figures that allowed them to memorise the data without the use of elaborate maps—arguably a better system than we have today. Their system involved a stylised representation of major geographical features and the relationships between them. The simplified form, recorded on pillars and other monuments, was immediately accessible, once you realised what you were looking at. (In hugely simplified form, it is as if a map-maker decided to represent London as a circle and Edinburgh as a square placed above it. Once you know what the two geometric symbols represent, you can tell at a glance that Edinburgh lies north of London. If the map-maker were to standardise the proportions of his "map" you could also determine the actual distance between them—all from two easily remembered symbols.)

An important part of the system was a prime meridian that split the country exactly in half longitudinally. Cities such as Memphis and Thebes and numerous temples were deliberately located at round-figure or simple-fraction distances from this meridian.[12] The pre-dynastic capital of Egypt was located right on it. Many obelisks weighing up to 1,000 tonnes were set up throughout the country as special markers. So too were *omphales*—geographical "navel" stones, marked with meridians and parallels, that indicated the distance and direction of the next *omphalos*.

The obelisks, temples and *omphales* have long been known to Egyptologists and can be seen on any conventional map of Egypt's antiquities. Stecchini's unique contribution has been to show that they were not randomly located, as was the assumption of early Egyptologists and remains the assumption of modern Egyptologists unfamiliar with Stecchni's work, or unwilling to accept his findings.

As if this were not impressive enough, Stecchini unearthed evidence that the geographic knowledge of Ancient Egypt was so respected that other countries adopted its prime meridian as the basis of location for several of their own major cities . . . a phenomenon that extended all the way to China with the siting of the ancient capital An-Yang.

The point of all this is not that the Egyptian system was sophisticated—which it was—but that its development must have taken centuries and its application millennia. Since the results were *already* in place in earliest dynastic times, this—like the Palette of Narmer—implies the existence of a highly developed culture before the dawn of Egyptian history as we know it.

It also suggests the existence of a highly developed science of astronomy. The accurate measurements shown in Egyptian texts could not have been made without it.

DATING THE TEMPLES

Sir Norman Lockyer (1836–1920) was a British astronomer best known for his detection of helium—an unknown element at the time—in the atmosphere of the sun. He is also credited with the initiation of spectroscopic observation of sunspots, discoveries about the nature of solar prominescences, and the founding of *Nature* (still one of the most respected scientific journals in the world).

Between 1870 and 1905, he conducted expeditions abroad to observe solar eclipses. Several of them took him to Egypt where he initiated a detailed study of its ancient temples. What he found was little short of incredible—so much so that most Egyptologists have chosen to disbelieve it to this day. Far from being simply places of worship, he concluded that Egyptian temples were precise astronomical instruments, capable, among other things, of determining the exact moment of the solstices and the length of the year to four decimal places.

This was achieved by carefully aligning the temple axis so that at sunrise or sunset on the solstice (the longest or shortest day of the year, depending on the season) a beam of sunlight passed through a passage into the darkened interior. Massive ornamental pylons screened the ray to create a concentrated beam. Egyptian architect-astronomers clearly realised that, by elongating the temple axis, they could narrow the beam and increase the accuracy of their measurements.

Once the beam hit the inner sanctuary—which needed to be as dark as possible—it would gradually build to a peak, then decrease to a glimmer before disappearing altogether. The whole process would take two minutes at most. By noting the peak, astronomer-priests could, and did, calculate the exact length of the year as 365.2422 days. Lockyer described the temple of Amen-Ra at Karnak, built to capture the sun at the summer solstice, as "a scientific instrument of very high precision."

Such an instrument would not remain precise indefinitely. The tilt in the Earth's axis shifts with time, moving its relative position to the sun. But the shift is slow—no more than a single degree every 6,000 or 7,000 years. None the less, the Egyptians were dissatisfied with anything less than pinpoint accuracy and actually rebuilt their temples on a new axis when the instrument began to fail. By calculating the shift in the Earth's tilt, Lockyer calculated that the Karnak temple must have been originally constructed in 3700 BC. Egyptologists have, naturally, ignored him because the date was 600 years earlier than their estimate of the foundation of Egyptian civilisation.

Alongside sun-oriented buildings, Lockyer discovered temples aligned to certain stars. In the temple at Tyre, for example, he was convinced that the twin pillars of gold and green stone described by Herodotus were quite capable of reflecting the light of Alpha Lyrae, a star now more commonly known as Vega. There were two particularly interesting aspects of these star temples. One was that, as astronomical instruments, they were considerably more sophisticated than the sun temples. The other was that they were earlier. It was as if the Ancient Egyptians showed a greater grasp of astronomy the further back in time you went—the complete reverse of what might have been expected.

Star temples would maintain their accuracy as astronomical instruments for a far shorter period than sun temples—a matter of only 200 or 300 years. This was due to the precession of the equinoxes (a phenomenon caused by a slow wobble in the axis of the Earth). Thus, far more realignments of star temples would be expected . . . something which Lockyer discovered time and again. The temple at Luxor, for example, shows signs of four major changes of orientation. And when Lockyer investigated temples in Karnak he found that courtyards and pylons had been added and realignments made in both frontage and sanctuary so that priests could continue to observe the dedicated star. He believed other temples were sometimes adjusted to begin observations of a new star when precessional movements rendered their original alignment useless.

Given his massive scientific reputation, one would have thought that the record of Lockyer's findings, *The Dawn of Astronomy*, would have been welcomed eagerly by Egyptologists when it was published in 1894. Instead it was arbitrarily dismissed and is largely ignored to this day. One Egyptologist remarked patronisingly that Lockyer should stick to his own speciality. The problem was not the temple orientations, which had been noted before. Nor was it even Lockyer's claims about the Egyptian obsession with precision. His cardinal sin was using his observations to date the original construction of the temples.

In one case he believed he had found evidence of a temple alignment to the star Dubhe which would have dated the building at 6000 BC. In another, an alignment to Canopus yielded a date of 6400 BC. Acceptance of either date by establishment scholars would have been tantamount to an admission that the orthodox dating of Egyptian civilisation was grossly in error.

DATING THE PYRAMIDS

The ancient pyramids at Giza and at Dahshur are among those built on limestone pavements. Airline pilot Ralph Ellis was sightseeing at Giza in the mid-1990s when his wife asked him curiously why there was a line running along one of the pavements there. Ellis examined the line and came to an interesting conclusion which he explains in his book *Thoth: Architect of the Universe* (Edfu Books, Dorset, 1998).

When you visit the Great Pyramid today, you do not see it as it was originally built. There are only remnants left of a highly polished white limestone casing that once covered the entire structure. In common with many other pyramids, the outer reaches of the casing stones fell short of the edge of the pavement. From the moment the pyramid was built, a process of erosion began on the exposed part of the pavement. Sand particles, weather and the feet of visitors all began to carry away its surface layers. The process was gradual, extremely slow, but quite inevitable.

The day eventually came when the lower terraces of casing stones were removed, leaving a new area of pavement freshly exposed. This area, protected by the casing stones, had not been subject to erosion. It more or less maintained its original surface which was marginally higher than the remaining weathered surface, so that a line was discernible between the two. Although the newly exposed surface began to erode in its turn, erosion continued on the rest of the pavement keeping intact the relative differences between the two areas. Thus the line between them remained and can be seen today.

As Ellis worked all this out, an idea struck him. Since the time when the casing stones were removed is now known—at least approximately—might it be possible to use the erosion differential to date the overall structure? He thought about it and decided that if you could establish the original level of the pavement, you would indeed have a wholly new method of determining the age of the pyramid.

But then it occurred to him that it *was* possible to establish the original level of the pavement by reference to the few casing stones left. It would be an approximate measurement to be sure, but one that would allow at least a ball-park figure for the pyramid's age. Ellis began to take measurements.

By the time he had finished, Ellis had figures for both the Giza and Dahshur pyramids. The casing stones were vandalised in the eighth or ninth centuries AD—roughly 1,000 years ago. At Dahshur, the erosion of the newly exposed surface was approximately 5 mm in that time. The erosion of the original exposed pavement was 50 mm. At Giza, the erosion of the newly exposed surface was again 5 mm, but the differential in the original surface was very much greater—it had eroded to a depth of 200 mm.

As Ellis points out, the dividing line separates two areas of the same paving stone, so we can assume a similar rate of erosion.[13] But if we know that rate to be approximately 5 mm per 1,000 years, this gives a date of 8000 BC for the construction of the Dahshur pyramid.

The same methodology reveals a construction date of approximately 38,000 BC for the Giza complex.

CHAPTER 4

BUILDING PYRAMIDS

JUST as there are indications that Egypt is far older than Egyptologists currently allow, so there is substantial evidence that this ancient civilisation reached a far higher level of technological competence than is currently believed. For the most obvious example, we need only return to the Great Pyramid, where the problems of who built this structure and when, are compounded by the problem of how. This additional mystery is independent of the puzzle we have already examined—how such a structure could have been completed in twenty-three, thirty or fifty years. The fact is, we are not at all sure how it was completed at all.

Although the *average* block of stone used in its construction weighs 2.5 tonnes, there are casing stones at the base that weigh as much as 15. But even these are lightweights when compared with the massive granite beams that roof the King's Chamber. These are estimated to tip the scales at between 50 and 80 tonnes; Unlike the interior blocks from Giza and the limestone casing which was quarried across the Nile at Tura, these granite giants had to be transported 800 km (500 miles) from Aswan.

Even the most dogmatic Egyptologist admits that the question of how the pyramids were built has not received a wholly satisfactory answer. But the admission tends to be qualified by the introduction of Egyptology's current consensus theory. According to this hypothesis, the Egyptians (who lacked tackle and pulleys for lifting heavy weights) employed a sloping embankment of brick, earth or sand. This was increased in height and length as the pyramid rose. The stone blocks were hauled up it by means of sledges, rollers and levers.

It is an idea that is accepted as plausible by Egyptologists. Engineers take a different view.

THE SHORTCOMINGS OF THE THEORIES

Peter Hodges was trained at the School of Buildings, Brixton. He served with the Royal Engineers during the Second World War and worked for a number of building firms before taking over and managing one of his own. Some time prior to 1989, he visited Egypt and promptly fell ill in his Cairo hotel. With a fine view of the Great Pyramid, he idled away the time calculating the engineering parameters of the ramp theory. Three days later he decided it was nonsense.

There are two types of ramp used in building—the short and the long. The short ramp is by far the more efficient since only the load is moved along it. Workmen stand at the bottom or on a level platform at the top. But, efficient or not, the short ramp could not have been used for a structure the size of the Great Pyramid, except for the first course or two. Beyond that, the platform becomes too small to hold the workers.

So far Hodges found himself in agreement with the

Egyptologists, who almost always use a long access ramp to illustrate their theory of how the pyramid was built. But he noticed that the drawings usually showed a 1:3 gradient and wondered if the "experts" had ever troubled to walk up a ramp set at such a pitch. His army experience had taught him that a 1:3 gradient was hard work—such hard work, in fact, that hauling tons of stone up it could be virtually ruled out. He thought a 1:10 slope might just possibly be workable, but only if you could find some means of reducing friction between ramp and load, while at the same time maintaining a good purchase for the workers' feet. Even then, such a ramp would have to be so long that it would stretch well beyond the Giza plateau.

Conventional Egyptologists were well enough aware of this latter problem and postulated *spiral* ramps as the solution. As an engineer, Hodges did not buy this for a variety of reasons. His main concerns were firstly that it would be impossible to drag stones around the sharp corners formed as the ramp wrapped around the pyramid; and secondly that, as the ramp rose, it would obscure more and more of the pyramid, making it impossible for the builders to check their work.

Further difficulties arose when he put his mind to the material that would have to be used in a ramp. Egyptologists dismiss this point as of small importance, suggesting earth, gravel or mud-brick ramps as a matter of course. Hodges examined these options and was forced to abandon each in turn.

Mud brick was the first to go. Flinders Petrie, the father of modern Egyptology, did the calculations in the nineteenth century and realised that mud bricks were not strong enough for the loads they would have to bear. A mud-brick ramp would simply crumble away. Regrettably, despite Petrie's eminence, his fellow Egyptologists paid scant attention to his conclusions.

Earthen and gravel ramps—with variations such as

sand and rock mixtures—brought up fresh problems. Used loose, these materials would tend to obscure the pyramid as the ramp rose higher, giving rise to exactly the same objection as a spiral ramp: the builders could no longer check their work. If, on the other hand, the material was buttressed to keep its shape, vast quantities of wood would be required and even then there would be a limit to the height the ramp could be raised before it collapsed under its own weight. That limit fell far short of what would be needed to complete the pyramid.

In Hodges' opinion, the only possible ramp material would have been squared stone. But this greatly exaggerated a further problem his engineering experience had permitted him to pinpoint: what do you do with a ramp when the pyramid is finished? This problem arises whatever material you use. At its greatest height, any ramp would have a volume three times that of the pyramid itself. This is a vast amount of spoil to get rid of when the job is done—enough stone to build three walls around the whole of France. The local quarries could not handle it and, even if you simply spread it out across open ground, it would bury the entire Giza plateau almost 2 m (6 ft) deep. It would also leave clear signs . . . but there is no archaeological evidence of ramp spoil at all.

Hodges decided the ramp theory so beloved of conventional Egyptologists would have to be abandoned. He pointed out that while some pictures depicting hordes of men dragging massive stones on wooden platforms have survived, all of them show transportation on a level surface.[14] It's also worth noting that none of these pictures is contemporary with the pyramid itself.

Even the movement of the local limestone blocks across the Nile from Tura is something of a mystery. Egyptologists have long maintained that they were floated across the river on rafts.

A group of Japanese engineers received permission

from the Egyptian government to attempt a duplication of this feat.

Their raft sank.

FEATS OF ENGINEERING

If the sheer bulk of stone in the pyramid creates the mystery of how it was built, several other aspects compound it.

The Great Pyramid's base covers 5.3 hectares (13 acres), more than six times larger than the Great Court of the British Museum in London. Surveyors have calculated that to build the Great Pyramid to the precision it now displays, the entire area of the mile-square rocky plateau first had to be levelled to within 2.1 cm—less than an inch. This is an extraordinary undertaking, which could probably be duplicated today, but only at vast expense and using laser technology.

How did the Ancient Egyptians manage it? As Egyptologists see it, they used manpower to clear away the accumulation of sand and gravel all the way down to the bedrock, then levelled the bedrock by "removing protuberances and filling in depressions."[15] In other words they levelled the bedrock by . . . levelling the bedrock. According to R. L. Engelbach, a former Keeper of the Cairo Museum and pupil of Flinders Petrie, the remarkable degree of accuracy was achieved by surrounding the 5.3 hectare (13 acre) site with mud walls and flooding it with water. He believed the levelling was then facilitated by cutting a network of trenches—a concept of which, in my engineering ignorance, I can make no sense whatsoever.

As we know, the Great Pyramid was originally faced with 9 hectares (22 acres) of polished limestone casings which had been transported 32 km (20 miles) from the quarries facing Memphis. Almost all of these have long since been hacked off and dragged away, apparently to construct the mosques of Cairo.[16] But a few remain, mainly near the pyramid tip. These show that the casings—weighing up to 15 tonnes each—were set with optical precision. They deviate from absolute true by less than a hundredth of an inch.[17] You couldn't slide a playing card between them.

This is a feat of engineering that we would find difficult to duplicate today. As author Desmond Leslie was already pointing out in the 1950s, once you put down a 15-tonne block, it stays down. There's no question of gently tapping it into place. The orthodox picture of sweating workers manhandling huge blocks up a ramp ignores the precision of the casing stones altogether. There is simply no known way they could have been positioned by manpower alone.

ANCIENT HYDROGEN BALLOONS

Retired electrical engineer and Fellow of the Royal Astronomical Society Eric Crew has made the intriguing suggestion that hydrogen balloons may have been used to lift the stones and convey them from the quarries, using winches from the gondola or on the ground.[18] He points out that the manufacture of hydrogen is a relatively simple process. In our own era, it was made (before the use of helium) by passing steam over hot scrap iron in a retort. In ancient times it might have been produced—admittedly much more slowly—using solar or other power for electrolysis. (As we shall see later, another engineer, Christopher Dunn, claims hydrogen may have been manufactured in Ancient Egypt by a chemical reaction such as hydrated zinc chloride and a dilute solution of hydrochloric acid.)

As Crew envisaged it, the gas would have been stored

in clusters of inflated bags, so that if one leaked the others would provide enough lift to avoid a disastrous accident. Although balloons experience problems with changes of air pressure as they reach higher altitudes, their use at Giza would not have been much higher than the pyramid itself. Temperature changes also affect lift, but Crew feels this would have been manageable.

Radical though this idea might appear, there are reasons why it deserves serious consideration. The first of these is the surprising discovery that the Ancient Egyptians were excellent chemists. It has been known for some time that they used fire-based technology at least as early as 2500 BC in order to manufacture blue pigment. But in 1999, a French team of chemists led by Dr. P. Walter published an article in the prestigious journal *Nature* describing a much more startling discovery.

They had found 4,000-year-old black, green and white powders—used for cosmetic purposes—in an exceptional state of preservation in their original vials of alabaster, ceramic and wood. Dr. Walter and his team obtained samples for analysis. At first their results contained no surprises. Some of the cosmetics were made from crushed galena and cerussite, both naturally occurring lead ores. But then laurionite and phosgenite turned up.

These latter compounds also occur in nature, but so rarely that the French team concluded they must have been created artificially in order to explain the quantities found. The only way to do this involves a difficult and repetitive process of wet chemistry of considerable sophistication. Against this background, it is no longer outlandish to suggest that the Egyptians may have been capable of manufacturing hydrogen as well—a point that lends additional support to both Crew's and Dunn's ideas.

Of further relevance to Crew's balloon theory is the variety of Egyptian texts that refer to "solar" or "celestial" boats by means of which Pharaoh could "ascend to the heavens." Most Egyptologists take these references to be statements of religious faith or mythic descriptions of pharaonic power, but this is no more than a convention. We have no means of knowing whether or not the references were meant to be taken literally. Crew claims that they were. He believes the celestial boats were modified copies of the gondolas of airships.

In fact, known Egyptian technology was quite capable of creating at least a primitive airship, once you accept the ability to manufacture hydrogen. As Crew points out, control methods did not have to be particularly complicated. Directional lift could have been accomplished by sliding a weight along a track below the centre line of the airship, thus tilting the nose. The weight may even have been something as simple as the crew moving from one end of the ship or gondola to the other. Rudders were familiar technology from Nile craft. Anchors would have been brought into play to tether the airship and enable loads to be removed.

Although a more sophisticated means of propulsion cannot be ruled out (as we shall see later), the ships might have been moved by men on the ground using natural fibre ropes to guide the balloons. Even in recent times, animal skins have been used in the manufacture of airships, another pointer towards the ease with which the Egyptians may have made one. The main technical effort involved today appears to be the provision of vast sheds for their construction and storage. But in Egypt these enclosures might not have been necessary, as the weather was generally calm and dry.

The realisation that it was technically possible for the Egyptians to have constructed airships does not, of course, prove they ever did. All the same, Crew's theory receives additional support from an unexpected source. There is an ancient hieroglyphic carving in Abydos that seems to depict exactly the sort of craft he postulates.

AIRSHIPS OR INSCRIPTIONS?

Abydos lies west of the Nile 10 km (6 miles) outside El-Balyana, a small town 145 km (90 miles) north of Luxor, midway between the provincial capitals of Qena and Sohag. It was once a royal necropolis and centre of pilgrimage for the worship of Osiris. Today, it is one of the most important archaeological sites in Egypt.

Part of its importance lies in the massive Osireion, a cyclopean structure of indeterminate age with an underlying reservoir it would be difficult to duplicate today for all our modern engineering skills. John Anthony West has pointed out that what is now taken as bedrock is actually compressed silt from the Nile.[19] Thus it seems reasonable to assume that the Osireion was not originally the semi-subterranean structure it is today, but was built on level ground and subsequently buried by the silting of Nile floods. Such high-level floods date back to 10,000 BC, which would give the Osireion an antiquity of more than 12,000 years. Its underlying reservoir might be older.

None the less, conventional Egyptologists confidently date the nearby Temple of Osiris to the New Kingdom Pharaoh Seti I and insist he built the Osireion as well. Whatever the truth about this, a ceiling support beam inside the Seti temple is carved with some of the most remarkable hieroglyphs found anywhere in Egypt.

Hieroglyphs are a peculiar form of writing in that they can be used both as letters of an ancient alphabet and as pictograms which represent directly the thing depicted. Thus an oval may be read either as the letter "R" or as representing a mouth. One of the hieroglyphs in the Seti temple seems to depict a device that could easily be the sort of airship suggested by Eric Crew. A blimp-like shape with a prominent tail fin floats above a structure that looks suspiciously like a gondola. This shape is like none of the standard hieroglyphs found in Egyptian papyri or inscrip-

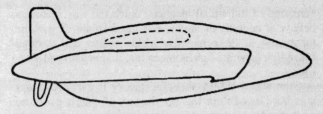

Airship hieroglyph, Abydos

tions elsewhere and thus seems to be a pictograph, rather than an alphabet letter.

Dr. Johannes Fiebag is among the experts who believe the hieroglyphs are no more than "superinscripted inscriptions of Rameses II and Sethos I," an expression I still find bewildering after two years study of hieroglyphic script. Although hieroglyphics *can* be written one above the other as well as side by side, the fact remains that several of the Abydos glyphs, including this one, bear no resemblance to standard alphabetical hieroglyphs. Despite this, scholars like Fiebag continue to maintain that the inscriptions must be standard forms and thus have nothing to do with any sort of technical vehicles. But even if Crew is wrong about his airships, we are still left with the mystery of how the Egyptians managed to move those massive stone blocks.

THE MAGNET THEORY

Edward Leedskalnin claimed it was all done by magnets.

Leedskalnin, who died in 1952, was a Latvian émigré to the United States who believed—and often loudly said so—that modern scientists were wrong about almost everything. He was obsessed by the idea that the universe contained magnets. Indeed, he believed matter actually consisted of individual magnets, much the way scientists believe it consists of atoms. For Leedskalnin, it was the movement of these magnets within matter and through space that generated phenomena like magnetism and electricity.

This was a cranky-sounding theory if ever there was one, but Leedskalnin was not the sort of elderly eccentric who shuffles along rambling about the cosmic secrets he's discovered. After his arrival in the United States he decided to put his insights to practical use. Incredibly, they worked.

At his home near Florida City, he made himself a rock garden decorated with, among other massive ornaments, a 20-tonne stone obelisk. He claimed—and no-one ever disproved it—that he had transported these megaliths single-handed, without the aid of machinery.

One evening while at work in his garden he was mugged. The experience unnerved him so much he decided to move house. He selected the town of Homestead in Florida and called in a local trucker to help with the megaliths. They began with the obelisk. When the truck was in position, Leedskalnin asked the driver to leave him alone for a moment. The man moved a short distance away. There was a resounding crash. Concerned there might have been an accident, the driver ran back to find that the 20-tonne obelisk was now on his truck and Leedskalnin was ostentatiously dusting off his hands.

The performance was repeated, a little less hurriedly but even more spectacularly, when they arrived at Homestead. Leedskalnin asked the driver to leave his truck overnight and promised not only that he would unload it, but would also erect the obelisk on its new site. It seemed an impossible task, but when the driver returned next morning, the obelisk was off the truck and in place.

Author and engineer Christopher Dunn visited Homestead in 1982 and again in 1995 to find ample evidence of Leedskalnin's extraordinary way with stone. Dunn describes how Leedskalnin's love of coral led to the construction of a veritable Coral Castle comprising 1,100 tonnes of rock.[20] The structure included a 3-tonne rocking chair, a 9-tonne gate, a 22-tonne obelisk, several blocks weighing between 22 and 23 tonnes each, and a massive 30-tonne slab crowned with a gable. All were Leedskalnin's own, unaided work from quarrying stage to final erection. The average weight of the stones used in this astonishing construction is actually greater than the average weight of the blocks in the Great Pyramid.

A great many engineers and even representatives of the United States government visited Leedskalnin during his lifetime in the hope of discovering his secret. None succeeded. But Leedskalnin himself was convinced his methods were identical to those of the Ancient Egyptians. We have no way of knowing whether he was right, but his approach is the only one so far examined that fits into a manageable time-scale. Over a period of twenty-eight years, Leedskalnin managed single-handedly to quarry and erect 1,100 tonnes of stone. This means that if the Egyptians really *did* use his methods, a team of 5,000 men could have built the Great Pyramid in under thirty years.

But there are other possibilities.

CHAPTER 5

WORKSHOP OF WONDERS

A surviving photograph of John Keely reveals a genial, middle-aged individual, conservatively dressed and sporting the spectacular mutton-chop whiskers so popular in Victorian times. He looks the sort of man you would trust instinctively, but the author of his entry in the *Encyclopaedia Britannica* gives him short shrift. John Ernst Worrell Keely is described bluntly as a "fraudulent American inventor."

Keely's career supports the judgement. To this day, it is astonishingly difficult to find accurate information on even the most fundamental aspects of his life. He was born on 3 September 1927 or possibly 1937, in Philadelphia or perhaps Chester, Pennsylvania. It's fairly certain that he lost both parents in childhood. His mother died soon after he was born, his father before he was three years old. No one seems sure what school he attended, although it was probably in Philadelphia and there is some consensus that he left it by the age of twelve to become a carpenter's apprentice.

According to one source, Keely remained a carpenter

until 1872. Another claims he became the leader of an orchestra. (His grandfather, a composer, led the Baden-Baden Orchestra in an earlier era.) Yet others say he was a circus performer, physician, pharmacist, plumber, plasterer, stonemason and upholsterer. Keely himself records that even before the age of ten he had begun his researches into "acoustic physics" and claims a specific incident set him on his life's path—without, however, explaining what the incident was. Clara Bloomfield-Moore, the woman, who became his patron in later life, wrote that he was intrigued by the discovery that no two seashells gave the same tone when he held them to his ear . . . but this may be a romantic fantasy.[21] Cynics feel the most relevant piece of information about his early years was that he took up conjuring.

In 1873, Keely's life became more public, better documented and, paradoxically, even more obscure. This was the year when he announced a new source of energy— the "intermolecular vibrations of ether." At the time, the concept of ether, an invisible universal field acting as the carrier for electromagnetic waves, was widely shared by physicists. It was not until 1881 that experiments began to weaken the theory, which was abandoned after the publication of Einstein's special relativity theory in 1905. Nevertheless, Keely had been working with it for at least two years (and possibly longer), mainly in relation to the influence of sound vibrations on air and water. "Specific reactions" released a "hitherto undiscovered force" which Keely believed resulted from his "imprisoning the ether."

His next task was to design a machine that would run on the "new force." Between 1871 and 1875 he made six of them—the independent flywheel, the Globe Motor, the dissipating engine, the multiplicator, the automatic water lift and the hydro-pneumatic-pulsating-vacuo engine. None of these appear to have had much practical application. And for some reason he only patented the fly-wheel.

While Keely was working on his generator in 1873, he felt a cold vapour on his face. He tried to wipe it off and found his face was dry. Not one whit shaken by the concept of a dry vapour, he announced the discovery of a "hitherto unknown gaseous or vaporic substance" which could be used as a power source.

In 1874, Keely established a workshop for himself at 1420, N. 20th Street in Philadelphia, in order to construct his generator—a bewilderingly complex arrangement of tubes, taps and valves built around a series of cylinders similar to those used today for the storage of oxyacetyline gas. There he seems for the first time to have demonstrated his remarkable machine to the public—or at least that segment of the public represented by wealthy businessmen. Although once again the source material is contradictory about who was involved, the result was the flotation of a new corporation, the Keely Motor Company. A total of $10,000 worth of stock was subscribed at the initial meeting. It was no more than the first trickle of what became a financial torrent.

An integral part of the arrangement to form the Keely Motor Company was a legal undertaking by Keely to disclose the secret of his motor. Although he happily signed up to clauses of this type throughout his life, Keely revealed precisely nothing. When put under pressure to comply, the most he would do was explain the technicalities to a nominated expert who was in turn bound by a nondisclosure agreement. One such expert, a shareholder named Boekal, was prepared to aver that "Mr. Keely has discovered all that he has claimed." The journalist Charles Fort, an indefatigable commentator on the human condition, remarked that he thought "Mr. Boekal was reduced to a state of mental helplessness by flows of hydropneumatic-pulsating-vacuo terminology."

It is difficult to disagree. Keely's own descriptions of what he was up to were peppered with terms like *octave resonator, mass chord, sympathetic etheric force* and *condensed atomic vibration*, none of which made much sense to his fellow engineers. While millions of dollars flowed into the coffers of his company, Keely declined to take out patents on a series of marvellous inventions and absolutely refused to explain publicly how they worked. What he *did* do, at intervals, was demonstrate his machines in action and make grandiose claims about their commercial application—a course of action that usually sent share values spiralling upwards.

But it couldn't last forever. By 1880, still without patents, explanations or a commercial product, the shareholders lost patience, the company lost value and Keely lost his stipend. Unable to pay his bills, he was saved from bankruptcy only by the intervention of Clara Bloomfield-Moore, the wealthy—and some would say impressionable—woman who funded his activities for many years to come.

During those years, Keely went briefly to jail for contempt of court (occasioned by his refusal, yet again, to divulge the secret of his engines), conducted experiments for the U.S. government, and was subjected to investigation by an English physicist whose report so disillusioned Mrs. Bloomfield-Moore that she withdrew her patronage.

It was not the last such disillusionment. After Keely's death in 1898, his landlord, Daniel Dory, sent in men to clean out the building that had housed his workshop. Officials of the Motor Company had already taken away the tools and machinery, but Dory's men discovered tightly fitting trapdoors in the floor of the workroom, a hidden compartment beneath an anteroom and, buried beneath the main workshop, a 2-tonne hollow steel sphere with brass connectors, securely set on a stone foundation. It was immediately clear to many people that the sphere had once contained compressed air which was the real driving force behind the marvellous machines—a suspicion borne out by the discovery of "many small tubes imbedded in the walls and concealed under floors." Keely was, at long last, conclusively branded a fake. Yet doubts remain . . .

FRAUD OR GENIUS?

Potted biographies of Keely, including the one you've just read, tend to give the impression that the millions flowing into the Keely Motor Company ended up in his pocket. The reality was very different. Keely survived on a relatively small stipend.

There were intermittent grants from the company, but almost every cent of these went to pay his suppliers—mainly fabricators of machine parts. Even when faced with bankruptcy, he only took half the $10,000 offered by Mrs. Bloomfield-Moore. Since he lived modestly and seemed to spend almost all his time in his workshop—where he built some 2,000 machines during his lifetime—it is difficult to see the financial motive for fraud.

Then, too, there are problems with the compressed air theory. The first of these is *how* Keely compressed the air that was supposed, to have been stored in the steel sphere. There was a compressor in his workshop, but it was known to have been inoperative for several years and, besides which, made so much noise in operation that it would have been easily detectable. Even Keely's critics did not believe he used it. They maintained he worked instead with silent hand-pumps.

This suggestion was met with derision by professional engineers. One of them, William F. Rudolf, stated:

> I never heard such nonsense. I would like to see the person who could pump up a pressure of more than

300 pounds in a 60-gallon reservoir, the size of the old sphere found, with no more than hand pumps. It's plain the force of the air inside would be too great to pump in more air by hand.[22]

Rudolf also remarked that even a compressor would have to work flat out for half a day to fill the sphere.

Compounding the problem were the concealed tubes that were supposed to have carried the compressed air to Keely's machines. Most of them were no thicker than wires and appeared to mechanics quite incapable of carrying the pressures they were supposed to. Dismissing the claims of fraud, Keely's supporters—including several engineers who worked with him—said the tubing was actually used to carry his unique "etheric vapour."

Etheric vapour sounds so unlikely that it is tempting to conclude it never existed outside Keely's imagination, but here again there is verification in that it was examined by others than himself. They found it "pleasant to the touch" and without any perceptible smell. A man called Henry C. Sargeant actually drank it without ill-effect, as recorded in Theo Paijmans' book *Free Energy Pioneer: John Worrell Keely* (1998).

Even Keely's bizarre terminology had an explanation, at least according to his supporters. It arose from sheer desperation. The man was so far in advance of the science of his day that he was forced to invent new terms to describe his discoveries. The claim may have been partisan, but some of his terms now seem to refer to states of matter that have since been confirmed by modern physics. If this is correct, Keely was the first to suspect the existence of quarks (sub-atomic particles).

Alongside all of this, there were reports of demonstrations in conditions that appear to rule out fraud completely. One of the most intriguing was recorded by the writer R. Harte.

The story began in Keely's laboratory with a gathering of twelve mining magnates, all concerned with finding the fastest, cheapest and most efficient means of extracting gold from rock. Keely claimed he had a new technique under development. When the men arrived at his workshop he produced a small, handheld machine and led them to several large blocks of quartz-bearing rock. As he held the machine to each block, it disintegrated into dust, leaving its embedded lumps of gold behind.

The miners were excited, but cautious. One promised funding for an industrial version of Keely's device if he was prepared to demonstrate it "under natural conditions" on rock of the miners' own choosing. Keely agreed and the party subsequently gathered in the Catskill Mountains where the men pointed out a face of rock for him to work on. Keely asked them to time the operation, then drilled a tunnel 1.4 m (4½ ft) in diameter and 5.5 m (18 ft) long in less than 20 minutes.

It seems the jury is still out on John Worrell Keely.

DEFYING GRAVITY . . .

Keely claimed that the device which disintegrated quartz was an accidental discovery originally designed to "overcome gravity."[23] This was something that obsessed him. As early as 1881, he told a reporter that a closed room in his apartment contained a secret device he had invented for a Californian gentleman to lift heavy weights. Three years later, he was promising to devote the rest of his life to the problems of "aerial navigation" which he saw in terms of "vibratory lift."

Exactly what this meant was demonstrated in the spring of 1890 when he succeeded in raising a small model airship, by means of an unknown force. The model, which weighed about 3.6 kg (8 lb) was attached to a thin wire to one of his machines, after which it rose, landed and even hovered on demand. One text—the Snell Manuscript (written in 1934 by C. W. Snell of Detroit and unpublished until the 1990s)—records Keely as saying, "An airship of any number of tons weight can, when my system is completed, float off into space with a motion as light as thistledown . . ."

Soon reports began to circulate that he had gone beyond small models in his experiments. One by William H. H. Harte, former Attorney General of California State, told how he had introduced a certain force to an iron cylinder weighing several hundredweight, after which he was able to lift it up on one finger and carry it round "as easily as if it were a piece of cork." Another, passed on by Mrs. Bloomfield-Moore, claimed he had been seen to carry a 500 horsepower engine single-handed from one part of his workshop to another through the use of a belt and "certain appliances" he was wearing at the time.

In a statement to a Philadelphia newspaper, an eyewitness named Jefferson Thomas insisted that he had seen Keely levitate a 2,700 kg (6,000 lb) metal sphere—apparently the same one his critics later claimed was used to store compressed air. Here again a thin wire connected the sphere to a device small enough to be worn on Keely's lapel.

How did he do it? Keely himself was typically obscure in his explanations:

A small instrument, having three gyroscopes as a principal part of its construction, is used to demonstrate the facts of aerial navigation. These gyroscopes are attached to a heavy, inert mass of metal, weighing about one ton. The other part of the apparatus consists of tubes, enclosed in as small a space as possible, being clustered in a circle. These tubes represent certain chords, which were coincident to the streams of force acting upon the planet, focalizing and defocalizing upon its neutral center. The action upon the molecular structure of the mass lifted was based upon the fact that each molecule in the mass possessed a north and south pole—more strictly speaking, a positive and negative pole—situated through the center, formed by the three atoms which compose it. No matter which way the mass of metal is turned, the poles of the molecule point undeviatingly to the polar center of the earth, acting almost exactly as the dip-needle when uninfluenced by extraneous conditions, electrical and otherwise. The rotation of the discs of the gyroscopes produces an action upon the molecules of the mass to be lifted, reversing their poles, causing repulsion from the earth in the same way as like poles of a magnet repel each other.[24]

The first hint of what was really going on came during a series of demonstrations in 1890 witnessed by, among others, Professor Joseph Leidy of the University of Pennsylvania.

Keely began by attaching a platinum wire to one of his devices which he called a "transmitter." The other end of the wire was fastened to the metal cap of a large glass jar standing on a wooden table about 1.5 m (5 ft) away. Leidy examined the jar, which stood about 1 m (40 in) high and was 25 cm (10 in) in diameter, and found it had a solid glass bottom. The jar was filled with water and contained three grocer's weights. These too were examined and weighed: they were 225 g (8 oz), 450 g (1 lb) and 900 g (2 lb) respectively.

Once everyone had determined that no trickery was involved, Keely took some string from his pocket, wrapped it round a brass spindle on top of his transmitter, then jerked it to set the spindle spinning. There was a harp-like instrument housed in the base of the transmitter which Keely next began to play by plucking the strings with one hand while he struck some resonant rods with the other. He explained that when exactly the same note was struck by both the strings and the rods, a force would be generated that would influence the weights. After a time he coaxed a simultaneous deep, clear note. Immediately, one of the weights floated up to the top of the jar.

Three years later, Jacob Bunn, a Vice-President of the Illinois Watch Company, was describing how Keely could set heavy steel balls moving through the air "simply by playing on a peculiar mouth organ."

One of the most detailed descriptions of such a demonstration was left by the Boston scientist Alfred H. Plum who visited the Keely workshop on several occasions. The first time, he was introduced to Keely's Liberator—a disc-shaped device on a stand, pulley-driven and with a series of central radiating metal spokes. Plum discovered that when these spokes were flicked, they gave off a sound like a tuning fork.

Attached to the Liberator by a wire of gold, platinum and silver was something called a "resonator." I can find no pictorial record of this device, but Plum describes it as a series of standing metal tubes inside a metal cylinder case. A brass cup on top housed a compass, pointing, naturally enough, to north.

Keely twanged the spokes of his Liberator until they emitted a sustained sound. Using a knob on the side he turned this note until it sounded something like a trumpet. At this point, the compass needle began to spin and remained spinning for up to three minutes, although no magnetic field had apparently been introduced into the experiment.

For his second demonstration, Plum saw what appeared to be a musical zither supported on metal tubes. This was attached by a silk cord to a moveable framework of iron rods that supported a small copper globe on another table.

Keely walked into an anteroom and blew a trumpet through an open window between the two. The globe began to spin. Plum noted it spun faster as the note grew louder and slowed to a halt when the note stopped or when the silk cord was cut.

Keely also demonstrated the use of his Liberator to drive a wheel which continued to spin so long as a trumpet note was sustained. Most impressive of all, he levitated a 900 g (2 lb) metal sphere inside a jar of water, again using the Liberator and a brass horn. In this variation of his grocery weight experiment, the ball continued to float "like a cork" after the horn was silenced and could only be persuaded to sink when a different note was sounded.

This description and several others leave little doubt about two things. The first is that John Worrell Keely had learned how to influence the weight of certain objects to such a degree that they floated in water and, sometimes, even in air. The second was that he used sound to do it.

The question is whether Egypt's ancient pyramid builders might have done the same.

CHAPTER 6

ꙮSONICS IN THE
ꙮANCIENT WORLD

SOONER or later, every bible student learns the Old Testament story of Joshua. As Moses' minister he quickly gained an enviable reputation as a warrior and was eventually sent to take Jericho, one of the most strongly fortified cities in the ancient world.

As he scouted out his objective, Joshua met with a "captain of the host of the Lord" who promised he would take Jericho if he was prepared to follow certain instructions:

> And ye shall compass the city, all ye men of war, and go round about the city once. Thus shalt thou do six days. And seven priests shall bear before the ark seven trumpets of rams' horns: and the seventh day ye shall compass the city seven times, and the priests shall blow with the trumpets.
>
> And it shall come to pass, that when they make a long blast with the ram's horn, and when ye hear the sound of the trumpet, all the people shall shout with a great shout; and the wall of the city shall fall down

flat, and the people shall ascend up every man straight before him.

JOSHUA 6:3–5

Joshua passed on the instructions to his priests and soldiers, warning all of them to make no sound apart from the trumpet blasts until he gave them the word to shout.

So the ark of the Lord compassed the city, going about it once: and they came into the camp, and lodged in the camp.

And Joshua rose early in the morning, and the priests took up the ark of the Lord.

And seven priests bearing seven trumpets of rams' horns before the ark of the Lord went on continually, and blew with the trumpets: and the armed men went before them; but the rereward came after the ark of the Lord, the priests going on, and blowing with the trumpets. And the second day they compassed the city once, and returned into the camp: so they did six days.

And it came to pass on the seventh day, that they rose early about the dawning of the day, and compassed the city after the same manner seven times: only on that day they compassed the city seven times.

And it came to pass at the seventh time, when the priests blew with the trumpets, Joshua said unto the people, Shout; for the Lord hath given you the city. . . .

So the people shouted when the priests blew with the trumpets: and it came to pass, when the people heard the sound of the trumpet, and the people shouted with a great shout, that the wall fell down flat, so that the people went up into the city, every man straight before him, and they took the city.

And they utterly destroyed all that was in the city,

both man and woman, young and old, and ox, and
sheep, and ass, with the edge of the sword.

JOSHUA 6:11–16/20–21

This vivid, detailed account seizes the imagination. Anyone who has actually heard a ram's horn trumpet will have
experienced the deep vibrations generated by the sound.
Multiple trumpets could indeed set up the sort of sympathetic vibration that sometimes destroys bridges today.
And it is tempting to conclude that the loud shout by
scores of simultaneous voices might just be enough to
finish the job . . .

Excavation at Jericho has shown that the city's massive
walls did indeed collapse at one time, although whether
or not this coincided with Joshua's attack is an open question. Archaeologists have decided the most likely cause
was an earthquake. But the fact remains that the Joshua
story is our best-known reference to the use of sonics in
the ancient world. It is not, however, the only one.

A City Built by Sound?

At latitude 16 degrees 37 minutes south and longitude 68
degrees 41 minutes west on the high Bolivian Altiplano,
you can find the monstrous ruins of Tiahuanaco, one of
the world's most mysterious cities.

Tiahuanaco is situated in a long, shallow valley some
5 km (3 miles) wide, bordered by low hills. The valley is
384,000 m (12,596 ft) above sea level, yet there are clear
signs that the ruined city once functioned as a port. There
is water on the Altiplano in the form of a series of interconnected lakes. But the closest—brackish Lake Titicaca—
is more than 19 km (12 miles) away and 27 m (90 ft)
lower in elevation.

Archaeological finds made in 1995 show that Tiahuanaco was once the capital of an ancient empire that extended across large portions of eastern and southern Bolivia, northwestern Argentina, northern Chile, and southern Peru. Nobody knows quite when the city was founded. The most conservative scholars claim that building started around 150 BC, while others believe it should be dated anything up to 2,000 years earlier. One archaeologist, Arthur Posnansky, used astronomical techniques to date it to 15,000 BC. The German astronomer Rolf Müller, who studied his findings, suggested they might also point to a date of 9300 BC, but admitted that 15,000 BC was possible.

Whatever its age, the size of the Tiahuanaco buildings is astonishing. A fortress-like structure measures some 198 × 183 m (650 × 600 ft)—roughly equivalent to the Tower of London. At 134 × 180 m (440 × 590 ft), the Sun Temple is as large as Trafalgar Square.

The builders had a fondness for enormous blocks of sandstone and andesite. Doorways in the city are monolithic, rather than formed by uprights and lintel. A typical andesite slab measures 2.9 × 1.6 × 0.8 m (9 ft 5 in × 5 ft 2 in × 2 ft 11 in) and weighs 8 tonnes. But this is by no means the largest block found. They can go right up to 65 tonnes. There are 100-tonne fragments 1.6 km (1 mile) southwest of the main site. Experts estimate the original unbroken block must have weighed around 400 tonnes.

How blocks this size were shaped, transported and erected is something of a mystery. There are no chisel marks on the stone. The largest blocks—those that originally made up the 400-tonne monster—are sandstone and were quarried 16 km (10 miles) away. The andesite was quarried from the slopes of an extinct volcano 80 km (50 miles) away. Since the horse was only introduced by the Spanish Conquistadors and there is no indication at all that the wheel was known, the conventional assumption is that the builders must have used human muscle to drag the blocks.

While this seems unlikely, it is perhaps possible. But the idea that those giant blocks were dragged to 396 m (13,000 ft) and then manhandled into position strains credulity to breaking point. At this altitude the air is so thin that the smallest effort leaves one gasping.

In an earlier book, I suggested that the city (whose unique "jigsaw" construction makes it earthquake-proof) must have been built *before* it rose to 396 m (13,000 ft) in a sudden cataclysmic rise of the Andes Mountains—a theory that incidentally explains what a port is doing so far from the sea.[25] But local legend proposes an even more peculiar idea. The Aymara Indians told a Spanish traveller shortly after the conquest that the stones were miraculously lifted off the ground and transported by the sound of a trumpet.

LEGENDARY SOUND BUILDERS

The Maya people once occupied an enormous sweep of territory that included Mexico, Guatemala, Belize, Honduras and El Salvador. Mayan architecture is similar in many ways to that of Ancient Egypt. Like the mystery builders of Tiahuanaco, they had a fondness for monumental buildings made from massive slabs of stone. They even built pyramids, constructed elaborate tombs and embalmed their dead like the Egyptians.

The Uxmal temple complex on the Yucatan Peninsula is decidedly Mayan, but local legend attributes it to a prehistoric pigmy race who also controlled the movement and placement of massive blocks through the use of sound. In this case trumpets were not used. Instead the builders simply whistled in order to set the stones in their correct position. Both the technique and the people themselves were lost in a great flood.

On the other side of the Atlantic, Greek mythology tells the story of Amphion, son of Jupiter, who was able to move huge stones by strumming on a lyre. The *Argonautica* describes how Amphion and his twin Zethus laid the foundations of Thebes. Zethus did it the hard way, lifting "the peak of a steep mountain" on his shoulders, but Amphion strolled after him, "singing loud and clear on his golden lyre . . . and a rock twice as large followed his footsteps."

Stories of this type are far from rare when it comes to explaining how large blocks of stone got to be where they are. Even Stonehenge has attracted one. According to Geoffrey of Monmouth, the entire circle was transported from "Killarius" in Ireland by the Druid Merlin. The legend claims every stone flew to its present position when the wizard chanted a spell.

The question is, are these widespread legends pure fantasy or do they represent a distorted memory of something real?

MEGALITHIC ULTRASOUND

According to folk wisdom, only the pure in heart can hear the squeak of a bat. Like so many old sayings, this one contains a grain of truth. As we get older—and presumably less pure than we were as children—our ears find the higher registers of sound more and more difficult to discern. A bat's squeak is extremely high-pitched and, while most children can hear it easily, adults beyond middle age usually cannot.

But even children are hearing only the lower frequencies of the call. Much of the sound a bat makes moves well into the ultrasonic range and can be detected only by specialised instruments. In the early 1970s, a zoologist studying bats with the relevant equipment happened to pass a group of standing stones on his way home around dawn. To his astonishment, the instruments detected a strong, regular and rapid pulse as the morning sun struck the stones.

The zoologist told the story to Paul Devereux, an intrepid investigator of earth mysteries. Devereux in turn passed it on to the Institute of Archaeology at Oxford. There it was picked up by a research chemist named Don Robins, who happened to be a member of a group of scientists and engineers actively investigating megalithic sites across the British Isles.

The project group assembled its own broad-spectrum ultrasonic detector and Robins took it to the Rollright Stones in Oxfordshire just before dawn on a morning in late October 1978. As the sun rose, his equipment picked up a regular rapid pulse around the Kingstone—an isolated menhir some distance from the circle proper.

For the next four years, the project team scanned further megalithic sites across the country and found that they too broadcast ultrasonics. By now, the equipment they were using was capable of excluding radio interference and stray signals from local energy sources including geological faults. Comparative readings taken at modern structures like streets and bridges, or areas of natural woodland, showed no more than the anticipated random background noise. None of it showed anything remotely like the dawn pulse effect of the megalithic circles. The discovery suggested that the sites had actually been created to generate the ultrasound—in other words, the pulse was purposeful.

As the work continued, more and more evidence was gathered to support this tentative conclusion, some of it very surprising indeed. First, the pulse was quite independent of weather conditions. It could be measured at dawn on any day, rain or shine. Next, the pulse transformed into a veritable ultrasonic howl lasting several hours on the mornings of the spring and autumn equinoxes. These effects were curious enough, but far weirder results were to follow.

On one occasion Robins and his team moved into a circle with their detectors and found no ultrasound at all. This was an impossible reading, since open countryside has a standard background of ultrasound generated by the movement of grass, the rustle of leaves and even the activity of the team members themselves. The scientists decided, reasonably enough, that their equipment had malfunctioned, but tests quickly showed that it was working perfectly. The great stone circle was somehow generating an ultrasonic screen that left its interior utterly silent.

Intrigued by their findings, the team extended their measurements to include radioactivity. Anywhere in the country will produce a level of background radiation detectable by a Geiger counter. And the stone circles were no different. Where they differed was that they somehow generated "hot spots" where the radiation was far higher than background. But when the counter was moved to the centre of the circle, just the reverse was found. There the scientists detected "cold spots" where the radiation dropped below normal background levels.

Engineer Charles Brooker extended the measurements still further by examining the Rollright circle with a portable magnetometer. This showed a seven-ring spiral of diminishing magnetic intensity. The circle was screening out electromagnetic radiation.

Although these findings have not been widely publicised outside specialist literature, they almost undoubtedly point to a sophisticated knowledge of ultrasound and various types of radiation in ancient times. At least some of Britain's megalithic stone circles seem to have been constructed as radiation shelters—although to what end is difficult to imagine.

The ultrasonic aspect of these ancient structures gives clear support to legends of a sonic technology lost in the depths of prehistory. But the evidence of megalithic Britain stops short of demonstrating that the ancients could use sound for construction purposes. For that we have to go further afield.

MONASTERY CONSTRUCTION, TIBETAN-STYLE

In 1934, a German named Theodore Illion became one of the few European travellers to penetrate Tibet. He approached—illegally—through Russian Turkestan, having been refused permission by the Soviet government. Then he entered Chinese Turkestan with the help of local Kirghiz chiefs and from there made his way, still illegally, on to the high Tibetan plateau.

Illion travelled in disguise. While he spoke the language reasonably well, he did not believe he was sufficiently fluent to pass as a native, so he pretended to be deaf and dumb when approached by anyone he thought might betray him. Surprisingly, the ruse worked and he travelled widely throughout the country, meeting many lamas and holy men.

Some years later he returned to Germany and began work on *Ratfelhaftes Tibet*, a book about his adventures that revealed him to be a man fascinated by the esoteric who none the less cultivated a healthy degree of scepticism. The first edition was published in Hamburg in 1936, with an English translation brought out by Rider & Co, in London a year later.

Among the illustrations in a more recent edition of the work are two diagrams by a Swedish aircraft designer named Henry Kjellson. The first shows a particular placement of people before a cliff face. Inset is a sketch of a monk beating an enormous drum which hangs suspended in a wooden frame. The second is a simplified version of the first, but in addition it shows the trajectory of a stone block as it is lifted up the cliff.

Neither of these diagrams is mentioned anywhere in the text of the book, nor is the operation they illustrate. The only explanation is contained in two captions. The first explains that the drawing shows a monastery under construction in the Tibetan style. On the right is a steep mountain side. In the centre is a stone block, and on the left are the priests and musicians. The key reveals "S = big drum, M = medium drum, T = trumpeter." The inset shows the method used to suspend a drum and gives an idea of its size. Kjellson says the 200 priests were waiting behind the instruments to take up their positions in straight lines of 8 or 10, "like spokes in a wheel." The caption concludes "Unlikely as it may seem, this operation has an intriguing precision, made slightly more so by Kjellson's meticulously detailed description."

The second caption is briefer but more enlightening and explains that Kjellson's sketch shows Tibetan monks levitating stones by using an acoustic levitation technique with the aid of drums.[26]

The inclusion of the sketches in Illion's book suggests that he actually witnessed stone levitation in Tibet, but this does not seem to have been the case, Henry Kjellson did not see it either. Both captions are misleading. The sketches were actually made by an anonymous Swedish doctor whose experiences Kjellson reported. The report is not, unfortunately, easily accessible. He told the story in his book *Försvunnen teknik*, published in Sweden in 1961. To date, as far as I am aware, no English-language translation has been produced. There was, however, a Danish edition *Forsvunden Teknik* (Nihil, Copenhagen) issued in

1974, and the British author Andrew Collins used this as the basis of his own account.[27]

It makes fascinating reading. The Swedish doctor in question was referred to simply as "Jarl" in Kjellson's book. Some time in the 1930s, Jarl was invited by a Tibetan friend to visit a monastery southwest of Lhasa. While there, he was taken to a nearby cliff where the lamas were engaged in a curious construction project. Some 250 m (820 ft) up the cliff face was a cave entrance fronted by a broad ledge on which the monks were building a stone wall. It was not an easy site to reach. The monks had to climb down ropes hung from the top of the cliff. How they raised the huge stones used in the wall was anybody's guess.

About the same distance from the base of the cliff as the ledge was above it, there was a large, flat, bowl-shaped stone embedded in the ground. Some distance behind it was a group of monks, some of whom were equipped with massive drums and trumpets. Among them was a monk who was using a knotted rope to measure out precisely where each of the others should stand.

As Jarl watched, the monks positioned thirteen drums and six trumpets in a 90 degree arc around the bowl-stone. Some eight to ten monks formed a line behind each instrument. At the centre of the arc were three monks with drums. The one in the middle had a small drum hung on a leather sling around his neck. The monks on either side of him had larger drums hung from wooden frames.

On either side of these two drums came monks supporting 3 m (10 ft) long trumpets. Beyond them were more drums slung from frames, including a pair of the largest drums Jarl had ever seen. Even further out along the arc were alternating placements of trumpets, drums, trumpets and finally two of the largest-sized drums. He noticed that each drum was open at one end and this end was invariably pointed towards the bowl-stone.

As the doctor watched, a yak-drawn sled dragged a 1.5 × 1 × 1 m (4 × 3 × 3 ft) stone block to the bowl-stone. A group of straining monks manhandled it off the sled and, with difficulty, into the depression. When it was in place, the monk at the centre of the arc began to chant rhythmically and beat the small drum. The sound it made was so staccato that it hurt Jarl's ears. The rhythm was taken up by the trumpets, then by the larger drums, which the attendant monks struck with leather-headed sticks.

The rhythm was slow at first, but gradually increased in pace until, to Jarl, the sound seemed continuous. Even so, the beat of the smallest drum remained discernible through everything else.

For three or four minutes, nothing else happened. Then, to Jarl's astonishment, the block in the centre of the bowl-stone wobbled suddenly. He saw the monks slowly tilt their trumpets and drums upwards. As they did so, the block rose with them as if lifted by invisible hands. The sound never faltered. The heavy block speeded up as it followed an arced trajectory towards the cave-mouth 250 m (820 ft) up the cliff. When it reached the edge, the sound cut off and it crashed down in a spray of dust and gravel. The yak-sled then dragged another block to the bowl-stone.

Jarl discovered that the monks could raise five stone blocks in an hour using their trumpets and drums—sometimes even six when they were working efficiently. Occasionally a block would shatter when it was dropped on the ledge, but the pieces were simply pushed over the side by the monks at the cave-mouth.

FURTHER ADVENTURES IN TIBET

Kjellson claimed to have found further evidence of sonic levitation in the experience of an Austrian movie-maker he called "Linauer."

Linauer, like Jarl, visited a remote Tibetan monastery in the 1930s. There he was shown two curious instruments. One was a gong 3.5 m (11½ ft) in diameter, comprising a centre section of gold, ringed firstly with iron and then brass. When struck, the soft gold emitted a short, dull sound. The second instrument was an oval bowl 2 m (6 ft) long and 1 m (3 ft) wide, also cast using three different metals, although Linauer was not told what they were.[28] Strings were stretched across it and the whole thing was supported in a sturdy wooden frame.

The gong and the bowl were used (together), in conjunction with two large screens, to form a triangle with the instruments. When the gong was struck, it set up a sympathetic vibration in the strings of the bowl. The sound was then directed by the screens towards a large stone block.

The monk who demonstrated the device to Linauer showed that after striking the gong repeatedly he was able to lift the stone block with one hand. While the sound had not levitated it like Jarl's trumpets and drums, it certainly seemed to have reduced its weight dramatically. The monk explained that instruments such as these had been used long ago to build defensive walls "round the whole of Tibet."

It was also claimed that similar devices could be made to emit sounds that would shatter stone and even dissolve matter completely.

SONIC DEMOLITION

How seriously can we take all this? Kjellson did not reveal the real names of his witnesses—a fact that must leave a question mark over any account. Yet there is support for the idea that sound can have destructive potential. Dr. Lyall Watson tells of a Professor Gavraud who was on the point of giving up his job at an engineering institute in Marseilles because he had recurrent nausea attacks in his office.[29] He suspected that something in the environment was making him ill and tested the office for chemical pollutants and even radioactivity. He found nothing to explain his symptoms. Eventually, however, while leaning against the wall he realised that the entire room was vibrating at a low, inaudible, frequency, in sympathetic resonance with an air-conditioning plant on the roof of the building opposite.

The phenomenon intrigued him and he decided to build infrasound equipment in order to investigate it further. The first such device was a giant whistle some 2 m (6 ft) long, powered by compressed air. Gavraud based his design on the French police whistle which generated a range of sound—including ultrasound—by means of a dried pea. When the device was tested, it killed the technician who switched it on. A post mortem showed that his internal organs had turned to jelly.

With Gallic aplomb, Gavraud pressed on with his experiments. He carried out the next test in the open air and built a concrete bunker to protect the observers. He also turned on the air very gradually, but even so managed to break windows 1 km (½ mile) away from the test site.

Despite this unpromising beginning, Gavraud eventually got his monster under control and went on to build smaller generators that continued to produce dramatic results. He discovered that infrasound could be directed at specific targets, and that if two generators were focused simultaneously they were capable of demolishing a building up to 8 km (5 miles) away.

The structure collapsed as if it had been shattered by an earthquake.

EVIDENCE FROM INDIA

Anyone who has witnessed a soprano shatter a wine glass must have some degree of belief in the destructive power of sound. But its use to levitate stone is an entirely different matter. Yet there is supporting evidence for this phenomenon as well. It is provided not by anonymous Swedes or Austrians, but by the first-hand account of an Englishwoman currently living near Bath.

Patricia (Paddy) Slade is now widowed. In 1961, she was living with her army husband Peter, stationed in Iraq under the regime of King Faisal. During a period of leave, Peter, who was born in India, decided he wanted to show his wife where he had been brought up and gone to school. The two of them set off on an overland trek using Land Rovers, ponies and camels according to local conditions.

Travelling via Uzbekistan, they visited Samarkand, then entered Pakistan by way of the Khyber Pass. They toured various places in the subcontinent and eventually came to Poona in India. They had been there only a few days when a friend advised them to attend a local religious ceremony that promised to be interesting. Paddy and Peter did so.

The ceremony took place in the open air and involved an enormous rock which Paddy Slade now estimates must have weighed at least 40 tonnes. A group of eleven white-robed priests appeared and began to circle the stone slowly, chanting. Today Paddy has forgotten the first word or words of the chant, but she does recall it made use of the commonplace prayer fragment *Ali Akbar*. Despite this, she does not believe the priests were Moslem and feels the rhythm of the chant was more important than the actual words.

After the priests had circled the stone eleven times, one of them gave a signal and all eleven stopped, placed a fingertip on the rock and lifted it shoulder-high. After holding it triumphantly for something in the region of twenty seconds, they gently set it down again.

It was an impressive display. Even allowing that the weight of the rock was distributed between eleven men, it still meant that each one was lifting substantially more than 3 tonnes with his fingertips. But an even more impressive demonstration was to follow. The priests called for volunteers who would lift the stone for themselves. To her husband's horror, Paddy stepped forward at once.

Along with a small party drawn from the spectators, she circled the stone chanting the *Ali Akbar* mantra. When the signal was given, each participant placed a fingertip on the rock and lifted. To Paddy's surprise, it rose up as easily as it had with the priests. They were not expected to hold it at shoulder height for as long as the priests had, but none the less it was elevated for what felt like quite a long time. Then they too set the rock gently down.

Although it is impossible to be certain, Paddy Slade's opinion was not that the chant somehow increased the strength of the participants, making them capable of the near-superhuman feat of lifting tonnes of rock. Rather, she believes that something in the ceremony influenced the weight of the stone itself—a first-hand experience of the power of directed sound to levitate rock.

CHAPTER 7

ʃSONICS IN EGYPT

THE fact that sound may have been used as a building tool in the ancient world does not necessarily mean it was used in Egypt. All the same, there are indications.

An Arab legend claims the pyramids were constructed using sound. Egyptian priests wrote spells on sheets of papyrus, which were slipped beneath the massive stone blocks. When a priest wished to move a stone, he struck it with a special rod that caused it to glide forward "the length of a bow-shot." In this way, even the heaviest granite was transported with ease from distant Aswan. Desmond Leslie, who recorded this legend, speculated in conversations with the present author that the "rod" mentioned functioned as a type of tuning fork, generating a resonance that lifted the stone.

Sound was also apparently used in the building process. Conclaves of priests "sang" the stones up the stepped terraces as the pyramid gradually rose towards the sky. Workmen manhandled them into place, their job made easy by the fact that each block was now light as thistledown. Contrary to common sense and modern expectations, the blocks *were* tapped gently into place.

This legend is just one of many myths that have surrounded the Great Pyramid for centuries.

Nobody takes it seriously.

THE MYSTERIOUS SWAN-NECKED VASES

Some 30,000 of the 40,000 artefacts found beneath the Step Pyramid at Saqqara were swan-necked vases made from rose quartz, diorite and basalt. The vases were potbellied in shape, with, as the name implies, long narrow necks. They were thin as card, demonstrating an astonishingly high level of craftsmanship and artistic skill. When they were first discovered, not only did no one know how they were made, no one knew how they *could* be made.

Rose quartz is a particularly attractive rock crystal with a delicate pink hue. But it is a difficult material to work because of its tendency to shatter. Basalt is a tough, volcanic stone. And Nubian diorite is one of the hardest substances in the world. To make a vase by hand, you begin with a single block of your chosen material and shape it externally. With basalt and diorite this is not an easy task. Today you would chip the stone with steel chisels, then smooth the surface with an abrasive. It would be a long, tedious task, requiring a great deal of patience. But there is no indication at all that the Ancient Egyptians had steel chisels. The *only* tools so far found are made from copper, a soft metal totally incapable of working stone.

Conventional Egyptologists deny there is a mystery. Copper tools harden with use and the suggestion is that old tack might have been called into play on the stone. It is a suggestion backed by no experimental evidence I can find. But, even if the Egyptologists are wrong about the hardened copper, they have a fall-back position. A handheld lump of diorite might be used to chip fragments from virtually any stone—even another lump of diorite. This is true, but fails to take into account the high degree of precision shown in the making of the vases: chipping with a diorite lump is a crude, clumsy process.

What's more, the problems of shaping the outside of the vase are minuscule when compared with the problem of shaping the inside. Whatever material you use, the riddle is how you design a tool that will hollow out the bulbous middle while at the same time being slim enough to fit through the narrow neck.

Where the neck is short, one proposed solution involves a series of L-shaped tools of different sizes. The first of these is used as a drill to open up a bore-hole the width of the neck down through the entire vase. The second tool of the series, which has a slightly longer leg to the L, is inserted at an angle and used to begin hollowing out a portion of the interior. When this is done, further tools in the series (each progressively longer of leg) are snaked through the neck to hollow out more and more. When the widest point of the vase is reached, you revert to tools with progressively shorter legs until the whole job is completed.

This approach has been shown to be effective when you are working with metal, but only when the tools themselves are attached to a power-lathe. Nobody has yet tried it with stone, a notoriously more difficult substance, but calculations suggest hand-pressure on the L-shaped tools would be nowhere near enough to cut through a substance like diorite. It is doubtful whether even machine-driven tools could replicate a short-necked Egyptian stone vase. Where the vase is designed with a long neck, the doubt vanishes completely. Nothing works: the L-shaped tools cannot be inserted. Thus the long-necked vases discovered at Saqqara remained an absolute enigma throughout most of the twentieth century.

But the time came when our technology advanced sufficiently to duplicate these artefacts.

Ancient Egypt's swan-necked vases could be manufactured today by using—and *only* by using—our most advanced ultrasonic drills.

MIRACULOUS TOOLS

Flinders Petrie was a young man of twenty-seven when he arrived in Egypt in 1880. By the time of his death in 1942, he had been knighted, achieved world fame and established Egyptology as a reputable branch of archaeology. One reason for the latter triumph was his insistence on careful, accurate measurements and a strictly scientific study of the evidence. Much of his approach was inherited from his father, a successful civil engineer.

Unlike many of his fellows, Flinders Petrie had a genuine regard for the country's ancient past. At a time when, as we have already noted, gunpowder was routinely used for excavations, he was more interested in preserving than exploiting . . . or exploding.

It was Petrie who discovered that the base of the Great Pyramid at Giza was a surface levelled to the tolerance of 0.6 cm (¼ inch) across an area of 5.3 hectares (13 acres). (For most of the area the tolerance was even less—no more than 0.25 cm (¹⁄₁₀ inch).

It was Petrie who discovered the curious fact that the pyramid was an architectural expression of the value *pi* which defines the relationship of a circle's circumference to its radius . . . and was believed to have been first used by the Greeks, not the Egyptians.

It was Petrie who noticed the bewildering blend of superb and shoddy workmanship in the structure.

It was Petrie who recorded that the average thickness

of the joints between the casing stones was only 0.5 mm, despite the wafer-thin layer of mortar between them.

And it was Petrie who published evidence that the Egyptians sawed stone.

Inside the Great Pyramid, in what is called the King's Chamber, there is a lidless sarcophagus created from a single block of chocolate-coloured granite. It retains to this day the marks of its manufacture. There are distinct saw tracks on the exterior, and on the west side of the northern face there are signs that the saw used was withdrawn and repositioned twice before making its final cut.

This is a bizarre discovery and another of the firsts ascribed to Flinders Petrie. From the evidence he assembled, he concluded the saw must have been no less than 2.7 m (9 ft) long. Clearly, such an implement is far too large to be used by one man, and even a two-handed saw of such proportions is difficult to visualise. To begin with, how could the blade be controlled? It is also hard to imagine how a saw of bronze—the hardest metal Egyptologists will allow was in use at the time—could slice through stone.

Petrie's own suggestion was that this massive implement must have had jewelled teeth. It was the only way he could account for the fact that it actually worked. The engineer in him wanted to insist that the jewels were diamonds, the hardest of all gemstones. Diamond-tipped bits and drills are widely used in industry today. But diamonds were unknown in Ancient Egypt, so he could not quite bring himself to make the definitive suggestion. Instead he contented himself with the typically Victorian fudge that, were it not for their scarcity, "one might be convinced" that diamonds had been used.

But none of this addresses the real mystery of the saw cuts on the sarcophagus. With or without diamond-tipped teeth, a two-handed saw requires a lot of backward and forward motion before it will even begin to dent the surface of a granite slab. How then did the Egyptian work-men manage to make an incorrectly placed cut of sufficient depth for it to remain visible several thousand years later—despite attempts to polish it away? And man-age it not once, but twice?

It is perfectly possible—even easy—to misposition a saw. But to achieve a substantial cut with a hand-saw requires a lot of effort. The mystery is why the workmen kept on making that effort long after they must have dis-covered their mistake. Had they been working on some-thing soft, like wood, what happened would be perfectly understandable. But they were working on granite. Such visible mistakes are inexplicable.

Petrie soon discovered another mystery. There were finds of hard diorite bowls with hieroglyphic inscriptions so finely wrought that there was no question of their being chiselled out with copper or bronze tools. The only thing Petrie could imagine doing the job was an engraving tool with a jewelled tip. Once again, "only considerations of the diamond's rarity in general and absence from Egypt . . . render the tough, uncrystallised corundum the more likely material." Clearly, Petrie really thought that only diamond was up to the job.

Here, the real problem is not the jewelled tip, but rather the degree of pressure and control that would be needed to incise such precise and clearly defined hieroglyphs. They were, according to Petrie's observations, "always regular and uniform in depth and equidistant."

They were, in short, the sort of engravings we would today expect to be carried out using machine tools.

There *were* machine tools—of a sort—in Ancient Egypt. When Petrie examined the diorite bowls he dis-covered that their concave surfaces were cut using two different axes—a clear indication that they had been turned on a lathe. He was also convinced the Egyptians had used circular saws.

Both finds are extremely interesting since they shatter the familiar picture of craftsmen cautiously chipping away at the diorite in much the same manner as their Stone Age ancestors chipped flint. At the very least we must now visualise some sort of machinery: perhaps a bow to drive a drill, and some sort of pedal-driven gearing to the lathe and circular saw.

But Petrie's discoveries went further still. When he examined the sarcophagus in the King's Chamber, he found it had been hollowed out by drilling. He then calculated how much pressure would have been needed to penetrate the hard granite, which was heavily flecked with feldspar, quartz and mica particles. To his surprise, he found the drill must have exerted a pressure of at least 2 tonnes. That sort of figure obviously could not have been achieved by a bow drill or any sort of treadle, however ingenious. It could not, in fact, have been achieved by any method believed to have been available to the Ancient Egyptians.

Egyptologists of a later era than Petrie solved the problem by ignoring it.

They have also ignored the evidence that tubular drills were used to hollow out the sarcophagus. These drills produced a tapering hole with a cylindrical core which was later broken away. Neat rows of the holes lined up to allow the craftsmen to complete the job. Petrie again concluded that the drill used was jewel-tipped and may have been aided in its objective by the use of an abrasive slurry—probably a sand and water mixture.

The mystery is the same as that of the saw marks. Several of the drill holes have gone too deep. As with the saw marks, the workmen tried to disguise their mistakes by polishing. As with the saw marks, they still remain visible to this day. And, as with the saw marks, the puzzle is how a (presumably) hand-powered drill got so out of control as to gouge through solid granite deeper than it should.

Although Petrie's first evidence of circular gem-tipped drills related to the Old Kingdom, he later came across similar finds which dated back to the depths of predynastic times. Although astonishingly advanced, the technology seemed ancient indeed. Just how advanced was demonstrated by the drill cores Petrie found. They exhibited perfectly formed machine grooves that spiralled evenly and without interruption. Curiously, the core samples all tapered towards the top, while the drill-holes from which they were removed tapered the other way—towards the bottom.

The discovery of drill cores added to the collection of mysteries. The granite from which the cores were extracted contained numerous flecks of quartz and feldspar. In his usual conscientious way, Petrie noted that the grooves were deeper when they passed through the quartz than they were when they passed through the feldspar. This is quite bizarre, since quartz is substantially harder than feldspar. If the drill was assisted by an abrasive slurry, the quartz should, logically, have exhibited shallower grooves. If a diamond tip really *was* used, then the grooves should have been of equal depth in both the feldspar and the quartz. What he actually found made no sense at all.

Nor did the rate of drilling. In one of the granite cores, the spiral sank to a depth of 0.25 cm ($\frac{1}{10}$ inch) over a 15 cm (6 in) circumference. Christopher Dunn, the author who visited the Coral Castle of Edward Leedskalnin, calculated that to achieve such a depth the Egyptians would have had to use diamond-tipped drills 500 times more efficient than the most advanced power tools in use today.

Dunn is an expatriate British engineer now living in Illinois. He was so intrigued by this problem that he decided to investigate further. The result was a conclusion he found so personally incredible that he passed the facts on to several other engineers and asked them to describe what sort of technology could account for them.[30] Most eventually replied that it couldn't be done.

One of them, Roger Hopkins of Massachusetts, confirmed Dunn's own verdict: the Egyptians must have used ultrasonic drills. "I do enough core drilling to know that the embedded scrape marks would not be the result of ordinary core drilling," he said in an email to Dunn (quoted in Dunn's book *The Giza Power Plant*, Bear & Co, Santa Fe, 1998).

CHAPTER 8

ƧELECTRIC EGYPT

FLINDERS Petrie is universally acknowledged as the father of Egyptology. The quality of his work was such that his books remain one of the foremost reference sources up to the present day. Subsequent discoveries have done nothing to diminish his reputation. If anything, it stands higher than ever within the Egyptological community. Yet his ideas about drills, lathes and circular saws are generally dismissed as worthless.

You don't have to look far for the reason. The saws and drills proposed by Petrie developed speeds and pressures far beyond anything that could be created by hand or by simple mechanical means. Whether he realised it or not, Petrie was speaking of power tools. Dunn's conclusion that ultrasound came into the picture does not change this. In fact, it makes power tools even more of a necessity. An ultrasonic drill works because a high-frequency sound—much higher than can be detected by the human ear—causes the bit to vibrate at exceptionally high speed. For the sort of control evident in the Egyptian core samples, such a sound would also require a power source.

It is not always realised how inventive our ancestors were when it came to the practical application of energy. Some time prior to the birth of Christ, for example, the Chinese had evolved a startlingly ingenious method of drilling for brine. They would first dig a borehole with spades until they reached bedrock. The borehole was then filled to ground level with a series of stone discs, open at their centres. This had the effect of creating a stone-lined shaft from ground level to bedrock. A heavy metal drill head was lowered into this shaft, suspended from a derrick. The bamboo "cables" that held the head were attached to a long lever. One man jumping on the lever could raise the head, which then crashed down again when he jumped off. Astonishingly, this simple, tedious method allowed the Chinese to bore brine wells to a depth of 259 m (850 ft).

Closer to Egypt, it is known that the Ancient Romans were familiar with the use of water power. A water-mill at Venafro, near Pompeii, was buried in the famous Vesuvius eruption of AD 79, while centuries earlier, according to the Greek historian and geographer Strabo, another was built at the palace of King Mithridates on Turkey's Black Sea coast.

In Egypt itself, both hydraulic and steam power were in use 2,000 years ago. Around AD 100 an individual named Heron described their principles in an extraordinary list of inventions that included a slot machine, a surveyor's theodolite, a syringe, a solar-powered fountain and a mechanical singing bird.[31]

Heron's hydraulic drive was applied to the automatic opening of temple doors. A priest would light a small altar fire outside the building and the doors would slowly open as if by magic. But the magic was mechanical. The fire heated a metal globe half-filled with water and hidden in the altar. When the air inside the globe expanded, it forced water through a siphon tube into a large bucket attached to the doors by a system of weights and pulleys. As the bucket filled, it became heavier and steadily dragged the doors open. When the fire was put out, the globe cooled down, the air inside contracted and water was drawn back out of the bucket through the siphon. The result was that the doors slowly closed again. A modification of the basic design produced an even more impressive effect. As the doors opened, a trumpet sounded eerily.

The first steam engine was not devised by James Watt in the nineteenth century (as taught in our schools). It was actually described in detail by Heron in Egypt nearly 2,000 years earlier. He called the device an *aeropile*. It was created by heating water in a large sealed metal cauldron. Two pipes carried steam from the cauldron into a metal sphere fixed on pivots above it. Protruding from this sphere were two angled narrow-gauge pipe outlets. Steam escaping from these outlets spun the sphere at 1,500 revolutions a minute. As Dr. J. G. Landels of Reading University has pointed out, this device and elements such as pistons, valves and cylinders from various other machines described by Heron could easily have been combined to create the sort of steam engine that powered Britain's industrial revolution in the Victorian era.

While there is some controversy about Heron's origins (the name is Greek, but some scholars argue that he was a native African), he is known to have worked with the square roots of negative numbers and is credited with the invention of a multitude of mechanical marvels. But whether he deserves the credit remains an open question. It may be significant that he was a citizen of Alexandria, famous throughout the ancient world for a library reputed to contain texts preserved from the great lost civilisations of prehistory.

The library was founded at the beginning of the third century BC, and survived until the civil war that occurred under the Roman emperor Aurelian in the late third century AD, so Heron certainly had the opportunity to browse its contents, including texts believed to describe ancient technologies.[32]

But even if the very earliest Egyptians did have access to steam or water energy sources, this would still not account for the power and efficiency of the drills and saws they must have used.

For that they would have needed electricity.

A BRIEF HISTORY OF MODERN ELECTRICITY

According to conventional wisdom, serious study of electricity did not begin until William Gilbert investigated the relationship between static electricity and magnetism at the end of the sixteenth century AD. Gilbert, who was physician to both Elizabeth I and James I of England, spent seventeen years working with magnetism and electricity. He concluded that the Earth was a huge magnet and showed that friction generates electricity in several common materials. But it took another 150 years or more before scientists came to realise that lightning was electrical in nature, thanks to the kite-flying experiments of America's Benjamin Franklin.

By Franklin's day, early investigators had recognised the two fundamentals of electrical usage—insulators and conductors. An insulator is a material that holds an electrical charge, but does not transmit it. A conductor is something that can transmit a charge from one body to another, although it won't store a charge unless it is insulated from its surroundings.

At the beginning of the nineteenth century, Count Alessandro Volta invented what was believed to be the world's first battery. (He called it an "electric pile.") Others quickly developed it into a practical source of current, while Volta's name was commemorated in the electrical measurement of "volts."

One of the earliest applications arose in 1807, when Sir Humphrey Davy isolated metallic potassium from fused potash by passing a current through an electrolyte solution. It was an obscure enough experiment in its day, but it led to the development of electroplating. A year later, Davy showed that electricity could produce light and heat when he persuaded an arc to jump between two charcoal electrodes.

The discovery of a direct relationship between electricity and magnetism had to wait until 1820 when Hans Christian Ørsted noticed that a compass needle was deflected by an electric current. He concluded (correctly) that the current produced its own magnetic field. Eleven years later the great Michael Faraday showed the reverse was also true. A magnetic field would generate an electrical current when applied to a moving conductor—the basic principle of the dynamo. In 1864, James Clerk Maxwell discovered that electricity and magnetism were actually just aspects of a single force, electromagnetism.

It's fair to say that very little of this impinged on the general public, but that was to change dramatically thanks to the work of engineers in the second half of the nineteenth century. Zenobe Théophile Gramme found you could carry electric power from place to place by means of overhead wires. Thomas A. Edison invented the light bulb. Nikola Tesla created alternating current. In 1881, Edison opened the world's first power station and began to distribute electricity to a select group of customers in New York City. The new energy was already powering the telegraph and telephone communications systems. Before long it was reaching widely into factories and homes.

This then is the history of electricity on our planet as taught to schoolchildren throughout the Western world today. There are substantial reasons for believing it to be inaccurate.

ELECTROMAGNETISM IN ANCIENT TIMES

The practical application of magnetism in the ancient world was, to say the least, impressive. Recently discovered fragments of the *Yung-Lo Ta Tien* encyclopaedia describe how China's very first emperor, Shih Huang Ti, used it to protect himself from assassination. The gates of the Ah Fang Palace in Hsienyang were made from lodestone generating a magnetic field of such intensity that no one wearing metal armour or carrying metal weapons could pass through them.

Shih Huang Ti is reputed to have protected his tomb in the same way. He built a vast subterranean palace beneath a massive tumulus near the city of Xian. Although only his famous terracotta warriors have so far been excavated, legend has it that the main complex is filled with wonders, including a scale model of his empire complete with mercury rivers. The same legend insists that the doorway to the tomb cannot be cut through with metal implements, since its magnetic stone would hold them fast.

More than 1,000 years ago, physicians of the Sung Dynasty were using the (supposedly modern) procedure of extracting metal splinters from the eyes and throat by using powerful magnets. By then the Chinese had discovered how to create artificial magnets, mainly for use in compasses, by heating iron needles, aligning them north, then hammering them vigorously.

There is also a suggestion that Ancient Greek medicine was in advance of our own in its use of powdered lodestone in various ointments, a practice attested in various Greek medical texts. The Greeks believed magnetic salves encouraged faster healing—an idea long treated as superstition by Western medicine which has only recently begun its first tentative experiments with the use of magnetism for healing and pain relief. This has led to the commercial production of magnetic bracelets and even magnetic dog collars, with numerous anecdotal reports of relief from conditions like arthritic pain.

But, according to the Roman writer Claudian (c. AD 370–404), the most spectacular use of magnetism appeared in Egyptian temples. During the Roman occupation, a temple at Alexandria housed statues of Mars and Venus made from iron and lodestone respectively. Their ceremonial use was magnificent. While music played, Venus was laid reclining on a bed of roses, then Mars was slowly brought towards her. As the magnetic field interacted with the metal, the two deities suddenly sprang together in passionate embrace.

Earlier still, Pharaoh Ptolemy II commissioned the Greek architect Timochares to create a metallic statue of his queen that would float in the air, suspended by magnets located in the ceiling and walls of its chamber. Although both the king and his architect died before the project could be completed, there is no doubt that it was practicable. According to Peter James and Nick Thorpe, in their book *Ancient Inventions*, an image of Ra floated in the Temple of Serapis at Alexandria until a Christian mob destroyed its magnetic magic in AD 391. There are also records of a magnetically levitated statue of Mercury in a Roman temple at Tréves, in France.

The original discovery of magnetism is ascribed to Thales of Miletus more than 2,500 years ago. The Greeks claimed it was first detected by a shepherd boy tending his flocks on the mountain slopes of western Turkey. He suddenly found he could not move because the nails in his sandals and his metal-tipped staff were held fast by magnetic forces in the ground. Although this is unlikely to be literally true, it is a fact that the environment of Magnesia—the setting for the whole delightful story—is rich in a magnetic oxide of iron. According to the Roman author Lucretius, the term "magnet" was derived from "Magnesia," but Pliny the Elder attributes it to the shepherd who was appropriately called Magnes.

Whatever the truth of all this, Thales—who lived quite close to Magnesia—was the one who took the trouble to experiment with the curious force. He found that magnetite attracted iron and noted the similarity between this action and the fact that, when rubbed, amber attracted feathers and other light objects. Since the latter reaction is the result of static build-up, the relationship between electricity and magnetism may have been suspected far earlier than we generally assume.

But whether or not this was the case, our own word "electric" comes from the Greek *elektron*, which means "amber," and there are hints scattered throughout ancient literature that the phenomenon was far more widely studied—and understood—than we now believe.

It is known, for example, that in ancient Babylonia electric fish were used as a local anaesthetic, following a similar principle to that of the modern T.E.N.S. machine which controls pain by overloading specific nerves with electrical current.[33] The Roman poet Claudian recorded that an electric ray was able to send a charge along a (presumably wet) fishing line to stun the unwary angler. Another Roman writer, Lucretius, was aware that electricity consisted of "minute and mobile particles" (anticipating the discovery by modern physics that electricity consists of a stream of tiny subatomic particles now called electrons).

The Greek love of amber may have been associated with its electrical properties and it is known that vast quantities of the fossil resin were being imported 4,000 years ago, long before those properties were supposed to have been discovered. Hoards of it have been found in the shaft tombs of the Mycenian kings and it was prized by generations of ordinary citizens for use in magical amulets and ornaments. In Europe, amber was traded extensively right back to the Stone Age and again seems to have been credited with magical properties. Such a history leads one to wonder whether the "magic" might not have had a basis in the reality of the electrical charge.

THE BAGHDAD BATTERY

Alongside indications that the ancients understood electricity better than we imagine comes clear evidence that they could put it to practical use. The point is illustrated by the discovery of a 2,000-year-old battery in Iraq. The story of the discovery has been repeated frequently in the literature dealing with historical anomalies, but the details, briefly, are as follows.

In June 1936, workmen constructing a new railway near Baghdad accidentally discovered an ancient tomb. Archaeologists were called in and soon unearthed an entire settlement dating back to the second century BC. There was a great deal of interesting material at the site, including engraved brick and glass, so it is not surprising that a plain clay jar received little attention . . . at least at first.

The jar, which seemed like a simple vase, was made from light yellow clay and was missing its neck. It contained a 9 cm (3½ in) copper tube, 26 mm (1/10 in) in diameter, closed at one end with an asphalt plug. Inside the tube was the rusted remains of an iron rod. There was a 3 mm layer of asphalt on the bottom of the jar. Similar finds had been made at Ctesiphon, another site near Baghdad, along with amulets and various magical artefacts. Not surprisingly, the jars were labelled "ritual objects," displayed and forgotten.

But the latest find was not forgotten. Wilhelm König, the German director of the Iraq Museum laboratory, realised it would only take the addition of acid or alkaline liquid to transform the jar into an electrical battery. Dr. Arne Eggebrecht took the trouble to duplicate the vase and added grape juice. It generated a measured half volt of electricity continuously for eighteen days.

The London Science Museum physicist Walter Winton was intrigued (although not at first impressed) by reports of the discovery and travelled to Baghdad more than thirty years after the find to examine it for himself. What he found was, in his own words, "completely obvious." The jar was indeed an electrical battery. Afterwards he went on record as saying:

> Put some acid in the copper vessel—any acid, vinegar will do—and—hey presto!—you have a simple cell which will generate a voltage and give a current of electricity. Several such cells connected together in series would make a battery of cells which would give enough current to ring a bell, light up a bulb or drive a small electric motor.[34]

The discovery of the "Baghdad Battery" might go some way towards solving a much more ancient mystery. Among the many finds unearthed by Egyptologists in the nineteenth century was a small Horus figure in what appeared to be solid gold. Closer examination, however, showed it was actually made from silver and gold-plated. The mystery was the high quality of the plating.

Gold-plating is an ancient technique and the means by which it was achieved are well-known: sheets of the precious metal were simply beaten on with mallets. The approach leaves a distinctive dimpled effect—the result of the hammer blows—that never quite disappears, however skilfully the artisan works. But the Horus figurine displayed no dimpling at all. Furthermore, the coating was far thinner than could be achieved by beating out.

Today, we could make an exact duplicate of the Horus figure . . . but only by means of electroplating. This technique, based on Sir Humphrey Davy's discoveries in 1807, involves placing the artefact in a solution containing suspended particles of the plating medium. Something called a cathode bar holds the object to be plated. An electric current is passed into the solution with the effect of dislodging negatively charged electrons from the bar. These transfer to positively charged ions in the solution, setting free single atoms of gold. The gold atoms collect on both the cathode bar and the object to be plated, gradually transforming into a wafer-thin layer of the precious metal.

This is a sophisticated process that results in artefacts exactly like the Horus statue, but its critical element is the availability of electric current. The assumption of Egyptologists has long been that the Egyptians, in common with all other ancient peoples, had no electrical knowledge whatsoever. They have clung to this assumption despite such evidence as the Baghdad Battery and the discovery by Greek archaeologist Chryssoula Kardara that, prior to 1100 BC, the Minoans of Crete set up metal masts on mountain peaks to attract lightning from passing storm clouds and thus produce much-needed rain.[35]

They have also ignored evidence from Egypt itself.

LIGHTING THE TOMBS

Among the most spectacular engineering works of Ancient Egypt are the tombs built for its kings, queens and nobility. Contrary to the official myth that pharaohs were laid to rest in pyramids, the real burials were almost always in subterranean rock-cut crypts known as "Halls of

Eternity." The name was not a whimsy. Belief in an afterlife was so strong that the tomb was seen—literally—as the place where you would spend your next few million boundless years and consequently needed to be as comfortable as you could make it.

Anyone who enters an Egyptian tomb for the first time is immediately struck by its sheer spaciousness. Typically it is a collection of roomy chambers, galleries and corridors that would originally have been packed with tables, chairs, replica servants and guards, ornaments, personal possessions and even food and drink. The walls and ceiling were often plastered, then painted brilliant white, before being decorated with hieroglyphic prayers and heroic accounts of the deceased's life.

Those white walls are something of a puzzle. Our picture of primitive Egypt includes the idea of tomb-builders lighting their way with torches as they worked the massive galleries. But in all the tombs so far discovered, not one of the white walls has shown a trace of smoke.

When Egyptologists realised that the facile explanation of torchlight would no longer do, they regrouped around one of two ingenious proposals. The first was that sesame oil lamps were used in place of torches. Sesame oil is a smokeless fuel that would certainly burn in the pottery lamps widely used in Ancient Egypt. But the amount of light generated is nothing like that of a flaming bitumen torch. Nor is it good enough to say that they simply increased the number of lamps. When tunnelling in a confined space, a multiplicity of burning lamps is unwieldy and quickly uses up the available oxygen, grossly impeding the progress of the work—an objection that might, indeed, be applied to the concept of torches as well.

The second proposal is that the trick was all done with mirrors. A strategically placed polished surface outside the tomb could be set to reflect the sunlight inside. As the tomb became larger and more complex, further mirrors might be positioned to divert the incoming light into the side chambers and passages. In the larger tombs, it would result in a complicated mirror system, but nothing that was beyond Egyptian ingenuity.

The mirror idea has a certain appeal if you are attempting to light a finished tomb during the hours of daylight. But it clearly doesn't work at night. For urgent projects, it is inconceivable that everything stopped at sunset. Some light source must have been used after dark and, as we have seen, it certainly wasn't torches. Nor do mirrors explain how the work was lit in the early stages. At that point—and in Egyptian mine shafts which show no sign of smoke blackening either—the workmen's bodies would have blocked the incoming light. Back-lighting was no good. What was needed was a light source that would illuminate the way ahead.

Had the Baghdad Battery been discovered in Egypt rather than Iraq, we would have a ready-made solution. An electric lamp would provide a low-heat, non-oxygen consuming, high-intensity light source that would allow the tombs to be constructed with no smoke blackening whatsoever.

But the battery was *not* discovered in Egypt. Nor, at the time of writing, has any similar artefact. Because of this, despite the evidence of electroplating, despite the indirect evidence of machine tools and despite the lack of smoke stains on tomb walls, Egyptologists insist that the Egyptians simply could not have known a thing about electricity.

They insist on this, even though (as we will see) there are hieroglyphic texts referring to electricity and surviving pictures of Egyptians using it.

The Horus Temple at Edfu flanks the Nile almost exactly midway between Luxor and Aswan. It is the best preserved example of ancient temple architecture in the whole of Egypt—arguably in the world. Although work began on the existing buildings in 237 BC, Edfu reflects a far earlier tradition. The original temple on the site was credited to Imhotep, the semi-legendary architect who designed Zoser's Step Pyramid at Saqqara, and may even have had a hand in the Great Pyramid at Giza.

Inscriptions at Edfu record that copper masts were built into its pylons. Copper is by far the most efficient electrical conductor known. Indeed, it is used so extensively in the wiring of our homes that world copper reserves are now running low. That the Egyptians were well aware of its properties is made clear by the ancient scribe who carefully cut the Edfu hieroglyphs that can be read to this day: "This is the high pylon of the god of Edfu at the throne of Horus the light-bringer. Masts are arranged in pairs *in order to cleave the thunderstorm* in the heights of the heavens [my italics]."

It would seem from this inscription that the Egyptians were at least as familiar with the properties of natural electricity as their Minoan cousins. There is also evidence to suggest that they knew how to make use of it.

THE ARK—SACRED ARTEFACT OR DEADLY WEAPON?

When Howard Carter broke into the tomb of the boy-king Tutankhamen in November, 1922, among the "wonderful things" he discovered was a series of ark-like vessels stored one inside the other like Russian dolls. With many far more exciting treasures on display, neither Carter nor anyone else paid particular attention to these artefacts, which were in any case duplicates of similar containers already found throughout Egypt.

But, though the point is seldom emphasised, the Egyptian vessels are actually design prototypes for a much more high-profile container—the biblical Ark of the Covenant.

The Old Testament insists that God himself gave Moses detailed instructions for the construction of the Ark:

> Two cubits and a half shall be the length thereof, and
> a cubit and a half of the breadth thereof, and a cubit
> and a half the height thereof . . . And thou shalt make
> a mercy seat of pure gold: two cubits and a half shall
> be the length thereof, and a cubit and a half the breadth
> thereof. And thou shalt make two cherubim of gold,
> of beaten work shalt thou make them, in the two ends
> of the mercy seat.
>
> EXODUS 25

Archaeological finds in Egypt show that these dimensions, if not the specific ornamentation, were similar to those of Egyptian arks. This is hardly surprising, since Moses was, by the biblical account, brought up in Egypt and, as a prince in the court of Pharaoh, would have had access to any priestly repository of knowledge he chose. What *is* surprising is the use to which the Ark of the Covenant was put.

Although described as a container for the Tablets of Law given to Moses on Mount Sinai, and as the seat of God himself, it is very evident from the biblical account that the Ark was primarily a weapon for the Israelites— and an extraordinarily dangerous one at that.

The evidence of its military use is presented in detail in my book *Martian Genesis*, but the point relevant to the present investigation is that the weapon seems to have been electrical in nature.[36] Description after biblical description points to this conclusion. It had to be covered with a special (insulating?) cloth for safety. Only members of a specialist order of priests—the Levites—were permitted to handle it. Others who touched it frequently died in a manner that suggests electrocution. It generated a localised field effect that was taken as a sign the Lord was present. It discharged "fire" that was somehow different from ordinary fire, yet capable of incinerating objects, animals and people.

The apparent dichotomy between what we would now call an electrical weapon and the Israelite perception of the Ark as a religious artefact is not nearly so extreme as it might seem. We have already seen how the electrical properties of amber led to its being considered a magical material in the ancient world. The gross electrical discharge represented by lightning was almost universally thought of as the work of deities. It takes very little imagination to understand how an electrical machine of immense destructive power might be seen as the seat of divinity.

If, as seems clear, the Ark really was an electrical machine, its basic design was almost certainly drawn up in Egypt.

FURTHER EVIDENCE FOR ANCIENT EGYPTIAN ELECTRICITY

The idea that the Ancient Egyptians created sophisticated electrical machinery may still seem incredible, despite the evidence of power tools and the rest. Yet it is supported by the controversial Abydos hieroglyphs already mentioned in Chapter 4, in relation to the theory that balloons or airships may have been used to help lift stone.

The "balloon glyph" is only one curiosity among the inscriptions found at Abydos. Others include what appears to be a representation of a helicopter ...

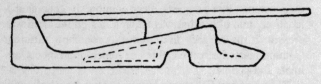

... a submarine ...

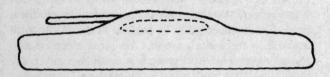

... and an aeroplane.

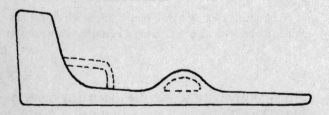

None of these machines uses electricity as its primary power source in their modern versions, but all have electrical components without which they could not function.

If these hieroglyphs actually represent what they appear to represent, they constitute yet another pointer towards the use of electricity in Ancient Egypt. So too does a most peculiar carving in a much-visited Egyptian temple. To understand its significance, one first needs to understand the workings of a radiometer (officially invented by William Crookes in 1875).

A Crookes radiometer consists of a glass bulb from which most of the air has been removed and a rotor mounted vertically inside. The rotor has four horizontal arms on a central pivot. At the outer end of each arm is a metal vane, polished on one side and blackened on the other. The polished surfaces reflect away energy that strikes them, while the blackened surfaces absorb it. This has the effect of raising the temperature of the blackened surfaces, heating the air above them and thus causing the rotor to turn. The instrument is used for detecting radiant energy. Wilhelm Röntgen discovered X-rays with it in 1895.

A Crookes radiometer looks like this:

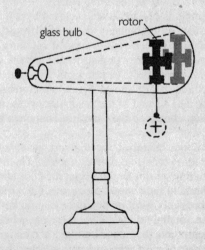

glass bulb   rotor

Diagram of a Crookes radiometer

The Egyptian temple mentioned earlier is in Dendera, an agricultural town on the west bank of the Nile. It is built on the ancient site of Ta-ynt-netert, the capital of Upper Egypt's sixth nome (one of the country's 42 administrative divisions) and a city dedicated to Hathor, the cow-headed goddess of the sky, women, fertility and love. Her temple remains a well-preserved tourist attraction to this day.

The present building originated in the Ptolemaic period but its oldest known stone block dates back to the Middle Kingdom (about 1900 BC), while the temple rests on the foundations of earlier structures dating back to at least 2600 BC. An inscription in one of the subterranean chambers states that the original Osirian temple was built "according to a plan upon a goatskin scroll from the time of the Companions of Horus." This suggests that the first temple on the site was built during the legendary prehistoric era of Zep Tepi, the First Time.

The temple is of sandstone, enclosed by a wall of mud brick. Inside, an elaborately decorated hypostyle hall is supported by eighteen Hathor-headed columns. The ceiling is carved with astronomical scenes and the walls with details of a royal visit. Leading off this hall is another, smaller chamber surrounded by six storerooms, and two vestibules. The second of the vestibules opens into a sanctuary which contained the image of Hathor in her sacred boat.

In an upper chamber, the topmost panel depicts two figures holding tube-like objects, each of which has a serpent extending its full length. From the base of each tube, a thick braided cable runs along the floor to terminate inside a box, on top of which sits an image of Atum-Ra, hands outstretched, with the sun-disc on his head. Each tube is supported by a djed pillar (a curious structure oddly reminiscent of some modern electrical transformers). On the floor underneath the right-hand tube two people kneel facing each other with their arms parallel and both hands touching. On the extreme right of the panel, a baboon holds a knife to the end of the nearest tube. This is not the only peculiar carving at Dendera. In one of the crypts, another panel portrays two standing priests facing each other, each holding a similar tube, again with an undulating serpent and cable connection to an Atum-Ra box.

On a wall panel opposite, yet another tube is depicted, this time with the arms of the djed pillar extended into the tube itself to support the serpent. Underneath are two kneeling people, while a third figure faces the djed.

In a separate panel two priests hold a serpent—without a tube—connected to the Atum-Ra box. Further panels show an upright tube with no serpent inside.

Several electrical engineers have commented on the curious resemblance between these instruments and a Crookes radiometer. One—America's Michael R. Freeman—believes that while the tube on the left of the first panel described is operating normally, something much more interesting is going on to the right of the carving. He takes the small box beside the baboon figure as an energy source and speculates that the Horus figurine on top of it supports an apparatus designed to collect static electricity.

In support of this idea, Freeman points out that if the tubes really were Crookes radiometers the static charge built up in the knife held by the baboon would divert an electron beam in the tube itself. If the snakes seen in the picture are symbolic representations of such a beam, it is noteworthy that the one on the right is turned away from the end of the tube, apparently repelled by the knife.

In other words, Freeman feels the carving depicts a complex technical experiment in static electricity.

Another electrical expert, America's Jon Jefferson, believes that, since the Temple of Dendera was a healing centre, the scenes show how electrically produced energy fields were used for radiation treatments.

Jefferson, who has a background in computers, physics, aeronautics and electronic engineering, points out:

> In one crypt scene, it clearly shows energy rays being transferred from the tube bottom to the top of the heads of two people sitting directly underneath. In fact, I believe the whole purpose of the djeds underneath the tubes was not so much for support, or even insulation, but was used to directly receive and store the energy being generated from the tubes.

ELECTRICITY AND THE GREAT PYRAMID

Several Arab legends claim that the Great Pyramid at Giza is haunted. Some describe a saturnine woman with sharp, vampiric teeth, but most refer to "ghost lights" that dance about the pyramid's peak.

The lights really exist—at least in certain weather conditions—but have more to do with static electricity than ghosts. It has been demonstrated that the pyramid generates at its summit an electrical charge strong enough to shock a grown man unconscious.

Today it is illegal to climb the exterior of the Great Pyramid.[37] Far too many tourists have fallen to their death for the Egyptian authorities to allow the practice to continue. But this was not always the case. In Victorian times, anyone with sufficient cash to pay a guide could make the heady trip and even ladies in crinolines could be seen perspiring their way upwards.

When Sir William Siemens made the climb, his guide demonstrated that a curious ringing sound could be heard at the top when he raised his arm. Siemens, an engineer who later founded the manufacturing empire that still sells household appliances under his name, was intrigued and suspected (correctly) that the phenomenon was electrical. He created a makeshift Leyden jar using an empty wine bottle and some newspaper. When he held the device aloft it generated a stream of sparks.

It proved an unwise demonstration. The guide was so upset that he accused Siemens of witchcraft and attacked him vigorously. Siemens lowered the bottle and knocked him unconscious with the accumulated charge.

Why the pyramid acts to generate electricity is not entirely clear, but a rather more important question may be whether or not the effect is accidental.

One engineer who thinks it's not is the ubiquitous Christopher Dunn (investigator of Egyptian power tools and other remarkable examples of ancient technology).

CHAPTER 9

PYRAMID POWER PLANT

THERE are a number of peculiarities about the Great Pyramid which challenge the consensus theory that it was constructed as a tomb.

First and most obvious, there is its sheer size. The pyramid covers an area of 5.3 hectares (13 acres) and rose originally to a height of 146 m (481 ft).[38] Some 866,495 cu m (30,600,000 cu ft) of material is incorporated in the structure. An estimated 2,300,000 stone blocks were used in its construction, each weighing on average 2.5 tonnes. Some of the casing stones at the base weigh up to 15 tonnes, while, as noted earlier, the granite beams in the roof of the King's Chamber vary between 50 and 80 tonnes each. If you add in the causeway, satellite pyramid, queen's pyramids and mastabas, you have a combined mass of 2,700,000 cu m (95,350,000 cu ft).

This is a lot of stonework just to house a corpse, even allowing for the Egyptian obsession with the afterlife. The orthodox explanation is that Pharaoh Khufu had an enormous ego.

(In this context, it's interesting to note that the interior

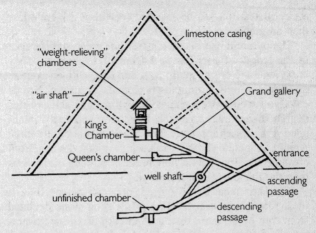

Cross-section of the Great Pyramid showing the passages and royal chambers

of the pyramid is nothing like as well-equipped for the afterlife as the Halls of Eternity hollowed out for generations of pharaohs in the Valley of the Kings. A cross-section of the pyramid shows a few passages and tunnels, but only three chambers and a Grand Gallery. The gallery bears comparison with the vast subterranean chambers of known pharaonic tombs, but the three chambers are relatively small. If Khufu—or whoever really did have the pyramid constructed—had an enormous ego, it did not drive him to provide much in the way of creature comforts for his afterlife.)

The next most obvious peculiarity about the Great Pyramid is the precision with which it was built. As we have already seen, the pyramid's base is huge. It covers the equivalent of seven New York City blocks in midtown. And, before building work began, this entire area of the rocky plateau had to be levelled to within 2.1 cm—less than an inch.

The pyramid itself is set square. The greatest difference in the length of its sides is 4.4 cm of 1¾ inches. They are oriented to north, south, west and east, with an average deviation of only 3 minutes 6 seconds of an arc. Nowadays you would use a magnetic compass to achieve this degree of accuracy. Yet the Egyptians apparently managed it with nothing better than astronomical observation. Again, as noted earlier, the casing stones deviate from absolute true by about a hundredth of an inch, rather less than the thickness of a fingernail.

That last measurement needs its own perspective. It means that each straight edge of a casing stone deviated from true by no more than a hundredth of an inch over a length of 190.5 cm (75 in). (Flinders Petrie compared this to the accuracy of an optician's straightedge.) The blocks were square and flat within the same tolerance.

But we are not just dealing with one or two blocks here. There were some 100,000 casing stones surfacing the pyramid when it was originally constructed. Every one that remains shows the same astonishing precision. To achieve such accuracy while cutting and dressing a single 2.5 tonne limestone block is remarkable. To achieve it in 100,000 blocks suggests mass production to a standard of accuracy far beyond anything we have today. We can manage it in a machine shop, but not on a building site. The commonly proposed idea that a stonemason's hammer and chisel could produce blocks of this quality is simply nonsense.

It is a mystery how such accuracy was achieved and a puzzle why. If a massive ego explains the size of the pyramid, nothing seems to explain its astonishing precision. The tolerances found in the structure simply aren't needed for a tomb—or, indeed, for any other type of building that springs readily to mind. The pyramid could have been constructed far more easily and quickly without them, yet it would have looked just as impressive and endured just as long.

MATHEMATICAL MYSTERIES

It was widely suspected in classical times that the Great Pyramid—in common with several other Egyptian structures—embodied measurements derived from geographical and geometrical absolutes. For a long time, this remained no more than an interesting theory due to the difficulties of measuring the pyramid accurately. (Early archaeologists had to content themselves with substantial quantities of rubble around the base.) Today, however, it is known that the suspicion was justified.

The man who discovered this was a Victorian newspaper editor named John Taylor. As a mathematician and amateur astronomer, he was fascinated by the pyramid's measurements and, in particular, why the builders had elected to use the angle 51 degrees 51 minutes for the faces rather than the more reasonable equilateral triangle of 60 degrees. He decided the choice was deliberate so that the faces would have an area equal to the square of the pyramid's height.

The conclusion had some interesting implications. One was that despite superficial similarities, there was no other pyramid in Egypt quite like the Great Pyramid. Once again, the mystery was why. Then Taylor discovered a second oddity. When he divided the perimeter of the pyramid by twice its height, he discovered the figure that resulted was equivalent to *pi* worked out to three decimal places.[39] In mathematics, *pi* is a constant that denotes the ratio of the circumference of any circle to its diameter. It is designated by the Greek letter "p" because it was believed to have first been discovered by Greek mathematicians long after the Great Pyramid was built, so its incorporation in the structure came as something of a surprise.

Several critics have suggested that Taylor's actual figure of 3.144 was not sufficiently accurate to be anything more than a coincidence. The known figure now is 3.14159 . . . calculated to more than 10,000 decimal points by our patient computers. But it is a curious fact that the optical proportion of the pyramid's faces—that is, the triangle you see due to perspective—gives a figure accurate to several more decimal points. If this is coincidence, it's a high one. *Pi* was not worked out to four decimal points until the sixth century AD and a further 1,000 years went by before just two decimal points were added.

Taylor himself had no doubts and in setting out to determine why *pi* had been incorporated in the pyramid, he began to wonder if the Egyptians had known that the Earth was round. On this premise he speculated that the perimeter of the pyramid might have been meant to represent the length of our planetary equator, while the height was a measure of the distance from the centre of the Earth to the pole.

In order to test his theory, he needed to know what unit of measurement had been used in the pyramid's construction. This took a lot of patient work, but he eventually concluded that the unit was a cubit of 63.5 cm or 25 inches, each inch almost equivalent to the inch used in Britain and America to this day. But the qualification "almost" is important. The actual size of the "pyramid inch" was 0.001 of an inch larger than the British inch. This gave a cubit 0.025 of an inch longer than 25 British inches. The measurement allowed Taylor to calculate that there were 365.24 cubits in the pyramid's base. Since 365.24 is the exact number of days in the solar year, Taylor declined to believe coincidence was involved here either. But his work was far from finished.

Using the measurements current in his day, Taylor discovered that his cubit was exactly one twenty-millionth the length of the polar axis. This was such an astonishing find (since it clearly indicated that the Ancient Egyptians had the ability to make planetary measurements of pinpoint accuracy) that his work was promptly dismissed as that of a crank. But, in 1957–58, satellite figures obtained during the International Geophysical Year confirmed Taylor's cubit to three decimal places.

Nevertheless Egyptologists continue to insist that the structure was simply a tomb.

A SCALE MODEL OF THE NORTHERN HEMISPHERE?

It was Flinders Petrie who discovered that the value *pi* was not only incorporated in the overall building, but in the King's Chamber as well. (The proportions of the room also showed that the ancient builders had been aware of the Golden Section and the Theorem of Pythagoras—both still tenaciously held to be Greek discoveries.)

Despite these finds, Petrie denied Taylor's earlier conclusion that the pyramid incorporated calendar measurements. But here, for once, he made an observational mistake. Each face of the structure is hollowed slightly— an effect not visible to the naked eye. By taking this into account, a Leeds engineer, David Davidson, came to some remarkable conclusions.

Although most of us think of the year in simplistic terms as 365.25 days, scientists actually work with several different "years." Among these is the orbital year (the time the Earth takes to complete a single circuit of the sun), the solar year (the time between two vernal equinoxes), and the sidereal year (the time taken by the sun to return to a specific point in its apparent journey against the background of stars). Davidson was able to show that values for the solar year (365 days 5 hours 48 minutes 46 seconds), sidereal year (365 days 6 hours 9 minutes 10 seconds) and orbital year (365 days 6 hours 13 minutes 53 seconds) were all incorporated in the pyramid.

Later calculations have also shown that the sum of the base diagonals give an approximation of the number of years in a total precession of the equinoxes (just short of 26,000). This approximation is as good as anything we have today, since there is no method of finding the figure exactly: astronomical considerations enforce an incalculable variation.

Faced with these enigmatic discoveries, Taylor and several others concluded that the Great Pyramid was built as a sort of repository for standard measurements.[40] None of them had a satisfactory explanation as to why the Egyptians took so much trouble when the measurements could have been recorded equally effectively in other ways at a fraction of the cost and effort.

Whatever the reason for its construction, the fact remains that the Great Pyramid at Giza is a stylised, but mathematically exact, scale model of the northern hemisphere. Its apex corresponds to the North Pole; its perimeter is equivalent to the equator; and its four plane surfaces accurately represent the four quadrants of the hemisphere. Claims to this effect, originally made by classical authors like Herodotus, were confirmed by fresh measurements made in 1925.

The pyramid's location exhibits two further peculiarities. It is possible to draw a specific line passing through the structure that will divide our planet into equal hemispheres of land and water. It is also possible to draw a second line that divides the planetary land mass into equal halves.

Thus we have a massive, precision-engineered model of one planetary hemisphere, exactly oriented to the car-

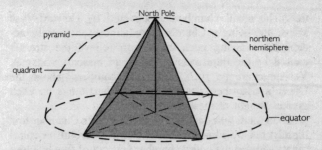

Diagram to show how the Great Pyramid is a scale model of the northern hemisphere

dinal points, built with an almost unimaginable investment of effort in what was clearly a specific location . . . and no one knows why.

Except perhaps Christopher Dunn.

THE MANY PUZZLES OF THE PYRAMID

When he began to investigate the Great Pyramid as a professional engineer, Dunn became aware of many more subtle examples of the structure's precision than its casing stones and orientation. There are, for example, small shafts leading out of both the King's and Queen's Chambers towards the exterior of the pyramid. These were once believed to be ventilation shafts, an idea now largely abandoned since they don't reach the open air. But whatever they were for, Dunn notes that, to make them, the builders had to cut the blocks at an exact angle and fit them together with exceeding care.[41] The King's Chamber northern shaft in particular presented formidable problems since it is not a straight-through cut, but veers to bypass the Grand Gallery, then veers back again.

Dunn's engineer's eye alerted him to other peculiarities. The small chambers discovered by Howard-Vyse above the King's Chamber are almost universally accepted as having been created to relieve the stresses caused by the thousands of tonnes of masonry above it. Yet there are no such "relieving chambers" above the Queen's Chamber, despite the fact that it has an even greater weight of masonry on top of it.

Then there was the damage to the King's Chamber first highlighted by Flinders Petrie. Petrie's careful measurements showed the entire chamber was out of true by close to an inch. He next observed that the massive granite beams to the south of the chamber showed every sign of having been wrenched from their original moorings. Some of them were cracked through. "On every side," Petrie wrote, "the joints of the stones have separated and the whole chamber is shaken larger."

Petrie assumed the damage had been caused by some ancient earthquake and generations of Egyptologists have agreed with him. It was left to Dunn to ask the obvious question: what sort of earthquake targets only one specific chamber in the Great Pyramid and no other?

Dunn also found himself wondering about things that had nothing to do with the engineering of the pyramid. One of the most mysterious was the thick coating of black powder discovered in the first "relieving chamber" immediately above the King's Chamber. Chemical analysis showed it to be a carbon substance and Egyptologists believe it is most likely to be the powdered remains of insect shells. But there were no insect remains found anywhere else in the pyramid, nor was there any apparent reason why thousands of insects should select this one small chamber in which to die.

Dunn eventually reached two conclusions. The first was that the orthodox tomb explanation of the Great Pyramid made no sense. The second was that any credible alternative would have to take into consideration *all* the puzzles thrown up by the structure. Major among these he listed:

Δ Why was granite—difficult to work and obtained 800 km (500 miles) away—used in the King's Chamber while the remainder of the pyramid was made almost exclusively from limestone?

Δ If the four small chambers above the King's Chamber weren't meant to relieve the weight of the masonry above, what were they meant to do?

Δ Why were huge granite monoliths used to separate these four chambers when simpler methods and materials would have done?

Δ What caused the "insect shells" in the first chamber?

Δ How was the King's Chamber damaged when the remainder of the pyramid was untouched?

Δ Why were the precision-engineered "ventilation shafts"—which weren't, of course, ever used for ventilation—actually constructed?

Δ Why was there a small, cramped antechamber to the King's Chamber?

Δ What caused the encrustations of salt on the walls of the Queen's Chamber discovered by early archaeologists?

Δ Why was there a corbelled niche cut into its eastern wall?

Δ Why was the Grand Gallery built when a simple passage would have done?

Δ What was the function of the small subterranean pit beneath the pyramid?

Δ Why did so many early explorers of the pyramid
   mention the presence of a foul smell?

Dunn was also intrigued by a discovery made by the
German engineer Rudolph Gantenbrink in 1993. Gantenbrink was the creator of Upuaut II, a robot camera and
laser pointer used to investigate the interior of the narrow
shafts leading from the Queen's Chamber. The northern
shaft turned out to be jammed by a steel tube (presumably) left by early explorers. The southern shaft ended with
a curious closure—a stone slab with two protruding copper fittings. Attention immediately focused on the slab,
which was universally referred to as a "door." Dunn found
he was far more interested in the copper fittings.

Dunn's list of mysteries was formidable, but he produced a solution that would fit them all. He decided the
Great Pyramid was built as an electrical power plant.

MAKING THE PYRAMID "SING"

If you take a quartz crystal point into a darkened room
and tap it sharply with a hammer at one end, you will see
a small spark flash from the other. The process that produces the spark is known as the piezo-electric effect.
Quartz has a natural ability to transform kinetic energy
(in this case the hammer blow) into electricity (the spark).

Although few people realise it, granite contains surprisingly large quantities of quartz. In Aswan granite,
quartz content runs as high as 55 per cent. The King's
Chamber and its four "relieving chambers" are constructed exclusively from Aswan granite.

Generations of tourists have noted that there are curious acoustics in the King's Chamber. It seems to amplify
even the softest, whispered conversations. And the granite
sarcophagus in the chamber rings like a bell when struck.

In March 1979, two American investigators, Rocky McCollum and Bill Cox, conducted musical resonance tests within the King's Chamber. Cox discovered that the entire chamber resonated sharply to an harmonic of 256 cycles per second. McCollum confirmed the vibratory effect not just in the chamber generally, but also in the granite sarcophagus.

After several experiments and considerable calculations, they concluded they had discovered a "master frequency" in the chamber of 640 cycles per second and concluded that the structure was deliberately constructed to this resonance, since a 640-cycle note produces a wavelength exactly equal in length to the Egyptian cubit—something they refused to believe was the result of pure chance. In a paper on their findings, McCollum observes that resonance is influenced by the nature of the gas through which a vibration travels.[42]

Christopher Dunn also refuses to believe that the resonances in the King's Chamber are accidental. He sees it as the heart of a massive energy generator in which every known feature of the structure plays an important part. His thesis, stripped of its technicalities, is as follows.

The Great Pyramid at Giza was designed to vibrate like a tuning fork. What we call the Queen's Chamber was actually a hydrogen generator. The corbelled niche inside was originally equipped with a cooling/evaporator tower. Chemicals—probably hydrated zinc chloride and hydrochloric acid—were introduced into the chamber through the northern and southern shafts. The reaction of these two chemicals produced hydrogen gas. Signs of the process remain in the (different) discoloration of the two shafts and the residue salts found on the Queen's Chamber walls. Any chemical waste flowed out of the chamber to drain down what is now called the Well Shaft into the subterranean chamber cut into the bedrock deep beneath the pyramid. The hydrogen gas rose to fill the Grand Gallery and the King's Chamber.

Tuned "Helmholtz" resonators set in the Grand Gallery took up the vibration of the structure as a whole and converted it into audible sound. (A Helmholtz resonator is a hollow short-necked sphere that has a single isolated resonant frequency and no other resonances below about ten times that frequency. These characteristics made it useful for the study of musical tones before the development of electronic analysers.) By means of these resonators the Great Pyramid began to "sing." The sound was focused through the passage leading to the King's Chamber, but only harmonics in sympathy with its basic resonance were allowed to reach the chamber itself. This was achieved by a series of filter baffles set in the antechamber.

When the sound reached the chamber with its positioned "sarcophagus," a massive, rhythmic heartbeat began. As Cox and McCollum have confirmed, specific sound frequencies caused the entire granite King's Chamber to vibrate. The whole design was aimed at minimising any natural dampening so that the vibration built dramatically. The moving granite created massive stresses in its component quartz. The piezo-electric effect generated an electron flow. Electrical energy began to be produced and was taken up by the hydrogen that filled the entire pyramid.

At this point, Egyptian astronomical knowledge came into play. The northern shaft of the King's Chamber was opened to become a conduit for the microwave signal contained in the cosmic radiation constantly bombarding our planet. This signal is created by atomic hydrogen, the reason why the Egyptians elected to use hydrogen gas as the carrier for their electrical energy in the first place. The signal, possibly amplified at some point in its passage, reacted with the energised hydrogen, causing a release of energy at the same frequency as the input. The realised energy was then beamed out of the pyramid along a track parallel to the input signal.

From an engineering perspective, a machine of this sort would work. We know the Egyptians were capable of building it, because they *did* build it. Recent finds suggest they had chemical knowledge of sufficient sophistication to create the hydrogen.

Even small details fit into the picture. The copper fittings in Gantenbrink's "door" may have functioned as sensors detecting when sufficient chemical solution had been added to the Queen's Chamber. According to Dunn, the chemicals themselves account for the bad smell that lingered in the structure. The damage specific to the King's Chamber could have arisen from a massive, accidental hydrogen explosion—which would also account for the black powder in the chamber above: not insect shells at all, but calcium carbonate "cooked" out of the core limestone.

Only one question remained for Dunn. How did the Egyptians persuade the Great Pyramid to vibrate?

SYMPATHETIC RESONANCE

If you set a pendulum swinging beside a second, similar but unmoving pendulum, the second pendulum will eventually begin to swing of its own accord. The phenomenon is known as sympathetic resonance and occurs because no object is completely static, however still it appears. Everything is subject to tiny, random motions generated by passing traffic, ambient sound, etc. These motions are known as "free vibrations."

Sympathetic resonance occurs when what's called the driving frequency—in this case the swinging pendulum—approaches the frequency of the static object. The result is a rapid take-up of energy, with an attendant growth in the amplitude of the vibration. Thus the static pendulum begins to swing.

The phenomenon is not confined to pendulums. Every artefact and natural object has its specific frequency and hence is theoretically subject to sympathetic resonance—although in practice only certain things will take it up to a noticeable degree. The amplitude of a sympathetic vibration does not, of course, increase indefinitely. It is limited by natural damping but, even so, the response can be very great. This is why soldiers marching across a bridge can set up sympathetic vibrations powerful enough to destroy it, just as opera singers can shatter wine glasses by creating a driving frequency with the right note.

In *The Giza Power Plant*, Christopher Dunn postulated that the Great Pyramid was constructed as a scale model of the northern hemisphere and located at its precisely balanced spot so that it might be subject to the driving frequency of the Earth itself. At the time he wrote his book—1998—the idea that our world might *have* a driving frequency was somewhat speculative. But in January 1999, *The Times* reported that a team led by Dr. Naoki Suda of Japan's Nagoya University had made a puzzling discovery.

For reasons scientists have yet to fathom, our planet vibrates with a steady hum below the level of human hearing.

CHAPTER 10

BROADCAST POWER

IF there is a weak link in Christopher Dunn's chain of logic, it involves the distribution of the electricity generated by his Giza power plant. Our own civilisation is heavily dependent on electrical power and anyone—in the Western world at least—can see the means of distribution by looking through the window. Unsightly pylons march across our countryside, while cables snake into every home, factory and office. We use so much wiring in this massive system that we have seriously depleted the copper reserves of the planet. If the Egyptians had anything remotely similar, one would expect traces of it to emerge in archaeological digs across the country. But even at the Great Pyramid nothing has been found to suggest a cable-based distribution.

Yet, looking at the evidence of powered tools and other machinery, it is clear that they must have had some form of distribution. So, is it possible that the Egyptians developed a different system? Dunn declined to speculate in the first printing of his book, but plans to deal with the question in a subsequent edition. He suspects the Egyptians may have used a form of distribution similar to that discovered by Nikola Tesla (one of the great pioneers of electrical technology), but never put to wide commercial use.

THE INVENTION OF ALTERNATING CURRENT

Tesla was born around midnight on 9 July 1856, in the Croatian village of Smiljan. His parents were Serbs and his father was an Orthodox priest.

In his second year at the Polytechnic School at Gratz in Austria, the school received a Gramoe Dynamo from Paris and Tesla watched fascinated while the professor demonstrated its use. The machine was slightly faulty and its metallic brushes sparked wildly. Tesla began to wonder if it would be possible to eliminate the problem by making a version of the dynamo without brushes at all. His professor assured him the idea was in the same category as perpetual motion, but Tesla wrestled with it throughout the remainder of his time at Gratz. It was this work that led him to develop his ideas about the practical use of alternating current.

In 1880, he moved on to the University of Prague where progress on his new-style dynamo was interrupted by a massive nervous breakdown which left him so highly sensitised that he could hear a fly landing on a table as "a dull thud in my ear." He recovered eventually and one afternoon, while walking with a friend in Budapest City Park, a passage from Goethe's *Faust* brought him to such a pitch of inspiration that he had a vivid mental vision of a wholly new type of brushless dynamo—a solution to the problem with which he had wrestled for so many years. It involved a rotating magnetic field and ran on alternating current.

Two years later, Tesla went to work in Paris for the

Continental Edison Company. It was the first step in a career that was to thrust him into the very forefront of the developing use of electricity and eventually lead him to be described as "the man who invented the twentieth century."

In 1883, he was sent to Strasbourg in Germany to sort out some serious problems with a lighting plant installed at the new railway station there. (A short circuit had blown out part of the wall and alarmed the German Emperor when he attended the official opening.) Tesla was promised substantial monetary reward if he succeeded. Germany did not suit Tesla. He found the red tape and official attitudes infuriating. None the less, he did the job he was sent to do and even managed to find time to construct his first induction motor, working after-hours.

By the spring of 1884, the lighting plant was accepted as functional by the German government and Tesla returned to Paris where the promised compensation for his efforts turned into an official runaround. In a fit of pique he resigned from his job, liquidated his modest assets and sailed for America. Somewhere en route he lost both his tickets and his money with the result that he arrived in New York with a pocketful of poems, plans for a flying machine and 4 cents in cash.

Despite these setbacks, he had lost none of his ingenuity and set out to make an impression on Thomas Edison, America's foremost electrical pioneer. Edison's company had installed a lighting system in the S.S. *Oregon*, the fastest passenger ship of its day, but around the time Tesla arrived in New York the system failed and sailing was delayed. Since the *Oregon*'s superstructure had been completed after the electrical installation, the machinery had to be repaired *in situ*, something that was causing massive problems for Edison's engineers. Tesla strolled on to the ship one evening, worked through the night and at five o'clock next morning was able to tell

Edison the repair was complete. Edison offered him employment as his assistant.

It was an uneasy relationship and when, for the second time, a promised bonus for work done failed to materialise, Tesla resigned. But his inventiveness was already attracting attention and he was approached almost immediately by backers who wanted him to form his own arc light company. He perfected an arc lamp system for use in factories and municipal lighting, and in April 1887 the Tesla Electric Company was formally incorporated with sufficient funds for a laboratory and workshop facilities. Tesla promptly forgot all about arc lights and set to work building the alternating current motor that had obsessed him since his student days.

The components went together exactly as he had visualised, and by 1888 an arrangement had been made with the Westinghouse Electric Company in Pittsburgh for large-scale manufacture. George Westinghouse bought the patent rights to Tesla's entire polyphase system of AC dynamos, transformers and motors, thus beginning a massive industrial struggle between Westinghouse and Edison.

Up to that point, Edison, in common with all the electrical pioneers of the day, had worked with direct current, a flow of electrical charge that does not change direction—the sort we still draw from batteries and fuel cells today. Alternating current, by contrast, is an electrical flow that reverses according to a set cycle. It might, for example, begin at zero, grow to a maximum, return to zero, then reverse, until it reaches its maximum in the opposite direction . . . then repeat the whole process indefinitely. The number of cycles per second is known as the frequency of the current. Normal domestic power operates on a low frequency—around 50 or 60 cycles per second—but vastly higher frequencies are now routinely used in television, radar and microwave communications.

Today AC electricity systems are so ubiquitous that few people imagine the power grids of our world ever ran any other way. Yet, for a time in the 1880s, the widespread use of AC electricity was by no means a foregone conclusion. Direct current is an extremely safe form of electricity—you can't electrocute yourself by gripping the terminals of a battery—and Edison, who had invested heavily in its development, was quick to brand AC a death trap. But until the 1960s, it was uneconomical to transform direct current into the high voltages needed for long-distance transmission. This cost factor, more than any other, led to the widespread adoption of alternating current despite the perceived safety hazards.

In a few years, alternating current was powering industry and lighting homes throughout the United States and later throughout the world. It became the driving force behind virtually every technical breakthrough of the twentieth century.

TESLA'S PUBLIC PROFILE

Although Tesla was an engineering genius, his business acumen left a great deal to be desired. Throughout his life, he continued to develop techniques, systems and devices that were nothing short of revolutionary, but routinely sold off the patents for a fraction of their real worth. The result was not only that he died in poverty, but also that the general public quickly forgot the massive contribution he had made to the development of modern technology. In 1915, despite widespread expectations, he failed to win a Nobel Prize and while, two years later, he received the highest honour that the American Institute of Electrical Engineers could bestow, it bore the name of his old employer. Tesla was handed the Edison Medal.

In the intervening years, Tesla's public profile has diminished even further. While the average schoolchild has definitely heard of Edison, very few could name a single one of Tesla's vital inventions. Following his death in 1943, an even more unfortunate development occurred. Tesla's life and works attracted a cult following who have since credited him with guidance from extra-terrestrials and the invention of all sorts of fantastic machinery, proof of which they say has been suppressed by various governments. Since there is just enough basis in reality to keep such speculation alive—Tesla *did* develop remarkable machines and once believed he had detected an intelligent radio signal from outer space—it has become increasingly difficult to take his name seriously.

Yet there is not the slightest doubt that he can and should be taken seriously. The list of his verified achievements is positively awesome:

Δ He experimented with shadowgraphs similar to those used by Wilhelm Röntgen when he discovered X rays in 1895.

Δ He worked on a type of arc light known as a carbon button lamp.

Δ He experimented with electrical resonance, and various different types of lighting.

Δ He gave exhibitions in his laboratory during which he lit lamps by allowing electricity to flow through his own body. (These demonstrations were a typically flamboyant response to Edison's allegations that AC electricity was dangerous.)

Δ In 1891, he invented the Tesla coil, still widely used today in radios, television sets and other electronic equipment.

Δ His system was used to light the World's First Colombian Exposition at Chicago in 1893.

Δ He won the contract to install the first power machinery at Niagara Falls—machinery which bore his name and patent numbers.

Δ In 1898 he announced his invention of a remote-controlled boat and proved his claims before a crowd in Madison Square Gardens.

In 1900 (as Marconi filed his famous wireless patent and fully a year before he conducted his experiments in long-range radio transmission), Tesla was already involved in the construction of the world's first broadcasting station based on discoveries he had made twelve months earlier. The station, located on New York's Long Island, was funded by the financier J. Pierpont Morgan.

Tesla secured Morgan's $150,000 loan by assigning 51 per cent of his patent rights in telephone and telegraph systems to the financier. Together they planned to provide worldwide communications, including, astoundingly, facilities for broadcasting pictures. Experts are agreed that Tesla had developed the technology to do it all, but the project was abandoned because of a financial crisis and labour problems, which led to Morgan withdrawing support.

With the collapse of his pet project, Tesla shifted his attention to other matters. But lack of funding ensured that his ideas never got further than his notebooks. He began a long slow decline. Throughout his life he had been prey to serious illness and now developed a progressive phobia of germs. He took to making grandiose statements about the possibility of communicating with other planets or the fact that he had invented a death ray capable of destroying 10,000 aeroplanes at a distance of 380 km (240 miles).

At first editors were inclined to take him seriously,

given his incredible track record, but when he claimed that one of his new developments would enable him to "split the Earth in two like an apple," he was quietly relegated to the lunatic fringe. All the same, engineers to this day continue to consult his papers for clues that might help them solve problems. In certain areas, Tesla is still taken very seriously indeed.

HARNESSING LIGHTNING

In the early months of 1899, when funds were at a low ebb, Tesla was approached by Leonard E. Curtis, of the Colorado Springs Electric Company, who offered him land and "all the electric power he needed" if he would locate his laboratory at Colorado Springs. Tesla was agreeable, but had no cash. Then his close friend John J. Astor, owner of the Waldorf-Astoria Hotel, advanced him $30,000. A temporary laboratory was built and Tesla moved in during May of that year. With him came some lab workers and an engineering associate named Fritz Lowenstein.

At this point in his career, Tesla was focusing on a unique area of research—the transmission of electrical power without the use of wires. While he waited for the necessary equipment to be built, he began a series of experiments with lightning. He was determined that if he *could* design a working wireless power transmission system, it would be capable of carrying millions of volts. Only lightning generated the sort of energy he needed.

He was in the right place for it. The mountainous area of Colorado where the new laboratory was located was subject to frequent electrical storms, generating lightning bolts of enormous intensity. Tesla quickly learned a great deal about the phenomenon, not all of it welcome—on one occasion a lightning strike almost destroyed his newly built laboratory. Tesla patiently rebuilt it.

The experimental station was a barn-like structure nearly 30 m (100 ft) square. From the middle of a 7.6 m (25 ft) high roof rose a wooden pyramid nearly 24 m (80 ft) above the ground. A 60 m (200 ft) high mast with a 90 cm (3 ft) diameter copper ball on top rose from the centre of the pyramid. A heavy-duty cable connected the mast to the apparatus inside the lab. Clearly Tesla was thinking big . . . and not just in the size of his equipment. His plan to broadcast electricity involved setting up vibrations in the structure of our entire planet.

Among the technical problems Tesla initially faced was whether or not the Earth was electrically charged. If not, it would absorb enormous amounts of electricity before it could be made to vibrate. But he discovered, to his relief, that the planet was indeed electrically charged—and to an extremely high potential. It also seemed to have some natural mechanism for maintaining its voltage.

It was while he was working on this problem that he made another discovery.

On 3 July, a violent storm broke to the west of the Colorado lab. After spending much of its fury in the mountains, it moved away over the plains. Huge arcs of lightning flashed almost incessantly. Tesla recorded the power surges on his instruments and noted how they faded to nothing as the storm moved further and further away. This, of course, was exactly the pattern common sense would tell you to expect. But Tesla, on the basis of earlier observations, suspected otherwise.

He waited, watching his instruments. Sure enough, in a little while they started to show indications of the storm again, growing stronger and stronger, despite the fact that the storm itself was still moving away. The instrument readings peaked, then faded back to nothing . . . only to begin again a little later. After watching the pattern recur again and again, Tesla came to the only possible conclusion: he was observing traces of stationary waves generated by the storm. This meant the planet itself was behaving like an electrical conductor.

It was a breakthrough discovery for his ongoing research. Tesla subsequently explained: "Not only was it practicable to send telegraphic messages to any distance without wires, as I recognized long ago, but also to impress upon the entire globe the faint modulations of the human voice, far more still, to transmit power, in unlimited amounts to any terrestrial distance and almost without loss."[43]

Tesla quickly arranged to duplicate the storm conditions artificially, planning to create man-made lightning at the top of his 60 m (200 ft) mast. He succeeded only too well. After generating lightning bolts 40 m (135 ft) long and creating thunder that could be heard 24 km (15 miles) away, he short-circuited the industrial power plant that was supplying him with electricity.

PLANETARY RESONANCE

What Tesla did that day at Colorado Springs was truly spectacular. His artificial lightning was generated by causing an electrical vibration in the Earth itself. This was achieved by pumping electricity into it with a rhythmic pulse. A resonance set up and, like soldiers marching across a bridge, the results were out of all proportion to the input. Moving waves expanded outward from Colorado Springs in ever-increasing circles until they passed over the bulge of the Earth. The waves then diminished in size, but increased in intensity, until they converged at a point between the Indian and Antarctic Oceans, directly opposite Colorado Springs on the other side of the planet.

This had the effect of building up an enormous electrical south pole, marked by a high-amplitude wave rising and falling in unison with Tesla's apparatus thousands of miles away in America. An electrical echo was returned to produce the same effect at Colorado Springs, causing the process to repeat and resonance to build up on a global scale.

Had the Earth been a perfect conductor, the resonance would have built up to such a degree that charged particles of matter would have been hurled outward with such force that the whole planet would have disintegrated. Fortunately the Earth is not a perfect conductor and pure resonance remains unattainable.

Tesla realised that once the Earth was set in oscillation an energy source was created everywhere on its surface. All that was required to draw it off was a relatively simple apparatus consisting of a tuning coil, a condenser, a ground connection and a metal aerial no higher than a house. This equipment would, in theory, allow electricity to be "beamed" into homes and factories with no intervening wires whatsoever.

Aware that theory and practice were two different things, Tesla set out to test his new discovery and succeeded in lighting 200 Edison lamps—10,000 watts of combined power—without wires, at a distance of 42 km (26 miles). It was this demonstration that persuaded J. P. Morgan to fund the abortive Long Island station which, it was hoped, would broadcast not only sound, pictures and messages, but eventually electrical power as well.

No one had succeeded in duplicating Tesla's achievements at Colorado Springs. He took no one into his confidence about the technical details while he lived and left no written records when he died. But the fact remains that this East European genius showed conclusively that broadcast power is possible.

Since Tesla's approach was based on the same principles of resonance that Christopher Dunn believes were used in the Great Pyramid, it seems possible that the Ancient Egyptians got there millennia before him.

If so, it may not be their only scientific achievement in advance of our own.

CHAPTER 11

EGYPTIAN MAGIC

EGYPT'S reputation as the sorcerous capital of our planet was well established in historical times. According to Sir E. A. Wallis Budge, onetime Keeper of Egyptian Antiquities at the British Museum, there was no land in the ancient world more renowned for magic. Magical interest and practice permeated the entire social structure. There was scarcely a man, woman or child who did not wear some sort of charm. Belief in the effectiveness of spells was universal.

Much Egyptian sorcery was the sort you would expect. For example, archaeologists have found wands carved from hippopotamus tusks and used to ward off poisonous snakes. Clearly this was a form of sympathetic magic which assumed that the great strength of the hippo would somehow frighten away the venomous reptiles.

An Egyptian text called *The Dream Tome* would not be out of place in the occult section of a modern bookshop. It listed many dreams and their meanings, categorising them in terms of good or bad omens. Dream of carving up a female hippo and you were due to receive a large meal from the palace. Dream of drinking warm beer and suffering was on the way—a sentiment that will be appreciated by beer drinkers to this day. Other texts described the portents of the day so that special calendars could be drawn up to guide people in their activities, rather like the horoscopes that feature in our daily papers.

Banned from the great temples of their state religion (which was administered exclusively by an initiate priesthood), the common people established shrines to household deities like Taweret and Bes. The former was a pregnant hippopotamus concerned, reasonably enough, with fertility and childbirth. The latter was a bandy-legged dwarf, a cross between a man and a lion, whose job was to attract happiness and protect from evil. Both appeared on plaques and amulets small enough to be worn or attached to objects that might benefit from their power.

But some experts are convinced that popular superstition and religious observance are only part of the story.

SCIENCE OR MAGIC?

In 1979, Bill Cox, the President of America's Life Understanding Foundation (an organisation, incorporated in 1976, dedicated to the study of ancient knowledge), delivered a paper on "Ancient Egyptian Technology" to a conference of the United States Psychotronic Association at the University of Houston in Texas. The thrust of his lecture was the "striking similarities between modern devices and ancient Egyptian hieroglyphs, trappings and . . . garments worn by royalty and the priesthood."

His audience listened enthralled as he presented example after example of Egyptian art, compared with modern drawings and photographs. At one point, hieroglyphic symbols were set beside a schematic diagram of the wiring for a battery-operated telephone, showing several identical elements. Cox went on to analyse the ubiquitous djed pillar, the looped cross or *ankh* (which the Egyptians used as a symbol of the life force), and various receptacles, items of headgear, carvings and hieroglyphs which, he claimed, could represent the use of electronic, sonic and electromagnetic equipment in Ancient Egypt. In many cases, this "equipment" was depicted being used in a "magical" context.

The British science fiction writer Arthur C. Clarke is said to have commented that "any sufficiently high technology is indistinguishable from magic." If, as seems to be the case, Ancient Egypt was capable of generating and using electricity, this may have been enough to attract its reputation for sorcerous power. It might even be that the Egyptians considered electricity a magical energy.

There is a language problem here. Until the Rosetta Stone was discovered in 1799, hieroglyphics were a closed book to Egyptologists. But even afterwards, difficulties arose in translation. For years, Egypt's highly developed science of astronomy was obscured by religious terminology. What scholars took to be mythic stories of the gods were actually accurate descriptions of planetary and stellar movements. To the Egyptians, heaven and the heavens were synonymous, gods and stars were one. The same problem has arisen in biblical references to the Ark of the Covenant. The real nature of this weapon was disguised down the centuries by the language used to describe it.

Although engineers suspect the carvings at Dendera (see page 105) depict electrical devices, they are devices operated by priests and associated with Atum-Ra, the sun god. An ape, traditionally associated in Egyptian religion with Thoth, the god of magic and communication, is also shown in one panel, underlining the fact that the Egyptians routinely used spiritual, religious or magical symbolism to describe what may well have been scientific activities. This means that, while much Egyptian "magic" never rose above the level of superstition, some of it may well have referred to electrical technology.

But for Bill Cox, electrical and sonic equipment in Ancient Egypt was almost hackneyed. Two years before the Houston conference, and in various papers since then, he has made it clear that his most enduring interest is what he believes to be the Egyptian use of psychotronics. This interest has been partly fuelled by some strange developments in eastern Europe.

WHAT IS PSYCHOTRONICS?

The term *psychotronics* was coined in Czechoslovakia during the 1960s. With the country then part of the Soviet Union and a Communist government in power that looked with huge suspicion on anything that smacked of religion or the occult, Czechoslovakian scientists interested in psychical phenomena were becoming desperate for recognition and funding. The introduction of the new name for their speciality—replacing the more familiar *parapsychology*—would, it was hoped, help to generate a more sympathetic climate.

The move worked. Within months of its introduction, the "new" field of psychotronics was attracting serious scientific attention. But the change of name also introduced a change of focus. Although a broad spectrum of research continued, Dr. Zdenek Rejdak, the Scientific Secretary of the Czechoslovak Co-ordination Committee for Research in Telepathy, Telegnosis and Psychokinesis, was moved to define his speciality in these terms: "Psychotronics is, in essence, the bionics of man. We're trying to study the psi phenomenon *in* man and secondly as an energy of its own."[44]

This definition was an early indication of a new way

of thinking. By 1968, Rejdak's group had issued a manifesto at the International Parapsychology Conference in Moscow proposing the existence of a hitherto undiscovered form of energy—inevitably referred to as "psychotronic energy'—which acted as the carrier for paranormal phenomena like telepathy, clairvoyance, psychokinesis and psychic healing. Rejdak reported that his team was trying to discover the nature of psychotronic energy and then isolate it so that it could be controlled and put to use.

Two American travel writers, Sheila Ostrander and Lynn Schroeder, who managed to get permission to visit the Soviet Union at the height of the Cold War, reported back on just how well the Czechs had succeeded in harnessing psychotronic energy. They were the first Westerners to see a Pavlita generator.

Pavlita generators are one of a whole category of contrivances that work without anyone having the slightest idea why.

MIRACULOUS MACHINES

A patent is a government grant of the exclusive right to make, use or sell an invention. It is typically issued, for a limited period, to new and useful machines, products or industrial processes and can also be granted for significant improvements to existing inventions. Patents usually last between sixteen and twenty years.

In most countries—and certainly in the United States—patents are granted only after the invention has been rigorously examined by trained inspectors. They ensure that no conflicting patent has already been granted and, more importantly, that the invention actually performs as claimed. Such inspectors are hard-headed individuals. There is no room in the Patent Office for flights of fancy masquerading as technological breakthroughs. If a patent is granted, one may be certain that the invention actually works.

On 27 September 1949, the United States Patent Office granted Patent No. 2,482,773 to Dr. Thomas Galen Hieronymous of Lakemont, Georgia, in respect of an electrical machine he had developed. The apparatus was also examined by British and Canadian patent authorities, both of whom also decided it was a workable device.

The machine was built around a broad-band voltage amplifier. In its original form, it was made using vacuum tubes and soldered wire connections. It was designed for the detection and analysis of metals or minerals, specifically as components of various alloys. If, for example, you were sold a gold brick that you had reason to believe might be fake, you could use a Hieronymous machine to determine its actual metal content.

Although patent applications are a tedious and often costly process, Dr. Hieronymous did not, so far as I am aware, put his device into commercial production. Or if he did, it was not a widespread success. One reason may have been a curious characteristic of the machine itself. While it worked effectively and consistently for most people, about 20 per cent of those who tried it could not persuade it to work at all.

This was not because the device was particularly complicated to operate. You simply place your test sample near a pick-up coil, tune the machine using a single control, and read the results with your fingertips on a detection plate, which changes its feel if the specific metal is present. None the less, for some people nothing at all happened. However diligently they followed the instructions, they could not operate the machine.

One man who *could* operate it was the American author and editor John W. Campbell Jr, who had a strong

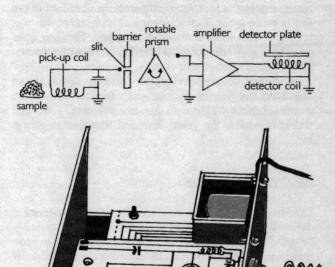

Block diagram of Hieronymous machine (above) and sketch of the inside showing the position of the prism and amplifier board (below)

interest in scientific discoveries. Campbell was intrigued by the machine's inexplicable "failure rate" and set out to test it using a broad cross-section of volunteers. He was hoping to find some common denominator between those for whom it would not work. During the tests he discovered something utterly bizarre.

A student volunteer set up the machine, tuned it and began his analysis of various test samples. The device worked perfectly. Then, to his astonishment, Campbell suddenly noticed the young man had forgotten to plug it in.

ELOPTIC RADIATION

Dr. Hieronymous, who invented the device, believed it detected a hitherto unrecognised radiation—he called it "eloptic"—emitted from metals and minerals. This radiation was initially picked up by an external coil which fed it to a terminal inside the casing of the machine. It was then refracted through a rotating prism to be picked up by another probe. From there, the signal was transmitted through an amplifier to a detector plate which comprised a wire coil underneath a glass plate.

Despite the conviction of the inventor, scientists have been slow to buy into the concept of "eloptic radiation." Their problem is expressed bluntly by engineer G. Harry Stine, who explains that radiation is a specifically defined physical phenomenon with specific characteristics "involving wave-length, frequency, propagation speed, energy content, ability to function either as a particle or a wave, and precisely defined relationship with matter." He continues by saying that radiation "may also behave in accordance with the principles of quantum mechanics. The principles of 'eloptic radiation' conflict with many of these known, proven and *used* principles of radiation."[45]

Stine also remarked that aspects of the machine made little sense in relation to standard physics.

But if the principles behind the machine remained obscure, John W. Campbell had little doubt that it was a conventional electronic gadget. During the year he had worked intensively with the device (1955–56), it had ceased to function when one of the vacuum tubes burned out, when the glass on the detection plate broke and when one of the soldered connections came loose. In other words, it behaved like normal electronic equipment.

Except that now it was working with no electrical input whatsoever.

Campbell might have been tempted to ignore the mystery, plug the machine back in and carry on as if nothing had happened. After all, an electronic detector that works without electricity is almost too weird for words. But in the event he remained true to his scientific training. First, he determined that the device *really was* functioning without electrical input by ruling out possibilities like static build up. Then he ran further tests to ensure that it would indeed continue to function without electricity. It did. The incident with the student volunteer was not a one-off.

Finally, he set out to find an explanation.

THE RELATIONSHIP BETWEEN THE PARTS

When a stage magician prepares to astound his audience, he often makes use of a technique known as "misdirection." That's to say, he acts in such a way that the watchers' attention is diverted away from the solution to the trick. After long, careful consideration, Campbell decided that the appearance of a Hieronymous machine—which masquerades as an electrical device—had to be an example of misdirection. Faced with an apparatus consisting of valves (later transistors) and circuits, it is only natural to assume that it must work on electronic principles. But clearly this was not the case. No machine that works on electronic principles can function without a power supply.

It is a regrettable fact that the majority of scientists and engineers faced with a device like the Hieronymous machine instinctively seek refuge in denial. They are perfectly well aware from their knowledge of electronics that such a machine *cannot* work. Consequently they decide that it *does* not work . . . and in many instances refuse to investigate it at all. Campbell side-stepped this common trap. He had seen the machine in action. He had used it himself. Since, despite all appearances, it could not be an electronic device, the machine had to work some other way.

Campbell's instinct was that the relationship between the various parts somehow functioned as a thing-in-itself. In other words, it was the relationship between the parts that made the machine work, not the parts themselves.

The theory made sense of a sort. If it was the relationship between the parts that was important, not the parts themselves, then electrical power became irrelevant. The machine should work equally well with or without it. But a broken plate, or a burned-out valve (which lacks a complete filament), or a loose connection would all be expected to influence performance since they each changed the original relationship to a greater or lesser degree.

This is a difficult idea to grasp, not because it is complex, but because it runs contrary to all our expectations. We expect machinery to work in a certain way so we look for explanations within that familiar context. When an explanation falls outside it, we have problems. There was an additional problem with Campbell's intuitive hypothesis. Absolutely nothing in orthodox physics had ever led anyone to believe that relationships could be seen rationally as things-in-themselves, let alone produce concrete results like metal analysis.

Nonetheless, Campbell decided to put his theory to the test. He constructed a Hieronymous machine in which the soldered circuits were replaced by a wiring diagram.

The machine still worked . . .

All this begins to sound like the sort of joke engineers like to play on new apprentices (when they're set to fetch glass hammers or other unlikely instruments). But there's much worse to come.

In 1957 Harry Stine, the engineer quoted earlier with regard to radiation, built his own version of a symbolic Hieronymous machine following instructions published by Campbell. His components were a dial, plate and coil identical to those used in a standard machine, a triangle of clear plastic replacing the prism of the original and a circuit diagram carefully inked on to white card. There was nothing in his entire engineering background to make him think that this hotchpotch could possibly detect anything. But, like Campbell's prototype, it worked perfectly.

Until, that is, his symbolic "batteries" went dead after several years of use. He had to re-ink them on the diagram to get the device running again.

CHAPTER 12

PSYCHOTRONICS TODAY

WHEN Sheila Ostrander and Lynn Schroeder, authors of *Psychic Discoveries Behind the Iron Curtain*, visited Czechoslovakia in the 1960s what they saw was, if anything, even more bizarre than the Hieronymous machine. "We were," they reported, "confronted with a gallery of objects—burnished and gleaming, rough and pebbled, steel, bronze, copper, iron, gold—'psychotronic generators' that do the impossible."[46]

These devices had been inspired, they were told, by archaic manuscripts and forgotten discoveries. They noticed at once that the collection included forms resembling the *ankh* (or looped cross) and the pyramid commonly associated with Ancient Egypt.

PAVLITA GENERATORS

When Ostrander and Schroeder first saw this collection of Pavlita generators, Robert Pavlita himself was in his mid-fifties, the design director of a Czech textile plant. He had been interested in the subtle use of energies since his twenties. Thirty years of research had taken him into several strange pathways, including a study of Ancient Egypt.

Several scenes depicted in tomb paintings and wall engravings intrigued him, as they have intrigued other engineers. A common representation of a priest offering a libation to Osiris, for example, shows the track of something emerging from a container and arching upwards over the god's head. A similar scene appears in a tomb at Thebes where the contents of a pot arc over the head of a mummy. Egyptologists routinely assume that what's shown emerging from the containers is liquid.

Bill Cox points out that, if this was so, the track of the liquid—which remains remarkably consistent in pictures of this sort—defies the laws of gravity, unless the liquid is pressurised . . . and this, given the containers shown, requires a source of energy. But there are doubts about whether liquid really is being depicted. The mummification process used in Egypt was designed to extract all moisture from a body and the last thing a servant would have done was pour liquid on a mummy.

If not liquid, then what? Cox speculates that the Egyptians were actually indicating energy tracks or energy fields. Robert Pavlita went further. He decided to see if some of the devices depicted might generate some sort of subtle energy in their own right.

It took him a long time to prove his point. He quickly discovered that it was nowhere near enough to create, say, a sculptured *ankh* and hope that some sort of energy would manifest automatically. The metal—or, more often, specific combination of metals—proved important and even then the device had to be properly primed in order to be any use at all. Nonetheless, he persevered, driven by what amounted to an obsession. Eventually he created a device that produced observable results.

Pavlita took his machine to Hradec Králové University

near Prague and persuaded a physicist there to put it to the test. The results were so dramatic that, within days, the entire physics department was involved. What Pavlita had carried in was a sealed metal box, through which passed a shaft attached to a small electric motor underneath. When the motor was switched on, the shaft revolved. The only other part of the machine was a small, shaped metal object in one corner of the box. This object wasn't attached to anything and did not seem to have any function whatsoever.

For their tests, the scientists balanced a T-shaped piece of copper on the top of the shaft. When the motor was switched on, the shaft rotated and so, predictably enough, did the T-shaped copper. A high-speed automatic camera kept track of the number of rotations.

Pavlita positioned himself about 2 m (6 ft) from the device and stared at it. After a moment, the copper T slowed, and then stopped, even though the motor was still running and the shaft still rotating. As the startled scientists watched dumbfounded, the copper actually began to spin in the opposite direction to the rotating shaft—an apparent impossibility.

The test caused a sensation in research circles, but was gravely marred by misreporting. Almost without exception, scientists assumed that what had been demonstrated was Robert Pavlita's natural ability as a psychokinetic medium—someone capable of exerting a purely mental influence on the physical world.

It was an easy mistake to make. From 1959 until his death in 1966, Dr. Leonid L. Vasiliev, a pioneer of Soviet psychical research, had conducted an intensive experimental programme in two research laboratories he had founded in Leningrad (now St. Petersburg). One of the most spectacular aspects of the programme was his work with a woman he referred to in his reports as Nelya Mikhailova. Her real name, revealed after her death, was Nina Kulagina.

Kulagina was a plump, dark-haired, dark-eyed woman with attractive Slavic features and an extraordinary "psychic" talent. She was able, on demand and under laboratory conditions, to move things with her mind.

This went far beyond any statistical effect. Kulagina could move matches, cigarettes, pieces of bread, even an apple. A journalist who interviewed her was treated to the spectacle of his lunchtime sandwich crawling across the table. Soviet scientists reported that she had successfully halted the pendulum on a wall clock . . . then started it up again. She had moved cups, dishes, glasses, plastic cases and even a water jug that was fully 450 g (1 lb) in weight.

After extensive experimentation, the Soviet scientific establishment was satisfied that Kulagina's ability was genuine. Dr. Ya Terietsky, who held the Chair of Theoretical Physics at Moscow University, went public in *Pravda* in March 1968 with the blunt statement that she "displayed a new and unknown form of energy." The Czechs naturally concluded that Robert Pavlita was exhibiting a similar natural talent.

But Pavlita was doing nothing of the sort. The small metal shape, forgotten in the corner of the sealed box, was the world's first functioning psychotronic generator—or at least the *modern* world's first functioning psychotronic generator. It was this device that allowed Pavlita to demonstrate his "impossible" effect.

PSYCHOKINESIS IN ACTION

Since that day, a great deal of experimentation has quietly taken place to determine the reality of mental influence on matter. In 1984, for example, three groups of Hungarian students from high schools in Szerencs and Budapest spent the month of December assisting in an experiment that produced results so astonishing they may one day shatter the current scientific paradigm.

Conducted by East European scientist Gy Egely, the experiment was set up to determine whether it was possible, under stringent controls and in repeatable circumstances, for the human mind to have a direct influence on physical matter. Such an influence is known technically as *psychokinesis* and had already been demonstrated as a statistical effect in dice-throwing experiments carried out in the United States. But Egely wanted to go much further. He wanted to *witness* psychokinesis in action, not simply infer its presence through statistics.

To this end, he devised an unusually simple procedure. He took a petri dish, of the type found in laboratories throughout the world, and filled it with water. Then, using metallic filaments, he laid fine trails of dye across the surface of the water as markers. This done, he covered the dish with a glass box to guard it against the influence of air currents.

The students selected to assist him were all fifteen- to seventeen-year-olds, divided into three groups. The first, mainly girls, were majoring in humanities and the arts. The second, mainly boys, were mathematics and physics majors. Both groups were marked by high intelligence and achievement. The third group, a mix of boys and girls, was much closer to the academic average. Students from all three groups were invited one at a time to place their hands on each side of the glass box housing the petri dish—there were curtains at the ends that allowed them do so. They were then told to *will* the liquid to rotate.

According to his published report of the experiment, Egely found the vast majority of the students interested and enthusiastic, although several of the young physicists found it hard to believe that such a result was possible.[47]

The high achievers turned the task into a competitive opportunity and vied to see who could do best.

When all other factors, such as heat, vibration, electrostatic fields and mechanical influence, had been eliminated, Egely discovered that a significant proportion of the students were able to rotate the liquid by willpower alone . . . and had the results on film to prove it.

The experiment turned out to be easily, although not straightforwardly, repeatable. That is to say, any representative set of students could be relied upon to generate a similar result in comparable conditions. But individual students who demonstrated their ability to move the liquid once were not necessarily able to do it again.

Successful students tended to be extrovert, optimistic, popular and easy-going. Strangely, the experimenter seemed to be a factor in the outcome—Egely noted that when he took personal charge results weakened. Most mysterious of all, nobody got results when it was raining.

But, despite the caveats and the puzzles, one thing was absolutely clear by the time Egely had processed some 500 experimental runs. It was possible for the human mind to exert a visible, recordable influence on physical matter under repeatable laboratory conditions. A talent that had long been thought of as "psychic" or even "magical" had suddenly emerged from the darkness.

But, exciting though these findings were, they proved tame when compared with the results of a second set of experiments Egely carried out with his colleague G. Vertesy. These showed conclusively that Pavlita generators would stimulate, or at least channel, a psychokinetic talent.

CHANNELLING PSYCHOKINETIC ENERGY

The experiments carried out by Egely and Vertesy were a great deal more complex than the water-moving tests involving the schoolchildren. What they tried to do was modify the known magnetic properties of various materials through mental action. Although we tend to think of magnetism as associated exclusively with ferrous metals, there are in fact many more materials, including wood and plastic, which exhibit magnetic properties. The difference is that they exhibit them at a level discernible only by careful measurement.

Like the water moving, this new series of experiments proved strikingly successful. According to the scientists, "The experiments unambiguously showed that in the majority of cases the activation procedure significantly changes the magnetic properties of the samples."[48]

But, interesting though it is, this categorical result conceals the most fascinating aspect of the experiment. The changed properties of the samples were achieved by means of Pavlita Activation Devices—a specific type of Pavlita generator.

Pavlita Activation Devices are smallish implements made from various combinations of steel, bronze, iron, brass and plastic parts.[49] They have no noticeable magnetic field, do not run on electricity or rely on chemical action. Until they are "activated," they might as well be ornaments.

Activation occurs when their operator engages in a specific mental process, parts of which are similar to yoga relaxation and concentration techniques. The process is not particularly simple but can, in principle, be learned by anyone willing to invest enough time to develop the disciplines.

Once activated, as Egely and Vertesy were to discover, the devices became capable of modifying the magnetic properties of various substances. Exactly *how* this effect was achieved remained something of a mystery.

PHOTOGRAPHING ENERGY FIELDS

The solution to the mystery may actually predate the mystery itself. During 1939, the year the Second World War broke out, Stalinist Russia was plagued by materials shortages. Money was scarce and new goods at a premium. When something wore out, it was typically not replaced but mended. This held good not simply for consumer items like shoes or clothing, but for technical equipment and even heavy machinery.

In the city of Krasnodar, close to the Black Sea in southern Russia, one of the most popular repairmen was an electrical engineer called Semyon Davidovich Kirlian. He had a reputation for reliability that brought him work from businesses, hospitals, laboratories, research institutes—anywhere in fact that had electrical apparatus in need of repair.

On a routine call-out to a medical clinic, Kirlian happened to see doctors treating a patient by means of a high-frequency electrotherapy machine. Either by accident or design, there was a flash between the electrodes and the patient's skin as the machine was switched on. Kirlian wondered idly if the flash could be photographed.

This passing thought gradually turned into an obsession—an obsession that was to change the course of his entire life. Since the electrodes in the clinic were made from glass, he realised any photographic plate placed between them and the patient's skin would fog due to ambient light before the flash could be generated. Opaque electrodes were obviously needed, but since these would have to be metallic there was a danger of producing a severe electric shock. Kirlian decided he could not subject the clinic's patients to this risk. He would have to become his own guinea pig.

This proved a sensible decision. The first time he threw

the switch on the machine, the metal electrode in contact with his hand gave him a severe burn. But he got his photograph. Oddly enough, it was not a picture of the flash. Instead, the developed plate showed an outline of his hand . . . with a curious luminescence radiating from the fingers.

Kirlian was not entirely sure what this meant. He asked around and discovered that he was not the first to observe the phenomenon. But others had attached no importance to it. They had noted its occurrence and left it at that.

Kirlian himself was far more curious. The picture he had taken seemed to suggest there was some sort of energy radiating from his hand. He determined to photograph it properly. With his wife Valentina he began to develop a whole new technology based on high-frequency electrical fields and within ten years he had invented an extensive range of instruments with which to detect this intriguing phenomenon. As other engineers and scientists grew interested, the process as a whole became known as "Kirlian photography."

But what did Kirlian photography actually show? Some of the very earliest experiments gave a clue. A leaf freshly taken from the tree showed an intriguing pattern of turquoise and reddish-yellow flares. When Kirlian took a section from the leaf, the overall shape remained intact in his high-frequency photographs. A ghostly outline, with its own dimmed pattern of flares, showed up where the missing segment had been. Clearly, Kirlian was photographing some sort of energy field generated by living matter.

This was quickly confirmed by photographing leaves that had begun to wither. The bright, vigorous flares of the fresh leaf were dimmed. A completely dried-out leaf showed nothing at all. "We appeared to be seeing the very life activities of the leaf itself," the Kirlians remarked later. "Intense dynamic energy in the healthy leaf, less in the withered leaf, nothing in the dead leaf."[50]

Animal tissue proved even more spectacular. Early Kirlian photographs of the human hand were likened to a starry cosmos of blue and gold, lit up by multicoloured flares and splashed by areas of cloud-like veils. When Kirlian's followers developed devices that would allow them to view the human body in motion and eventually to take moving Kirlian images, some astounding new information emerged. It appeared that the level of energy in the flares diminished dramatically when the subject was ill. With study, the patterns, colours and intensity of the photographed energy became an indicator not only of current illness, but of developing maladies that as yet showed no physical symptoms. The energy field was even sensitive enough to indicate mood swings. In one classic series of experiments, the Kirlian field of a male volunteer flared dramatically when a pretty young woman walked into the room. The phenomenon was reflected in the use of alcohol. A single shot of vodka caused the field to light up like a Christmas tree.

As news of the Kirlian discoveries spread, many were quick to point out that the idea of a human energy field was nothing new. Clairvoyants and mystics had claimed for generations that the body was surrounded by an "aura" which reflected—in its colouring and composition—the physical, emotional and even spiritual state of the individual. The artistic convention of drawing a halo around the head of a saint reflected this tradition: the aura of a highly spiritual person became so bright, particularly around the head, that it was supposed to create this nimbus.

Chinese acupuncture (which seems to have been developed in deep prehistory) is also based on the idea that an energy—known as *chi*—runs through the human body.

Interestingly, the traditional acupuncture points show up as flares in Kirlian photographs.

The *chi* energy of China has its counterpart in the *ki* energy of Japan. Hindus likewise accept the reality of *prana*, a subtle body-energy that can be strengthened by means of yoga. In Polynesia, Huna practitioners talk of *mana*, a similar force. The energy seems, in fact, to have been discovered again and again. But in each case, the scientific establishment has been inclined to dismiss the discoverers as woolly-minded mystics and relegate the mysterious energy to the realm of legend.

All that changed—at least in eastern Europe—once Kirlian was able to show his photographic proof:

> Soon the greats of the Soviet scientific world began to trek to Krasnodar. There were the famous and the curious. There were members of the Academy of Science, Ministers of the Government. Over some thirteen years, there were hundreds of visitors. Biophysicists, doctors, biochemists, electronics experts, criminology specialists all appeared at the door of the little [. . .] pre-revolutionary wooden house on Kirov Street . . . [51]

Western scientists were much slower to react to the Kirlians' groundbreaking discovery—and only partly because of the Soviet obsession with scientific secrecy. Even when the news did begin to spread, it was met with scepticism in the West. Aura photographs were altogether too occult to attract serious scientific attention.

The result was predictable. Research into the mysterious new bio-energy was more or less confined to eastern Europe.

Manipulating Subtle Energy

Virtually every tradition that deals with the human energy field claims it can be transferred, manipulated or used.

To mystics, it can be offered through the laying on of hands to effect healing. Yoga practitioners claim it can be diverted towards the brain to produce enlightenment. Acupuncture aims to control its flow through channels called meridians. Several of the Oriental martial arts attempt to concentrate *chi* in order to increase physical force and strength. The *mana* of the Polynesian Hunas is used to influence their environment in various ways, thus accomplishing "magical" or "miraculous" effects.

The Hungarian scientists Egely and Vertesy, who carried out the experiments we examined earlier, were of much the same opinion. They suspected that the biological field might be persuaded to influence the magnetic properties of other physical substances. The idea was not a million miles away from Egely's experiment with the schoolchildren either. Placing the hands on either side of the petri dish would put the water within the subject's energy field. Successfully willing the liquid to move might not indicate direct mental influence on matter, but rather mental influence on the subject's "aura," which in turn influenced the water.

Proof of this theory—or at least proof that a biological field played a part in some examples of psychokinesis—was eventually forthcoming, once again in Russia.

Nina Kulagina, the psychokinetic medium who moved small objects and stopped clocks, did so in much the same way as the schoolchildren persuaded the water in the petri dish to react. She concentrated. But did her mind directly influence matter? Soviet scientists very much doubted it and eventually hit on an experiment that proved they were right. A Kirlian "movie" was made of Kulagina in action. As she started to concentrate, the energy field around her body began to pulse. The pulsation became stronger and stronger with a corresponding increase of amplitude. Then, at what appeared to be a critical point, a "wave-front" extended from Kulagina's body to strike the object of her concentration. As it did so, the object moved.

Machines—of a sort—were developed to tap this subtle energy before Robert Pavlita came on the scene. As long ago as 1922, for example, the prestigious journal of the British Medical Association, *The Lancet*, carried news of a device called a "sthenometer" that could be set in motion by "vision or the proximity of the human body." Developed by Dr. Charles Ross, the sthenometer consisted of a needle suspended above a calibrated dial inside a transparent quartz shield. Dr. Ross claimed the needle showed a measurable reaction when stared at fixedly or when approached, clearly suggesting some form of energy transfer between the experimenter and the device.

Dr. Ross was not the first to develop such an apparatus. An even earlier version—called a "biometre"—was built in France by Dr. Hippolyte Baraduc to an almost identical design. In the biometre, a copper needle was suspended over a calibrated dial from the centre of a glass dome. Rather than simply gazing at it, the operator cupped both hands around the dome and sought to move the needle by "concentrated thought." The dial indicated to what degree he succeeded.

A modern version of these devices was designed by the American electronics engineer and author Gerald Loe who registered it as the Energy Wheel®. It consists of a 6 cm (2½ in) rotor (in the form of four ultra-light aluminum vanes) which is balanced on the point of a needle. Like Dr. Baraduc, Loe instructs experimenters to sit with their hands cupped on either side of the wheel (which may be covered with an inverted glass) and concentrate on making it spin. Most people quickly discover that not only can they set the wheel in motion, but they can cause it to slow, stop and reverse its direction of spin, all with purely mental commands.[52]

Loe, who is interested in spiritual healing, remains convinced that the Energy Wheel effect is not, strictly speaking, psychokinesis (which is defined as direct mental influence on the material world). Rather, he believes that the person's concentration influences their energy field, which in turn influences the wheel.

Michael Brown, a physicist from the UK, experimented with a device similar to Loe's and became convinced the motive power was provided by convection currents emanating from the back of the hands. (He used smoke to make the currents visible.) When the wheel was isolated under transparent plastic, he found the effect ceased.

But Brown's experiments did not address the apparent ability of some people to control the direction of the spin—although a biofeedback mechanism did appear to allow variations of the speed of rotation in free air. Because of the extreme sensitivity of the wheel, great care had to be taken to avoid background convection currents and draughts. Claims have been made in the United States that the wheel will continue to spin under glass, at least for certain people, and there have been many experiments in Russia claiming to rotate wheels under similar circumstances.

In 1924, the Viennese psychologist Wilhelm Reich became convinced of the existence of a universal energy which he labelled orgone and believed to be the power source of the nervous system. He felt mental illness was the result of orgone deficiency and attempted to combat this through the development of a special "orgone accumulator" into which patients were placed in order to replenish their energy supplies. Quite clearly Reich's concept of orgone is identical to the Chinese *chi* and the Hindu *mana*. His orgone accumulator consisted of a box fabricated from alternate layers of organic and inorganic material.

This same design can be found in several prehistoric mounds, including those of Newgrange, Dowth and Knowth in Ireland, suggesting that the knowledge of how to manipulate subtle energies was abroad in the ancient world.

CHAPTER 13

ζPSYCHOTRONIC
ξEGYPT

WHEN Ostrander and Schroeder visited Moscow on their marathon evaluation of psychical research in the Soviet Union, they were shown a movie featuring the Czech work on psychotronic generators. The documentary demonstrated a more up-to-date version of the first-ever psychotronic experiment, during which a needle was balanced on a revolving rotor. When Pavlita pointed a special device at it, the needle stopped turning. Another device turned into a "magnet" for non-magnetic substances and continued to work perfectly under water, thus ruling out the presence of static electricity. Yet another turned a small blade. The scientists tested to eliminate static electricity, air currents, temperature changes and electromagnetic fields. Still the blade turned.

Virtually every scientist they interviewed told them the same thing—the secret of psychotronic generators lay in their form. Something about specific shapes, coupled with precise mixtures of metals and other materials, interacted with human bioenergy—directed by will—to generate observable effects.

In the movie they watched, Ostrander and Schroeder saw examples of many different forms as the cameras tracked across a collection of generators, lighting up what seemed to be modern sculptures:

> Other objects looked like precision-cut components for machines that hadn't been invented yet, spare parts from 2001. Still other small metal and wood sculptures were reminiscent of those "ritual objects" set out by museums of the world, from the British Museum in London to the little dusty museums of Asian Turkey and southern Egypt.[53]

When they paid him a personal visit, Pavlita was reluctant to give away too many details of his marvellous inventions—a colleague explained there were difficulties in patenting them—but the documentary gave one broad hint about their inspiration. Without comment or commentary, the camera cut from the generators to shots of Egyptian hieroglyphic texts and wall carvings, tracking eventually to a prolonged examination of an ancient *ankh*.

ARCHAEOLOGY AND ANCIENT TECHNOLOGY

There is a problem with our investigation of the ancient world. Archaeologists, by and large, are trained as historians, not engineers. Thus examples of ancient engineering sometimes go unrecognised and are misclassified as ritualistic, religious, magical or ornamental objects.

If this can occur with known technology—as was the case with the Baghdad Battery—it is easy to see how dramatically the problem may be compounded when dealing with an obscure branch of knowledge like psychotronics, the technology of which is known intimately to no more than a handful of scientists, most of whom are confined to eastern Europe even today.

Without the "magical" ingredient of acid, the Baghdad Battery remains a simple clay jar. But the magical ingredient of a psychotronic generator is far more subtle—a particular action of the human mind. As Pavlita explained to the Hungarian researchers, anyone can use one of his generators . . . but only after training. A particular yogic state of mind must be achieved before these things will work. Perhaps some form of yoga practice was required of the Egyptian priesthood, who certainly experimented with psychotropic drugs. But, without knowledge of that state and the training needed to reach it, archaeologists might discover a thousand psychotronic generators in the ruins of Luxor and never see them as anything more than ornaments. It is, indeed, entirely possible that such generators *have* been found—metallic *ankhs*, perhaps, or delicately shaped containers—but they have remained inert without a trained mind to trigger them.

All the same, there is one psychotronic generator that has attracted attention in recent times, since it appears to produce effects independent of a specific user.

That generator is the most typically Egyptian of all geometric forms, the pyramid.

PYRAMID POWER

In the early 1970s, a story began to circulate concerning the observations of a French traveller named Bovis while on a visit to Egypt. Variations of the story appeared in several publications at the time, but the broad thrust of the account was as follows.

Some years before, M. Bovis found himself on the Giza plateau during particularly humid weather. Exhausted by the heat, he sought refuge in the Great Pyramid. Despite his tiredness, he made his way through the pyramid's internal corridors and along the Grand Gallery until he reached the King's Chamber, which is situated exactly one-third of the way up the structure from its base.

The authorities had installed refuse bins for the rubbish left by tourists. Bovis noticed that one of them contained the body of a dead cat and several other small animals that had apparently wandered into the pyramid, lost their way and died. But, while the creatures had clearly been dead for some time, there was no smell of decay. Intrigued, Bovis examined them more closely and found that they were dehydrated, despite the high humidity. Some sort of natural mummification process had taken place.

Like most orthodox Egyptologists, Bovis subscribed to the theory that the Great Pyramid was a pharaoh's tomb. He was also aware of the religious importance placed by the Ancient Egyptians on the preservation of the body after death and began to wonder if they had built some sort of fail-safe mechanism into this tomb in case the normal process of embalming proved ineffective. Since he could think of nothing else that would cause the natural mummification effect, he concluded that there was something in the pyramid shape itself that produced the curious result. The well-known precision of its construction and orientation convinced him that there might be something to the idea. He decided to experiment.

Bovis made himself a scale model of the Great Pyramid out of cardboard with a base about 1 m (3 ft) long. He set up a platform inside at the height of the King's Chamber and on it laid to rest a second conveniently dead cat. Then he waited. After a while, the cat mummified. Bovis then experimented with other organic materials, particularly those that tended to decay quickly. In each case they desiccated instead.

According to the reports, Bovis published his findings, although I have been unable to track them down. But a

Czech radio engineer named Karel Drbal had more luck and stumbled on the paper some time in the 1940s. He was fascinated by what he read and mounted a series of experiments of his own. He not only successfully duplicated the Bovis research but extended it by using different sizes and relative dimensions of pyramids.[54] He concluded that the shape of the space inside the container did indeed have a measurable effect on biological processes within it. They could not only be slowed (as in mummification) but also speeded up.

Some time after his biological experiments, Drbal engaged in an unlikely piece of lateral thinking that catapulted him into a whole new career. He recalled that, when he had served in the Czech Army, a common way of irritating unpopular soldiers was to leave their razors out in the moonlight. The cutting edge of a razor is crystalline in structure, and moonlight is polarised, which means it vibrates on one plane only. This influenced the crystal structure and dulled the edge. Drbal's imaginative leap was to wonder if the "mummification energy" accumulated inside a pyramid might have a measurable effect on a razor blade as well. He set up an experiment and discovered that, far from dulling the blade, the pyramid actually sharpened it.

At the time, good razor blades were at a premium in the Soviet Union and imported blades impossible to find. Most men used what they could get more than once and Drbal was no exception. But he knew that, after four or five shaves, the typical blade became so blunt it was uncomfortable. By placing his blade under the pyramid (at the level of the King's Chamber) after each shave, he managed to keep it going fifty times. Eventually he found blades that reacted so well he could shave with them 200 times or more. It suddenly occurred to him that he was sitting on a gold mine.

Drbal, who had pioneered radio and television in

Czechoslovakia, was no stranger to the world of commerce. He took his model of the Great Pyramid to the Patent Office in Prague on 4 November 1949. Three years later, following extensive tests, he was issued with a Czech patent, an abridged version of which reads:

> The invention relates to the method of maintaining of razor blades and straight razors sharp without the auxiliary source of energy. To sharpen the blades, therefore no mechanical, thermal, chemical or electrical (from an artificial source) means are being used . . .
>
> According to this invention, the blade is placed in earth's magnetic field under a hollow pyramid made of dielectric material such as hard paper, paraffin paper, hard cardboard, or some plastic . . . The most suitable pyramid is a four sided one with a square base, where one side is conveniently equal to the height of the pyramid, multiplied by p/2 [*pi* or 3.14/2]. For example, for the height of 10 cm, the side of 15.7 centimetres is chosen. The razor is placed on the support . . . [of a height] . . . between ⅕ and ⅓ of the height of the pyramid . . . [which] . . . could vary from the limits stated above. Although it is not absolutely necessary, it is recommended that the blade be placed on the support with its sharp edges facing west or east respectively, leaving its side edges as well as its longitudinal axis oriented in North South direction . . . This position improves the performance of the device, it is not however essential for the application of the principle of this invention.
>
> It is beneficial to leave a new blade in the pyramid one to two weeks before using it. It is essential to place it there immediately after the first shave, and not the old, dull one. But it is possible to use an old one, if it is properly resharpened. The blade placed using the method above is left unobstructed until the next shave.

The west edge should always face west. It improves the sharpening effect.[55]

The patent mentioned that the device enabled 1,778 shaves to be obtained from just sixteen blades. An average of fifty shaves per blade was achieved through the use of the pyramid—ten times what might be expected without it. The materials-conscious Czech authorities estimated that the invention would lead to an annual saving of 33.15 grams of steel per head of the male population. Soon a Prague factory was manufacturing the devices in their thousands. Later, production shifted from cardboard to styrofoam pyramids.

X-RAYING KHAFRE'S PYRAMID

The story of Bovis's cats and Drbal's razor blade enterprise followed hard on the heels of another rumoured pyramid mystery. In 1968, a scientific team comprising specialists from the United States Atomic Energy Commission, the Smithsonian Institute, the UAR Department of Antiquities and the Ein Shams University of Cairo launched a million-dollar project to X-ray the pyramid of Khafre.

Khafre's pyramid is built beside the Great Pyramid at Giza and, with a volume of 2,211,096 cu m (78,073,799 cu ft) and a height of 143:5 m (471 ft), is only marginally smaller. The project was set up under the direction of Dr. Louis Alvarez, a Nobel Prize–winning physicist, in an attempt to find hidden chambers. To this end, detectors were installed in a known chamber at the base of the pyramid and set to measure the amount of cosmic radiation penetrating the structure. Since a cosmic ray would obviously pass more easily through any hollow in the pyramid than it would through solid stone, it should theoretically reach the base with a slightly higher energy content than a ray that made its total journey through a solid mass of rock. The scientists believed that the difference could be analysed and the results stored. If their measuring devices were moved and the experiment repeated, a process of triangulation would allow any cavities to be accurately pinpointed. In this way a radiation map of the interior could be generated. Later it was proposed to drill small boreholes into any cavities discovered and examine them fully using advanced optical equipment.

The instruments were left in place for more than a year, with readings recorded twenty-four hours a day. Some two million cosmic ray trajectories were recorded by September 1968 and subjected to analysis by the IBM 1130 computer installed at Ein Shams. Initial results were encouraging. Dr. Lauren Yazolino, Dr. Alvarez's assistant, was dispatched to the United States to obtain further analysis of the tapes at Berkeley University, leaving a Dr. Amr Goneid in charge of the Egyptian operation.

According to a story that became current at the time, Dr. Goneid was visited in July 1969 by a London *Times* correspondent named John Turnbull, who subsequently filed a report claiming that each time Dr. Goneid ran the tapes through the local computer, a different pattern would emerge. Even known features of the pyramid failed to maintain standard patterns. It was, Turnbull quoted Dr. Goneid as saying, against all known laws of physics: something "scientifically impossible." He was further quoted as saying, "Either the geometry of the pyramid is in substantial error, which would affect our readings, or there is a mystery which is beyond explanation—call it what you will, occultism, the curse of the pharaohs, sorcery or magic: there is some force that defies the laws of science at work in the pyramid."

The rumours went on to insist that the report was flatly denied by Dr. Alvarez, who suggested Dr. Goneid—in whom he had every confidence as a physicist—had been misquoted and described the remarks attributed to him as "nonsense." Preliminary results showed no hidden chambers in the area scanned, although there remained the possibility of discoveries in other parts of the structure. Dr. Yazolino added that a malfunction in the equipment had produced areas which at first seemed to indicate a hidden chamber, but under further analysis were shown to have been due to a gap between two spark chambers.

Although there is a question mark about whether Turnbull's controversial report ever appeared at all—at least in the London *Times*—the story of the Khafre pyramid mystery was, like the story of Bovis in the King's Chamber, passed on in several publications.[56] The result was predictable. The early 1970s saw a dramatic upsurge of public interest in "pyramid power."

PYRAMID MADNESS

In a movement reminiscent of the table-turning fad that swept through Victorian withdrawing rooms, everyone, it seemed, began to experiment with pyramids. They were used to exert a mysterious influence on all sorts of things. A pyramidical hat was marketed as an aid to psychism. Pyramidical tents were sold as meditation aids. Pyramids were promoted as headache cures and stimulants to spiritual growth.

The hype, commercialism and downright silliness of the pyramid power movement went a long way towards obscuring an interesting fact. Properly constructed models of the Great Pyramid did indeed influence organic tissue and razor blades exactly as the original reports claimed. This is something you can easily test for yourself.

Cut four pieces of stiff card into identical triangles with the proportion of base to sides following the ratio 15.7 to

14.94. (The proportions remain the same, of course, whatever size pyramid you build but you may find it convenient to use a base measurement of 23.8 cm [9⅜ in] and a side measurement of 22.5 cm [8⅞ in.]) Tape the triangles together. You'll find the resultant pyramid has a proportional height of 10, equivalent to 15 cm (6 in) if you're using the suggested measurements.

Using a compass, align your cardboard pyramid precisely north-south and east-west. Place your pyramid well away from electrical fields (e.g. television sets, computers and microwave ovens). Construct a stand 3.33 of your proportional units high and place it inside the pyramid, directly underneath the apex. If you want to try sharpening a razor blade, position it on the stand so that the blade's edges face east and west. For mummification experiments use small pieces of meat or fish unless you have made a large pyramid. Typically, organic material will show a 66 percent dehydration between six and fifty days exposure.

Along with the mummification and razor effects, it is worth germinating seeds under a pyramid and contrasting their growth rate with similar seeds grown within a different type of container. These experiments will quickly convince you of the basic premise of modern psychotronics—shape really does have a mysterious but measurable influence on certain physical processes.

This discovery was made independently of Bovis and Drbal. A French company developed—and patented—a specially shaped yoghurt container which they found encouraged the growth of lactic cultures. And an East European brewing company stopped using a new form of maturation casks when they found the flavour of the beer was adversely affected. This too is an effect you can test for yourself. Try drinking your favourite beverage out of a square container rather than a familiar round glass and you will immediately notice a flavour change.

Despite all this, there was little real progress. Egyptol-

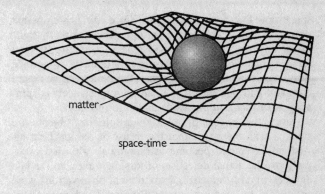

Distortion of the space-time continuum

ogists continued to insist that pyramids were tombs. And, outside eastern Europe, psychotronics remained a fringe area of investigation. Part of the problem was that not even the Soviets had a working theory of psychotronic energy. They knew from experience that certain devices worked, but they had no idea why.

Since then, however, some answers have started to emerge from the findings of modern physics.

TORSION FIELDS

Torsion field theory emerged from Einstein's General Theory of Relativity which indicated a relationship between gravity and distortions of the space-time continuum. The mathematician Elie Cartan developed this concept into a full-blown Torsion Field Theory, linking space-time distortions to geometrical shape. But little practical work was done in the field until 1980, when Russian scientists began to take a serious interest.

Simply stated, a torsion field is a twist in the fabric of

space-time that results from spin. Since spin is an inherent property of most subatomic particles, this means that virtually any physical object will tend to generate its own torsion signature. Where there is an alignment of particle spin—as in crystals or magnets—the field becomes more complex and pronounced. When the object itself is spinning, a further complexity is added to the field.

Since the largest of all known spinning objects are stars, it was inevitable that the thrust of torsion field investigation should become astronomical. This led eventually to the actual detection of torsion waves. In the late eighties to early nineties, astronomical observations were conducted by members of the Russian Academy of Sciences under the direction of Professor M. M. Lavrentiev.

Observation of a star is not altogether straightforward. The position we see it occupying is not its actual location in the universe, since the light reaching us is shifted slightly by a variety of factors. Because of this, the actual position of a star has to be calculated rather than observed directly. In the Russian studies, signals were detected coming from the visible position of each star and its actual position undistorted by distance. This was predictable enough, but the scientists also picked up signals from positions symmetrical to the visible position of the star and relative to its true position. There was no theoretical explanation of such observations, but in 1992 the experiments were successfully repeated by the Observatory of the Ukraine Academy of Sciences at Kiev and the Crimean Astrophysical Observatory where the results were finally interpreted as detection of torsion waves.

Torsion fields have really thrown a spanner into the works of modern physics, since they appear capable of propagating considerably faster than the speed of light. This has led to one of the weirdest of all developments: G. I. Shipov's Physical Vacuum Theory indicates that torsion fields can propagate not only in the future, but in the

past as well. Several hard-headed Russian physicists—
Yuri V. Nachalov and A. N. Sokolov among them—have
thus been forced to acknowledge the possibility that various paranormal phenomena, including precognition, are
connected with specific manifestations of torsion fields.

This is an extraordinary development and one which
suggests that Egypt's ancient reputation for "magic" may
not, after all, have been founded purely on superstition.
Meanwhile, work on torsion fields continues, with the
most promising results obtained from such shapes as cylinders, cones . . . and pyramids.

CHAPTER 14

THE EGYPTIAN MYSTERY

WHAT is happening here? On the face of the evidence, Ancient Egypt seems to have developed a body of knowledge and techniques that equals—and in some instances actually surpasses—the science and technology of modern civilisation. The list, as we have seen, includes advances in architecture, engineering, electricity, geography, astronomy, chemistry, sonics and the little-understood energies of psychotronics. The Rhind Papyrus, written by the scribe Ahmes around 1650 BC but copied from a much earlier document, even indicates a knowledge of the binary mathematics which drive modern computers.

There is clear evidence that much of this knowledge was in place from the earliest dynastic times, virtually from the very foundation of the Egyptian state. This would suggest that the knowledge itself was developed *prior* to 3100 BC, but conventional Egyptology insists that before this time the country had not yet emerged from the Stone Age.

But this is only *modern* Egyptology. The Egyptians

themselves had a very different picture of their early history.

ACCORDING TO PLATO . . .

Some time in the fourth century BC—the exact dates are uncertain—the Greek philosopher Plato began work on two texts that were to generate more controversy than all his other writings put together. The first of these was a major document he called *Timaeus*. The second, entitled *Critias*, was little more than a literary fragment. The controversial element in each was his description of a lost civilisation that, he claimed, had existed in the depths of prehistory on an island continent beyond the Straits of Gibraltar. This is the earliest known mention of Atlantis. Plato claimed its civilisation disappeared overnight when violent earthquakes sank the homeland beneath the icy waters of the Atlantic Ocean.

It was a story that seized the imagination. Lost Atlantis was widely discussed in Plato's own day and continued to be discussed long after he was dead. It remains a focus of interest in our own time. An estimate that some 20,000 books have been written on Atlantis seems, if anything, conservative. And a poll of U.S. journalists revealed that they considered the re-emergence of Atlantis to be a bigger story than the Second Coming of Christ.

But the sheer drama and interest of the Atlantis story has tended to overshadow the fact that Plato wrote about two other ancient civilisations in *Timaeus* and *Critias*—the martial city-state of Athens and an established culture of Ancient Egypt. This Egypt is clearly not the Egypt of our history books. What he wrote about was a culture that Egyptologists deny ever existed.

Plato's *Timaeus* reads like the minutes of meetings between four men. Although scholarly consensus suggests the meetings never took place and the ideas put forward were Plato's own, the named individuals were real enough. The first was the great philosopher Socrates, some forty years Plato's senior and a long-time friend and mentor. The others were the Sophist and politician Critias, his colleague Timaeus and the politician Hermocrates, who was leader of the moderate democrats of Syracuse in Sicily. All were Plato's contemporaries.

The text begins with some social chitchat, then the four get down to an intellectual examination of what would constitute the ideal political state. After a lengthy reprise of their conclusions so far, Hermocrates remarks that after their last meeting Critias had told the others of an "ancient tradition" possibly relevant to their discussion. He suggests Critias should now tell Socrates about it. Critias agrees, then describes in some detail the adventures of a man named Solon.

Like the others mentioned in *Timaeus*, Solon was real enough, although he was a historical personage rather than a contemporary. He was an Athenian statesman born almost exactly 200 years before Plato and known—with considerable justification—as one of the Seven Wise Men of Greece. He was also an ancestor of Critias and, more distantly, of Plato himself. Although a member of the nobility, he was far from wealthy and seems to have earned his living as a merchant.

Solon first rose to prominence at the age of thirty. At that time, the Athenians were on the point of losing a war with neighbouring Megara. The conflict arose from a land dispute about the island of Salamis. Solon decided to take an interest and arranged for the public recitation of a stirring poem he had composed, calling on the Athenians to rise and take the island. It had the desired effect. Military efforts were renewed, the Athenians won the war and Solon's reputation was assured.

Apart from this war, Solon lived in troubled times.

Athens was dominated by an aristocracy who owned the best land, monopolised government, and bickered constantly among themselves. As in feudal Britain, the poorer farmers soon fell into debt to their landlords and were reduced to serfdom, if not outright slavery. Their hatred of the aristocracy was mirrored by that of an extensive middle class who resented being excluded from government. Dissent fermented to a point where revolution seemed almost inevitable, but, rather than resort to violence, citizens of all classes agreed to ask Solon to mediate. He suggested reform and was given almost dictatorial authority to push his reforms through.

Solon set to with a will and history has judged his reforms as one of the great achievements of Ancient Greece, but they caused uproar at the time. Having asked for change, nobody really wanted it. The poor complained he hadn't done enough, the rich that he'd done too much. Solon couldn't be bothered to argue. He announced that he was leaving Greece and would not return for ten years.[57]

Among the countries he visited during this period was Egypt.

ANCIENT GREECE AND ANCIENT EGYPT

The Critias of Plato's dialogue heard the story of Solon's Egyptian trip as a child of ten. He was attending what sounds like an excruciatingly embarrassing family gathering. (The boys received prizes from their parents for reciting edifying poetry.) Among the set pieces were several composed by Solon, whose work was somewhat out of fashion at the time.

One of the relatives remarked that Solon was the noblest of poets. It was a comment probably designed to please the patriarch of the gathering, another, older, Critias who may have been the young boy's grandfather. The old man brightened visibly and remarked that, had Solon not been diverted by other interests, he might have become an epic poet to stand beside Homer or Hesiod if only because of a story he had brought back from Egypt. When pressed, the elderly Critias told the story of a war between the lost kingdom of Atlantis and an alliance of Greek states, led by Athens. But, like any good storyteller, he set the scene carefully.

Critias began by talking of Sais, a district of Egypt's Nile Delta which had a capital city also called Sais. The founding goddess of the city was Neith, whom the Egyptians believed to be identical to the Greek goddess Athene, patron deity of Athens. The people of Sais felt a great affinity towards the Athenians and believed themselves somehow related—a notion that must have helped assure Solon of a warm welcome. For whatever reason, Solon was received with great honour.

As a politician and scholar, Solon was interested in history and Egypt was renowned for having the most comprehensive and accurate historical records of the ancient world. These records were in the safekeeping of the Egyptian priesthood, with Sais itself a central repository. Solon lost no time in approaching the priests there in the hope of finding out more about events of antiquity. But he made a mistake when he tried to impress them with his own knowledge of the subject.

One can imagine the scene as Solon began to pontificate about Phoroneus, the "first man" of Greek mythic history, more or less equivalent to the Judaeo-Christian Adam. He then spoke of the Great Deluge, which was as much a part of Greek tradition as our own, and described how the Greek couple Deucalion and Pyrrha were the only two people to survive. The Egyptians listened to all this with enormous tolerance, but when Solon began calculating dates by adding up the lifetimes of Deucalion and

Pyrrha's descendants, their patience finally ran out. An elderly priest fixed him with a gimlet eye. "O Solon, Solon, you Greeks are never anything but children! There is not an old man among you," he said.

When Solon asked what the outburst meant, the old priest explained that it meant the Greeks had young minds, since they were not exposed to any ancient tradition or scientific knowledge. But there was a reason. The Egyptians firmly believed that humanity had come close to destruction several times in the remote past, sometimes by flood, sometimes by a fiery bombardment from the skies. When this occurred, the records kept in various countries were wiped out and their cultures, plunged into primitive barbarism, eventually forgot their historical heritage. But Egypt, by an accident of geography, had escaped all or most of these disasters, with the result that her ancient records had been preserved. According to these records, the city of Sais was fully 8,000 years old, while Athens had been founded 1,000 years earlier.

A great many authors have understood Plato's *Timaeus* to claim that Egypt was founded 8,000 years before Solon's visit, but this is a misreading of the text which refers explicitly to the city, not the country. Since Solon visited Egypt during the sixth century BC, this means building work first began at Sais some time before 8500 BC. Egypt itself was clearly founded earlier.

MANETHO AND THE TURIN PAPYRUS

Plato is not the only authority we have for accepting that the Egyptians believed their civilisation was founded in the depths of prehistory. Although all but the earliest hieroglyphic text of Egypt has been accessible to us since Thomas Young and Jean-François Champollion deciphered the Rosetta Stone in the nineteenth century, finds of actual Egyptian historical records have been surprisingly scarce. But two texts have come to light that support the Solon story.

The first of these is the *Aegyptiaca*, a history written in Greek by an Egyptian priest named Manetho. The whole work was probably prepared for Pharaoh Ptolemy I somewhere between 305 and 282 BC and, while the original has been lost, some narrative fragments were quoted by the Jewish-Roman historian Josephus, writing around AD 70. More importantly, Manetho's comprehensive tables of dynasties, kings and the lengths of their reigns have been preserved in three different sources—the works of Julius Africanus in the third century AD, Eusebius of Caesaria in the fourth century AD and the Byzantine historian George Syncellus in the eighth century AD.

It is generally agreed that Manetho relied on much earlier sources for his information and at least one of these has survived in fragmentary form—the so-called Turin Papyrus. This work was compiled during the reign of Ramses II (1279–1213 BC) and lists the kings of Egypt from the earliest times to the Nineteenth Dynasty.

Taken together, Manetho's work and the Turin Papyrus strongly support the theory of a truly ancient Egypt. The Turin Papyrus claims there were three distinct divisions in what is now thought of as Egyptian prehistory. The first was a line of pre-dynastic kings who ruled for 13,420 years. The second was a line of "Horus-kings" extending for a further 23,200 years. The third is described as a time of demi-gods, but the papyrus is damaged so we don't know how long they ruled. Manetho tells a somewhat similar story. He records that the pre-dynastic pharaohs went back some 13,777 years and gives a combined dating for the Horus-kings and demi-gods of a further 15,150 years.

Add these figures to a rounded date of 3000 BC for the establishment of the familiar dynastic era, and you can see that Manetho suggested a foundation date for Egyptian civilisation of 31,927 BC. The earlier Turin Canon goes even further. Allowing for the missing period of the demi-gods, it claims that Egypt was long established and flourishing at 39,620 BC.

There are substantial reasons for supposing that Egyptian civilisation was founded earlier than 3100 BC. They range from direct evidence (like Robert Schoch's geological dating of the Sphinx and Sir Norman Lockyer's astronomical dating of the temples) to the multiplicity of technical developments examined in this book, which simply could not have arisen without a far longer lead-time than Egyptology allows.

But the suggestion that any civilisation might have been founded more than 40,000 years ago runs contrary not simply to orthodox Egyptology, but to the entire Western scientific consensus about the evolution of the human race.

CHAPTER 15

DARWIN DISINTEGRATES

TODAY, the most widely accepted scientific view of humanity's origins is rooted in Charles Darwin's *On the Origin of Species*, published in 1859. This masterpiece, based on careful field work and observation, proposed an elegant theory of animal and human evolution, driven by a process that Darwin called "natural selection."

Although the evidence occupied several hundred pages, the theory itself can be simply enough expressed. Changes in physical function or structure occur from time to time in nature. Beneficial changes tend to be retained— in other words are naturally selected—leading gradually, over a long period of time, to the creation of a whole new species.

Today scientists have used Darwin's insights to construct their own ideas of how humanity came to evolve on our planet. The story begins in the forests which covered virtually every inch of the world's landmass 30 million years ago. Around that time, a four-legged, ground-dwelling creature about the size of a squirrel was in the process of evolving into the first of the primates.

Ten million years later, this evolution has proven so successful that many types of apes had become widespread throughout the forests. But around 15 million years ago, climatic change caused the forests to shrink.

By somewhere between 8,000,000 and 4,000,000 BP (Before Present), the disappearing forests had created a serious problem for their flourishing primate population: there simply wasn't enough food to go round any more. Faced with hunger, one group of forest apes made a critical change. They left their ancient habitat and moved out on to the African savannah in search of food.

In the new environment, natural selection favoured what we now think of as human characteristics. The tall grasses of these immense plains meant that any creature who could stand upright would see enemies approaching at a greater distance or spot more potential prey and hence improve its chances of survival. Elongated arms for swinging through the high branches would no longer be needed; nor, as the sun beat down without the protection of a leafy cover, would the fur that once kept the creature warm. Better eyesight would be selected for seeing at long distances. Changes in throat and larynx that allowed for more sophisticated warning calls would tend to develop, leading eventually to actual speech. Social behaviour, necessary for survival, might provide the driving force behind the gradual evolution of a larger brain. And so on. Once the primates came down from the trees, their evolutionary tendency was linear, one-directional and inevitable—they started, slowly but surely, turning human.

FIRST HOMINIDS

Australopithecines, in common with a few other species, are known as *hominids*, human ancestors who diverged from the simian ancestral stock somewhere between

5,000,000 and 8,000,000 BP. Hominids are found only in Africa and are distinguished almost entirely by their upright stance. That stance is important. It leaves the hands free to carry weapons and tools.

Those hominids who first made tools are now called *Homo habilis*—'handy man." They represent, so it is believed, the transition between Australopithecine stock and a more advanced ancestor of our species, *Homo erectus* (or "upright man"). Although both *habilis* and *erectus* are considered only proto-humans, they were still a far cry from the apes. Almost two million years ago, *habilis* was building his own shelters in Africa's Olduvai Gorge. He may even have been making his own clothes. A few hundred thousand years later, he was able to create fire. All three talents were important. The world was heading into the deep freeze of the Pleistocene Ice Age.

These early humans spread out from Africa to begin the population of the world. At first they clustered round the Mediterranean for much the same reason people go there today—good weather and great food. Later they spread throughout Europe and Asia. By 120,000 BP, the squat, powerful Neanderthal strain had evolved in western Eurasia. But it was back in Africa, the original cradle of humanity, that the final breakthrough came.

Somewhere around 100,000 BP, *Homo sapiens sapiens*—anatomically modern humanity—evolved around the southern tip of that great continent and quickly spread. Like their most primitive forebears, they too eventually left the ancestral home. Some time prior to 35,000 BP they were in Europe and presenting heavy competition for their Neanderthal cousins—so much so, in fact, that the Neanderthals dwindled, then died out. With nothing left to stop him, Cro-Magnon *Homo sapiens* strode out to conquer the world.

It was not an easy world to conquer. Some 2.5 million years ago, for reasons that are not altogether clear, the weather took a turn for the worse. Global temperatures plummeted. Vast ice sheets appeared. The largest of them was the Laurentide in North America which stretched all the way from southern Illinois to the Canadian Arctic and reached from the Rockies to Newfoundland. Another formed in western Alaska and stretched to northern Washington. There were glaciers and ice caps throughout the highlands of the western United States, Mexico, Central America and Alaska.

On the other side of the Atlantic, a Scandinavian ice sheet covered most of Britain, central Germany, Poland and northern Russia to the Arctic Ocean. There were smaller ice caps in the highlands of northern Siberia and Arctic Eurasia.

In the southern hemisphere, ice caps and glaciers developed throughout the Andes. Glaciers formed in New Zealand, Africa and Tasmania. Glaciers even formed on mountains that stood on the equator.

Worldwide, temperatures were anything up to 20°C colder than they are today. A 200 kilometre (124 mile) zone of permafrost clung to the southern border of the North American ice sheet. In Europe and Russia, permafrost extended many hundreds of kilometres south.

Sea levels fell. There was a land bridge connecting Alaska and Siberia. And the British Isles were part of mainland Europe. With lowered sea levels and colder oceans, there was less rainfall. Sand dunes multiplied and arid zones increased in Australia, Africa, India and the Middle East. As glaciation peaked, the world's deserts expanded by a factor of five and the world's oceans began to freeze.

Despite the difficulties, the new humans managed to expand their range, leading a nomadic, hunter-gatherer existence and somehow keeping body and soul together in the brute hope of better times to come.

THE NEOLITHIC REVOLUTION

Towards the end of the Ice Age, a few communities in areas of good geography and climate began to make the transition from Old Stone Age savagery to a more settled way of life. The population grew, as did the size of individual communities. There was a widening mastery of materials so that worked clay was used for pottery and brick, and woven fabrics began to take the place of animal skins for clothing.

For the most part, even the new communities depended on manpower, but domesticated animals were increasingly pressed into service for transport and the carrying of loads. Most experts believe small boats were first built at this time and some have suggested the sail might have been invented.

The period is now known as the Neolithic Revolution. It was a revolution that produced some comparatively sophisticated devices, like the wheel, the potter's wheel, the bow drill and the pole lathe. Somewhere around 8000 BC, the Ice Age ended as mysteriously as it had begun. Rainfall increased, and the tundra and desert were reclaimed by forest and grassland. Game animals multiplied.

In these softer times, there was an emergence of farming in the Fertile Crescent—a swathe from the Persian Gulf around the northern edge of the Syrian Desert to Palestine and the borders of Egypt—almost as soon as the glaciers retreated. Two thousand years later, agriculture had appeared in Mesoamerica and China. By 4000 BC, farming had become a way of life throughout most of the Old World.

Around this time, people began to settle in the southernmost part of Mesopotamia between the Tigris and the Euphrates rivers, in the area that later became Babylonia and is now southern Iraq. Their remains were first discovered near the modern village of Al-Ubaid, and the people themselves named Ubaidians for that reason. They drained the marshes for agriculture, developed trade, and established weaving, leatherwork, metalwork, masonry and pottery. Various Semitic peoples infiltrated the territory, adding their cultures to the Ubaidia. What resulted was the world's first glimpse of civilisation. By the third millennium BC the country included at least twelve separate city-states. A separate Egyptian civilisation sprang up soon after.

Against this broad background, it is easy to see that while the Egyptian state may have come into being a few hundred years earlier than Egyptologists currently envisage, there can be no question of its foundation some 40,000 years ago as the Egyptians themselves believed. At that time, the scientific consensus assures us, the most advanced communities on the face of our planet were beetle-browed tribal groupings of shambling Neanderthals. We will have to look elsewhere for a solution to our Egyptian mysteries.

Unless, of course, the scientific consensus is just plain wrong.

PROBLEMS FOR DARWIN

There are problems with Darwin's theory of evolution. Darwin spotted a couple of the more obvious ones himself. He was, for example, distinctly uneasy about the fossil record.

The importance of the fossil record is that Darwin's picture of one species evolving into another relies on the development of numerous intermediate forms throughout the long, gradual process of transformation. Thousands of these intermediate forms must have roamed the Earth at one time. When they died, their bones were just as likely to fossilise as those of any other creature. Consequently you would expect the fossil record to be full of them. Darwin certainly did . . . but never found them. This did not lead him to abandon his theory. He decided the reason why the missing links remained missing was that the fossil record was "less perfect than is generally supposed."

Darwin's supporters were happy to concur. Palaeontology was in its infancy in the nineteenth century so it was perhaps not altogether surprising to find transition species absent from the few fossils discovered at the time. But, since then, enormous resources have been devoted to filling in the gaps . . . and have failed miserably. Professor Niles Eldredge of Harvard is on record as remarking that, since no one had ever found any "in-between" creatures and the fossil record had failed to show up "missing links," many scientists have come to believe that Darwin's famous transitional forms never existed.

Among those "many scientists" is the internationally renowned Stephen Jay Gould, an American professor of zoology and geology, who claims bluntly, "The fossil record offers no support for gradual change." Others have noted what the fossil record *does* appear to show—that familiar species are actually astonishingly long-lived, with few if any evolutionary modifications.

But if the fossil record fails to show the missing links required by Darwin, what does it show? The answer is a little creepy.

Plants first appear in the fossil record about 450 million years ago. There is no indication of their having developed out of any earlier form. They simply appear. What's more, every major form of plant arrives together. This can only be explained in orthodox evolutionary terms if none of the millions of intermediate stages which led to this dramatic development ever fossilised. The chances against this are astronomical.

The first flowering plants also appear in the fossil record fully formed. Although we have an abundance of fossils of the earlier, non-flowering species, not a single one of these can be described as an intermediate form on the evolutionary path to flowers. At one point there were no flowering plants. At another, flowering plants were all over the place.

You find exactly the same bizarre pattern in the animal kingdom. The earliest fish with spines and brains appeared some 450 million years ago. In all the many curious life forms discovered in the sea, they had no apparent evolutionary ancestors. According to orthodox doctrine, the cartilaginous skeleton found in certain fish—like the ray— gradually evolved into a bony skeleton. The fossil record shows cartilaginous fish appeared (without apparent ancestors) 75 million years *after* bony fish.

Orthodox doctrine also insists fish with jaws gradually evolved from jawless varieties. The record shows nothing of the sort. Fish with jaws suddenly appeared, with no discernible ancestry. Furthermore, these jawed fish somehow evolved one jawless species—the lamprey—despite the fact that jawlessness is supposed to be a characteristic destined to be selected out of the life stream.

Darwinian theory suggests that lung-fish, capable of breathing both on land and under water, eventually evolved primitive legs out of their gills and crawled on to a beach to become the first amphibians. Amphibians certainly exist. What doesn't exist is a single intermediate fossil tracing the famous lung-fish gills-to-legs evolutionary sequence. Some 320 million years ago, fossils of fully a dozen orders of amphibians began to be laid down. All had well-developed limbs, shoulders and pelvic girdles. None showed the slightest sign of having evolved from fish, or from anything else that evolved from fish.

Fish species themselves show no signs of evolution. The shark who terrifies swimmers today is the same beast he was 150 million years ago. Oysters and mussels have been around unchanged for even longer—they appeared in their present form and were arguably just as delicious 400 million years ago.

Mammals appeared suddenly as well. The orthodox theory suggests they evolved from a single, tree-dwelling, shrew-like creature that expanded into the niche left when the dinosaurs perished. There was indeed such a creature, but the fossil record gives no indication that it evolved into anything. Instead, 10 million years after the dinosaurs disappeared, a dozen or so separate and distinct mammalian species turn up without warning in the fossil record . . . in areas as distant as South America, Africa and Asia. There are no intermediate fossils showing a connection between these mammals and the earlier shrew. There are no fossils showing any inter-species evolution either. Among the fossil mammals that appeared so abruptly at that time are lions, bats and bears that you would recognise immediately if you were chased by them today.

HUMAN ANCESTRY

The fossil record is equally unclear about humanity's ancestral heritage. We may be reasonably confident that the vast primeval forests gradually shrank. It seems equally clear that apes flourished in those forests that remained. But then, about 8 to 9 million years ago, they abruptly disappeared. Or at least the fossil record of this great primate evolution cuts off abruptly. Whether this reflects a reality of life at the time, no one really knows.

The period 8 million to 4.5 million BP is virtually devoid of primate fossils, although the fossilised remains of other animals have turned up in their tens of thousands. It is in this period, characterised by lack of evidence, that scientists believe the evolution of humanity took place. But the fossil record does not show that humanity evolved then. The fossil record has nothing to say on the matter. What the fossil record seems to show is that 8 million years ago the primates disappeared, then reappeared in all their glory—with humanity amongst them—3½ million years later.

The idea that our most distant ancestors came down from the trees to make their mark on the savannah is now being increasingly questioned.

It's all very well to say we first stood upright so we could see approaching predators over the tall grass. But, having seen them, such a stance positively ensured that we could not run fast enough to get away. This is inherent in the mechanics of upright posture. For any ape-like creature adapted to four-legged motion, standing upright steals energy that would otherwise be used in moving forward. Thus an upright stance on the savannah would not be the advantageous mutation it seems at first. Which may be why we have never witnessed its appearance in any known species of ape, despite similar pressures on their forest habitat.

Nor has any known species of ape lost body hair, developed a larger brain, or evolved the unique type of breathing that permits speech. It's as if the evolutionary pressures that produced humanity suddenly stopped working.

THE BEGINNINGS OF HUMAN HISTORY

Whatever else the fossil record may show, conventional experts believe it places the entire history of our species (*Homo sapiens sapiens*) in the Pleistocene and Holocene periods (roughly 2 million BP to the present day) and insist that modern man is probably little more than 100,000 years old. Unfortunately, this agreement is reached by ignoring or dismissing any evidence to the contrary.

In one of my earlier books, *Martian Genesis*, I surveyed just a few of the finds—rigorously excluded from the orthodox canon—which indicated that humanity has been on the planet for longer than is taught in our textbooks.[58] These included:

Δ A human skull fragment from Hungary dated between 250,000 and 450,000 BP.

Δ A human footprint with accompanying paleoliths (stones deliberately chipped into a recognisable tool type), bone tools, hearths and shelters, discovered in France and dated 300,000 to 400,000 years BP.

Δ Paleoliths in Spain, a partial human skeleton and paleoliths in France; two English skeletons, one with associated paleoliths, all at least 300,000 years old.

Δ Skull fragments and paleoliths in Kenya and advanced paleoliths, of modern human manufacture, in the Olduvai Gorge in Tanzania, dated between 400,000 and 700,000 BP.

Δ Neoliths (the most advanced stone tools and utensils) in China of a type that indicate full human capacity, dated to 600,000 BP.

Δ Hearths, charcoal, human femurs and broken animal bones, all denoting modern humanity, in Java, dated to 830,000 BP.

Δ An anatomically modern human skull discovered in Argentina and dated between 1 million and 1:5 million BP. (Eoliths—chipped pebbles, thought to be the earliest known tools—at Monte Hermoso, also in Argentina, are believed to be between 1 and 2:5 million years old.)

Δ A human tooth from Java yielding a date between
   1 and 1.9 million years BP.

Δ Incised bones, dated between 1.2 and 2.5 million
   BP, have been found in Italy.

Δ Finds of paleoliths, cut and charred bones at Xi-
   houdu in China and eoliths from Diring Yurlakh in
   Siberia dated to 1.8 million BP.

Δ Eoliths in India, paleoliths in England, Belgium, Italy and Argentina, flint blades in Italy, hearths in
   Argentina, a carved shell, pierced teeth, a pierced
   bone and even two human jaws all bearing a *minimum* date of 2 million BP.

Curiously enough, several of the very earliest artefact
finds show an extraordinary level of sophistication. In
Idaho, for example, a 2-million-year-old *clay figurine* was
unearthed in 1912. But this find does not mark an outer
limit. Bones, vertebrae and even complete skeletons have
been found in Italy, Argentina and Kenya. Their minimum
datings range from 3 million to 4 million BP. A human
skull, a partial human skeleton and a collection of neoliths
discovered in California have been dated in excess of 5
million years. A human skeleton discovered at Midi in
France, paleoliths found in Portugal, Burma and Argentina, a carved bone and flint flakes from Turkey all have
a minimum age of 5 million years.

  How far back can human history be pushed with finds
like these? The answer seems to be a great deal further
than orthodox science currently allows. As if the forego-
ing finds were not enough, we need to take account of:

Δ Paleoliths from France dated between 7 and 9 million BP.

Δ An eolith from India with a minimum dating of 9 million BP.

Δ Incised bones from France, Argentina and Kenya no less than 12 million years old.

Δ More paleolith finds from France, dated at least 20 million years ago.

Δ Neoliths from California in excess of 23 million years.

Δ Three different finds of paleoliths from Belgium with a minimum dating of 26 million BP.

Δ An anatomically modern human skeleton, neoliths and carved stones found at Table Mountain, California and dated at least 33 million years ago.

But even 33 million years is not the upper limit. A human skeleton found in Switzerland is estimated to be between 38 and 45 million years old. France has yielded up eoliths, paleoliths, cut wood and a chalk ball, the minimum ages of which range from 45 to 50 million years.

There's more.

In 1960, H. L. Armstrong announced in *Nature* the discovery of fossil human footprints near the Paluxy River, in Texas. Dinosaur footprints were found in the same strata. In 1983, the *Moscow News* reported the discovery of a fossilised human footprint next to the fossil footprint of a three-toed dinosaur in the Turkamen Republic. Dinosaurs have been extinct for 65 million years.

In 1938, Professor W. G. Burroughs of Kentucky reported the find of three pairs of fossil tracks dated to 300 million years ago. They showed left and right footprints. Each print had five toes and a distinct arch. The toes were spread apart like those of a human used to walking barefoot. The foot curved back like a human foot to what appeared to be a human heel. There was a pair of prints in the series that showed a right and left foot. The distance between them is just what you'd expect in human footprints.

In December 1862, *The Geologist* carried news of a human skeleton found 27.5 m (90 ft) below the surface in a coal seam in Illinois. The seam was dated between 286 and 320 million years BP.

It's true that a few eoliths, skull fragments and fossil footprints, however old, provide no real backing for the idea of prehistoric civilisations put forward by Plato and the Ancient Egyptians.

But some other finds do.

EVIDENCE OF PREHISTORIC CIVILISATIONS?

In 1968, an American fossil collector named William J. Meister found a fossilised human *shoe* print near Antelope Spring, Utah. There were trilobite fossils in the same stone, which means it was at least 245 million years old. Close examination showed that the sole of this shoe differed little, if at all, from those of shoes manufactured today.

In 1891, an 8-carat gold chain was found in a piece of coal in the USA. Non-carbon material is normally dated by reference to the strata in which it is found. In this case, the coal was laid down around 260 million years BP.

In 1897 a carved stone showing multiple faces of an old man was found at a depth of 40 m (130 ft) in a coal mine in Iowa. The coal there was of similar age.

A piece of coal yielded up an encased iron cup in 1912. Frank J. Kenwood, who made the find, was so intrigued he traced the origin of the coal and discovered it came from Wilburton Mine in Oklahoma. The coal there is about 312 million years old.

In 1844, Scottish physicist Sir David Brewster reported the discovery of a metal nail embedded in a sandstone block from a quarry in the north of England. The head was completely encased, ruling out the possibility that it had been driven in at some recent date. The block from which it came was 360 million years old.

On 22 June 1844, *The Times* reported that a length of gold thread had been found by workmen embedded in stone close to the River Tweed. This stone too was around 360 million years old.

Astonishing though these datings may appear to anyone familiar with the orthodox theory of human origins, they pale in comparison with the dates of two further finds.

According to *Scientific American*, dated 5 June 1852, blasting activities at Meeting House Hill, in Dorchester, Massachusetts, unearthed a metallic, bell-shaped vessel extensively decorated with silver inlays of flowers and vines. The workmanship was described as "exquisite." The vessel was blown out of a bed of Roxbury conglomerate dated somewhat earlier than 600 million years BP.

In 1993, Michael A. Cremo and Richard L. Thompson reported the discovery "over the past several decades" of hundreds of metallic spheres in a pyrophyllite mine in South Africa.[59] The spheres are grooved and give the appearance of having been manufactured. If so, the strata in which they were found suggest they were manufactured 2,800 million years ago.

INTERPRETING THE EVIDENCE

There are, of course, relatively few archaeological finds of artefacts and fossils dating back several hundred million years. This is predictable—the marvel is that anything would survive for such a long time—but it also urges caution.

The difficulty is one of interpretation. Professor Burroughs, who found the Kentucky footprints, decided they were made by a hitherto unknown saurian that just happened to have feet like a human and walk the same way. He might be right. Professor A. Bisschoff, a geologist at the University of Potchefstroom, decided that the South African spheres were limonite concretions. This is frankly unlikely for a variety of reasons, but it does remain (just) possible that the spheres are natural formations.

Experts determined to hold to the current consensus dismiss many anomalous finds as fakes. There are times when they're right about this too. Some so-called fossil footprints have been hand-carved in the hope of attracting tourists. Dating finds from the strata in which they are discovered is problematical, although it has been standard archaeological practice for more than a century. Bones or artefacts found in a million-year-old stratum may actually have been buried there much more recently. Unfortunately, whether or not a find is "acceptable" seems to depend on the preconceptions of the archaeologist. If it fits his idea of the time period, the stratum dating will be accepted without question. If not, the find will be listed as a recent burial.

Despite all this, there seem to have been more than enough discoveries to warrant revision of our consensus beliefs about the age and origins of humanity. But can we really be sure that advanced cultures existed in the depths of prehistory? Specifically, would we be justified in taking seriously the Ancient Egyptian claim that their civilisation was already more than 30,000 years old at the time of Narmer?

This is a much more difficult question to answer. When Robert Schoch questioned the conventional dating of the Great Sphinx at Giza, Peter Lacovara, assistant curator at the Egyptian Department of the Museum of Fine Arts, said the revised dating was ridiculous. Egyptology had the real chronology "pretty well worked out." It is difficult not to sympathise with Dr. Lacovara. Despite Schoch's findings, despite Lockyer's suspicions, despite the astonishing developments of Egyptian technology examined in this book, the archaeological record of the Nile Valley remains quite clear. There are no indications whatsoever of any widespread civilisation prior to about 3100 BC.

Furthermore, in some instances at least, Egypt's cultural development has run contrary to all logic. More than one historian has pointed out that Egyptian building techniques degenerated steadily from the time of the Great Pyramid. The Arab proverb that insists "Time fears the pyramids" refers only to the structures at Giza. Later pyramids—and many were built—are in many instances little more than hills of rubble now.

Orthodox Egyptology claims the ancient engineers "practised" on works like the Step Pyramid at Saqqara or the Bent Pyramid of Dahshur, then eventually got it right with the Giza complex. But after that, for reasons no one quite understands, it was downhill all the way. Less conventional investigators like Ralph Ellis suggest the engineering perfection of the Great Pyramid actually came first, with all other pyramidical structures increasingly flawed copies. Neither picture makes much sense.

These then are the central Egyptian mysteries. How did an extraordinarily advanced technical and scientific civilisation spring up out of nowhere in North Africa? And why did its technology decline so dramatically from an early peak?

Any theory that purports to solve the mystery of Ancient Egypt will have to answer both these questions.

CHAPTER 16

ʕANCIENT TRADITION

THE teachings of Tibetan Buddhism and Indian Hinduism—not to mention several other world traditions—support the anomalous archaeological findings in suggesting that humanity has a far longer provenance on our planet than Western science allows. This idea is preserved in Hinduism to the present day, especially in the doctrine of the *yugas*.

The term *yuga* means "age" and refers to the Hindu belief that humanity has lived on our planet during four separate and distinct time periods: the *Krita Yuga*, the *Treta Yuga*, the *Dvapara Yuga* and the *Kali Yuga*, the first three of which have already been and gone. The names of the ages are rooted in the Sanskrit terms for four of the sides of a die, with the *Krita Yuga* derived from the side showing the figure 4, *Treta Yuga* 3, *Dvapara Yuga* 2, and *Kali Yuga* 1. This reflects the Hindu conviction that the degree of righteousness in the world diminished in an arithmetical progression as time went on.

The *Krita Yuga* is seen as a primeval golden age, characterised by piety, peace and plenty. The world had one

God, one truth, one scripture and one rule. Fear was unknown, as was hatred, deceit or malice. This age lasted 1,728,000 years.

The *Krita Yuga* was followed by the *Treta Yuga* which was only three-quarters as righteous as the age before. Unity of religion still held sway, but now humanity no longer followed spiritual pursuits for their own sake, but rather in the hope of reward. The *Treta Yuga* spanned a further 1,296,000 years.

Next came the *Dvapara Yuga*, in which righteousness again diminished by a quarter. Now the single truth and single scripture fragmented into four. Humanity moved further and further from the ways of good and as a consequence found itself beset by disease and disaster. This age lasted 864,000 years.

Finally, humanity entered the *Kali Yuga*, the age in which we are living now. Once again righteousness was reduced so that in our present time we are only one-quarter as spiritual as our most distant ancestors. Most of humanity no longer makes sacrifice to the One God. Hunger and fear have become commonplace, as have natural and man-made disasters. This age is destined to last 432,000 years.

Adding the various figures together gives a human history of 4,320,000 years, but the total is deceptive, as Hindu spirituality was based on the idea of recurring cycles. Each round of the four *yugas* forms a *Mahayuga* (sometimes called a *Manvantara*) which is then repeated, with the final *Kali Yuga* giving way to a new *Krita Yuga* and so on.

But the cycle is interrupted eventually. A thousand *Mahayugas* constitute a full Day of Brahma, during which the world is in manifestation. This is followed by an equally long Night of Brahma, during which it is withdrawn into nothingness. As the Night of Brahma ends and a new Day of Brahma dawns, the sequence of *yugas* begins again, exactly as before.

A Prehistoric Golden Age?

The idea of a prehistoric golden age, like that of the *Krita Yuga*, is not confined to the Far East. Judaeo-Christian mythology tells how early humanity lived without hunger or death in the Garden of Eden. In the West, this is our most familiar allusion to a golden age, but the legend itself is universal.

The Norse myths of the *Völuspá* speak of multiple "creations'—an echo of the Days and Nights of Brahma—and insist that, after chaos was overcome in the first of them, humanity enjoyed a prolonged period of peace and plenty. The belief was also current in Ancient Rome where, again as in Hindu mythology, it was associated with recurring cycles.

The Celts mourned the loss of ancient Avalon, an enchanted archipelago which included the island of the Blest, larger than Ireland, where there was neither grief, sorrow nor death. The Greeks believed the god Chronos once ruled a world where no one worked, experienced pain or grew old. In Ancient Persia there was a strong tradition of four prehistoric kingdoms, the first of which was marked by peace and prosperity. In faraway China, a primeval golden age again forms part of the most ancient traditions.

The fourfold division found in the Hindu *yugas* turns up again in the Tibetan tradition of the creation, as does a variation on the theme of Brahma bringing the world into manifestation by means of breath. The primeval state of unmanifestation is described as a dark void before the beginning of time. This was eventually disturbed by a gentle wind which gradually intensified until it formed clouds. The clouds yielded rain which fell to form the great ocean *Gyatso*. The continuing action of the wind on the waters produced earth through a process analogous to churning butter.

Although the mythic geography of Tibet—which involves a four-sided column of precious stones, seven huge lakes and seven mountain rings—sounds bizarre to Western ears, there are more familiar elements in the idea of four worlds, the first of which was the most blessed.

Sometimes the world's traditions tell how fragmentary remnants of the primeval paradise endured long after the rest of it had disappeared. The Babylonian *Epic of Gilgamesh* describes how Gilgamesh finds a survivor named Utnapishtim on a mysterious island. According to Homer, Menelaus, the husband of Helen of Troy, went somewhere similar, as did Britain's legendary King Arthur, following his last battle.

As one of the world's oldest religions, the literary source of Hinduism—the hymns of the Rigveda—dates back to the second millennium BC, but there is evidence of even earlier antecedents derived from archaeology, comparative philology, and comparative religion. As the state religion of India, it is never referred to by name among its adherents. The term "Hindu" is Persian and translates simply as "Indian." To the Indians themselves, their religion is the *Sanatana Dharma*. The *Dharma* is the body of the faith, a term that roughly translates as "law" or "truth." *Sanatana* means "eternal and ageless." Since, unlike Christianity or Islam, Hinduism has no known founder, practitioners believe it has existed for all time. Although Westerners are reluctant to take this literally, it is clearly a tradition of great antiquity.

Curiously, this tradition contends that civilisation appeared on the planet long before conventional scholars will credit. Its epic scriptures even contain detailed records of prehistoric wars fought with weaponry so advanced it would not be out of place today.

The Sanskrit *Mahabharata*, for example, describes how the Asuras, a race who fought with the gods, built three aerial metal fortresses in order to attack specific earthly locations. The same account written today would, of course, describe satellite technology.

This source and the epic *Ramayana* also refer to undersea cities, military and commercial aircraft, not to mention weapons of mass destruction eerily reminiscent of lasers, high-explosive fragmentation bombs and atomic armaments.

VISITORS FROM THE HEAVENS?

Ideas of alien intervention are also mirrored in a surprisingly large number of world traditions, usually expressed in religious or mythic terms. Once again, the most familiar example of the belief is found in the first five books of the Old Testament—the Jewish Torah. Although the term "God" is used in English translations to describe the deity who walked and talked with Adam, the original Hebrew is *Elohim*, an unusual construction that is not only plural, but embodies both male and female forms. Thus a more accurate translation might suggest that godlike male and female creatures were responsible for the creation of humanity. Such an interpretation is given additional weight by two very curious verses in the book of Genesis:

> That the sons of God saw the daughters of men that they were fair; and they took them wives of all which they chose.
>
> GENESIS 6:2

> There were giants in the earth in those days; and also
> after that, when the sons of God came in unto the
> daughters of men, and they bare children to them, the
> same became mighty men which were of old, men of
> renown.

GENESIS 6:4

A fuller account of the tradition is given in the apocryphal book of Enoch which describes how a group of 200 beings from the sky decided to interbreed with humanity. Their leader, Semjaza, became worried, mainly, it seems, because he was afraid he would get the blame if they were found out. To reassure him, the group met together on Mount Hermon and swore to accept collective responsibility. They then put the plan into action. When matters went badly wrong, the worsening situation was reported back to God who put a stop to the whole sorry business with the Deluge, sparing only Noah and his kin.

The concept of intervention crops up again and again in various ancient traditions. In Tibetan doctrine, for example, our world is referred to as *Dzambu Lying*. For a time after it came into being, Dzambu Lying was empty of people, animals and plants. Then it was visited by creatures from "the centre of the universe." In Tibetan scriptures, these creatures are referred to as "gods." Their point of origin, *Rirab Lhunpo*, often goes untranslated, but it remains clear that the intent was to describe powerful and intelligent beings from some distant part of the galaxy.

These creatures established themselves on Earth and gradually adjusted to it. In the process they became human. After a period of war and turmoil, they selected a king named Mang Kur, who taught them the arts of building and agriculture.

Native North American folklore also insists that all people lived originally in the sky and subsequently visited Earth to establish humanity. In China, the legendary Yellow Emperor was taught agriculture, medicine and the erotic arts by a visitor from heaven. With 70,000 years of uninterrupted culture behind them, the Australian Aborigines have the oldest living tradition on the planet. They too believe Earth was visited by aliens in the distant past. They were called the Wandjina, or Sky People.

Hittite texts describe the outcome of an extra-terrestrial conflict which resulted in the loser fleeing to take refuge on Earth. The earliest of the world's great known civilisations—the Sumerian—produced texts packed with references to the Anunnaki, creatures from the heavens who colonised Earth. The first group of fifty landed in or on the Arabian Sea at a time when the Persian Gulf was no more than a marsh and came ashore to establish a settlement they called *E Ri Du*—"Home Far Away."

Thousands of kilometres away in Mali, Dogon tribespeople believe they were once instructed by a creature from the Sirius star system. Northwards in Egypt itself, there was a belief that the ancient founders of the state came from the sky and were specifically associated with the constellation Orion.

There may be differences in detail but the three major elements—the early appearance of humanity, alien intervention in the affairs of our planet, and the development of advanced prehistoric civilisations—all receive support from a multiplicity of ancient traditions worldwide.

This interesting fact may be of help in reconstructing the secret history of Ancient Egypt.

CHAPTER 17

EGYPT AND ATLANTIS

P LATO'S brief mention of Egypt's early foundation comes as an introduction to his famous story of Atlantis. It is clear from the context that he believed Egypt to have been in existence before Atlantis sank. He claimed Atlantis itself was destroyed "in a single day and a night" at a time of great earthquakes widespread enough to have swallowed up the Athenian army and destroyed an early version of this Greek city-state. Is it possible that Egypt could have been devastated at the same time?

Before even considering this question, we need to examine a far more urgent proposition: was the whole Atlantis story no more than a Platonic fable?

As Atlantis is first mentioned in a dialogue about the nature of an ideal state, we might assume that Plato created a fictional story to illustrate its characteristics—and there are scholars today who are happy to argue that this is exactly what he did. But there are problems with such a conclusion.

It is, for example, clear that Atlantis was *not* the ideal city-state. Plato claims it was ruled by a federation of kings who displeased their gods by growing corrupt and warlike. Furthermore, he attributed the story to Solon, a statesman of such prestige that it would have been unthinkable to use his name to support a fiction. In his own day, many of Plato's closest followers accepted the Atlantis story as history—or at the very least a genuinely ancient tradition presented as history.

That qualification raises its own problems. A tradition may be genuine and ancient without necessarily being true. The Atlantis story has many elements that seem entirely mythic. It tells of a civilisation far too advanced for the period in which it was set. According to Plato, its citizens wore tailored clothes, the horse had been domesticated, a vast navy built, metal mined and worked, writing invented, a central authority established—all at a time when science assures us our ancestors were primitive nomadic hunter-gatherers, living in makeshift shelters as they followed herds of reindeer over the chill tracts of a bitter Ice Age. Plato also describes international contact and trade, lush vegetation and tropical beasts—notably elephants—roaming the Atlantean plains at latitudes that must then have been extremely chill.

But the biggest objection of all to the validity of the Atlantis story is the description of the country's demise. According to Plato it sank beneath the Atlantic Ocean at a time of particularly violent earthquakes. Any geologist will confirm that this is just plain impossible. The most violent earthquakes ever recorded have managed to affect the elevation of only a few hundred hectares of land. They have not come remotely close to sinking a continent.

Tidal waves, earth faults or volcanic action don't fit the bill either. The mechanism that comes closest is volcanic, but even that is relative. A volcanic megaexplosion, like those on Krakatoa and Thera, might be expected to destroy portions of a small island. But no volcano—or chain of volcanoes—erupts with sufficient violence to destroy a continent.

EVIDENCE OF ATLANTIS?

All the same, evidence has come to light that suggests there really *was* a powerful maritime civilisation, now lost, in the depths of prehistory. The core of this evidence is a series of ancient maps, each one a copy of an original whose structure indicates that it was drawn in the Pleistocene Ice Age.[60]

These maps were analysed over a period of years by an American professor of the history of science named Charles Hapgood, who concluded that they originated with an unknown people, whose knowledge was inherited by the Minoans and Phoenicians. Most of the surviving charts are of the Mediterranean, but others show the Americas, the Arctic and the Antarctic. The latter continent—which we have always believed was not discovered until the nineteenth century—is accurately mapped, although it now lies under an ice sheet more than 1.6 km (1 mile) thick. Hapgood concluded that the ancient mapmakers visited the continent before the ice cap formed.

Professor Hapgood has gone on record with the opinion that his Ice Age civilisation was more advanced than the classical cultures of Ancient Greece and Rome. In areas like astronomy, navigation, mathematics, mapmaking and ship-building, it was actually more advanced: modern technology did not catch up until the eighteenth century. He believes the lost civilisation knew the exact length of the solar year and the circumference of the Earth. It had developed spherical trigonometry and knew the moons of Jupiter and Saturn, although these are invisible to the naked eye.

Although there is nothing in the evidence to show that

this ancient civilisation was based on Atlantis, it certainly fits well with Plato's contention that an advanced sea-going culture existed more than 12,000 years ago.

Further support for the Atlantis story is provided by archaeological evidence of a major war fought in the same period that Plato claimed Atlantis attacked the Mediterranean states. Recent finds also confirm that there were people wearing tailored clothing more than 20,000 years ago, metal was mined before flint in certain areas and writing seems to have been developed long before the first cuneiform tablet was inscribed in Sumer. There are cave drawings in France showing bridled horses, suggesting that the animal was indeed domesticated. Although still controversial, some archaeologists are now suggesting an astonishingly early date for certain monumental stone buildings, notably in South America. The revised dating, if accurate, would place them earlier than the supposed destruction of Atlantis.

It has to be admitted that none of this adds up to definitive proof. But it also shows that there is scarcely anything in Plato's story that can be dismissed as outright fantasy. If Atlantis itself did not exist in prehistory, there was certainly an advanced civilisation that did.

Or perhaps it would be more accurate to speak of an advanced culture, a term that is less dependent on a specific geographical location. Plato's account does not describe a single island kingdom surrounded by a world of barbarism. It is quite clear that he believed many more countries—Egypt and Greece are specifically named, others inferred—had achieved civilised status. Hapgood's evidence supports this. One of his maps was found carved on a stone pillar as far afield as China. That Egypt had a place in this international culture is also supported by hard evidence. While Egyptologists like Bob Brier continue to believe that "Egyptians developed their navigational skills on the smooth-flowing Nile and . . . remained river sailors, not tempted by the lure . . . of the open sea,"[61] an inscription on remote Pitcairn Island and scarabs found in Australia all show that the Egyptians ventured much further afield.

The question is, how was this ancient culture lost? If the geologists are right, there can be no question of its having been sunk by earthquakes in a day and a night. This would not account for the disappearance of a single continent, let alone a far more widespread level of civilisation.

Unless, of course, some unique set of circumstances triggered earthquakes of a magnitude no longer experienced today.

COSMIC CATACLYSM

In 1995, Gateway Books of Bath, England, brought out a scholarly work by D. S. Allan and J. B. Delair entitled *When the Earth Nearly Died*. It proposed a thesis that explained the destruction of Atlantis and the disappearance of a culture that extended far beyond its island shores. The theory was that Earth had suffered the effects of a close pass by a supernova fragment some time around 10,000 BC. Allan and Delair's ideas provided the inspiration for my own book on the subject, *The Atlantis Enigma*.[62] They may be summarised as follows.

Astronomers have long realised that we live in a damaged solar system. The "harmony of the spheres" so beloved of medieval philosophers was never more than a myth. A number of the outer planets and their moons show signs of having been violently disrupted in their orbits and there are experts who believe the asteroid belt between Mars and Jupiter is the remains of an exploded planet. Mars itself exhibits surface devastation and the innermost planet, Mercury, seems to have been subjected to an intense meteor bombardment.

What caused the damage is anybody's guess. But a consensus has formed that, whatever the cause, the event must have occurred millions of years ago. It is a consensus without rational foundation. The plain fact is that no-one knows when the damage was caused. There is absolutely no evidence related to the timing. Allan and Delair bravely postulated a relatively recent date. Their proposed engine of destruction was a fiery mass hurled off by an exploding supernova.

As it happens, there was a supernova that would fit the bill. It was located only 45 light years from Earth and flared sometime between 12,000 and 9000 BC.

Although 45 light years is just next door in astronomical terms, it is still a massive distance. And a supernova fragment would have taken centuries to cross it. Nonetheless, the figures still suggest it could have reached our solar system around the date given by Plato for the destruction of Atlantis.

The term "fragment" is deceptive. The postulated body would have been a flaming mass several magnitudes larger than the Earth. According to the current theory, its passage through the solar system was marked by a trail of devastation and a close pass to Earth.

There was no collision—you would not be reading these words if there had been—but the close pass set up massive gravitational and electrical interactions between the visitor and our planet. Among the predicted effects would have been intensive meteor bombardment, planet-wide earthquakes, volcanic eruptions and a tilting of the Earth on its axis.

But the most important and dramatic result would have been the creation of a mega-tide in the world ocean, drawing water inexorably northwards to create a massive standing wave hundreds of kilometres high. As the intruder continued its journey, gravitational influences weakened, the standing wave collapsed and the resultant drainage created flooding on a planetary scale.

Such a disaster would certainly have been extreme enough to sink Atlantis. According to Plato, it destroyed the earliest manifestation of Athens as well. Allan and Delair believe it came close to wiping out the human race: many species extinctions date to that time. The Egyptians themselves claimed to hold records of ancient catastrophes—Plato mentions it in his account of Solon's visit. They believed planetary disasters occurred more than once in the distant past and were convinced that Egypt's unusual geographical position had saved their culture from obliteration:

> There have been, and will be again, many destructions of mankind arising out of many causes; the greatest have been brought about by the agencies of fire and water, and other lesser ones by innumerable other causes. There is a story, which even you have preserved, that once upon a time Phaeton, the son of Helios, having yoked the steeds in his father's chariot, because he was not able to drive them in the path of his father, burnt up all that was upon the earth, and was himself destroyed by a thunderbolt. Now this has the form of a myth, but really signifies a declination of the bodies moving in the heavens around the earth, and a great conflagration of things upon the earth, which recurs after long intervals; at such times those who live upon the mountains and in dry and lofty places are more liable to destruction than those who dwell by rivers or on the seashore. And from this calamity the Nile who is our never-failing saviour, delivers and preserves us. When, on the other hand, the gods purge the earth with a deluge of water, the survivors in your country are herdsmen and shepherds

who dwell on the mountains, but those who, like you, live in cities are carried by the rivers into the sea. Whereas in this land, neither then nor at any other time, does the water come down from above on the fields, having always a tendency to come up from below; for which reason the traditions preserved here are the most ancient.[63]

To modern ears, this reasoning sounds naïve. But even if Egypt was fortunate enough to survive earlier—possibly localised—disasters, nothing in its geography is likely to have provided protection against the destructive force of a supernova fragment. Egypt did not disappear completely, like Atlantis, but its civilisation suffered a blow from which it took millennia to recover.

THE SECRET HISTORY OF ANCIENT EGYPT

What then is Ancient Egypt's secret history? The plain truth is that no one knows for sure. But circumstantial evidence can be pieced together to provide a reasonable reconstruction.

Sometime in the depths of prehistory, in a world very different from our own, civilisation appeared in North Africa, along the shores of the Nile. Conditions were certainly suitable. The area that is now desert was once lush savannah and the great river an unfailing supply of fresh water.

When did it happen? Geological examination of the Sphinx at Giza redates the monument to between 5000 and 7000 BC, so the civilisation must have been in place before then. Plato writes of a war between Atlantis and various Mediterranean states, including Egypt. Widespread archaeological finds of arrowheads and skeletal remains showing violent death throughout the Mediterranean indicate that a large-scale prehistoric war did take place in the area and date it between 10,000 and 12,000 BC. If this was Plato's conflict, Egypt must have been founded before 10,000 BC. Egyptian sources claim a much earlier provenance, something borne out by Ralph Ellis's ingenious dating of exposed stonework and the astonishing development of certain Egyptian sciences, notably astronomy, which required long periods of observation to reach the heights it did. Taken as a whole, available evidence suggests that the first Egyptian state was probably founded earlier than 40,000 BC.

The likelihood is that the Nile Valley culture was neither the world's first nor the world's only civilisation. Others may have existed in the Far East, on Atlantis (wherever that legendary land was located), in South America and, closer to hand, in that area of the Mediterranean we now know as Greece. Trade links probably sprang up between these various centres.

We should not assume that the world was civilised at this early time. Available evidence suggests that most of Europe and large tracts of Asia remained primal wilderness, inhabited mainly by small tribes of Neanderthals. While more extreme, the pattern was similar to what we have today: Stone Age cultures in Southern Africa and Central Australia coexist with high-tech computerised societies in the U.S., Britain, Europe, Japan and elsewhere.

For millennia upon millennia, the pace of life on the Nile was slow, civilised and conservative. Although conventional science places the old civilisation in the depths of the Pleistocene Ice Age, there are reasons to believe this view may be mistaken.[64] Almost certainly, Egypt enjoyed balmy, humid weather.

In time, the Egyptian civilisation developed impressive scientific and technical skills. These were particularly evident in engineering, astronomy, sonics and psychotronics. In three of the four areas—the exception is astronomy—

Egypt was as advanced as, if not more advanced than, the modern Western world. If Eric Crew is right, the Egyptians had manned flight in the form of balloons and one interpretation of the Abydos hieroglyphs suggests powered aircraft as well. Certainly they were deep sea sailors. To this day, some evidence of their presence is scattered across the globe. Egyptian investigation into the techniques of engineering and the benefits of electricity led to the construction of the Great Pyramid at Giza as a power source. The pyramid shape may have been chosen because its curious psychotronic effects enhanced the mechanical and chemical processes described by Christopher Dunn. With the development of broadcast electricity (the secret of which was rediscovered millennia later by Nikola Tesla), this single massive structure may have been able to supply the electrical needs of the entire nation.

Despite its technical excellence, it would be a mistake to imagine Egyptian civilisation as being similar to our own. Since the world was far less densely populated, cities and city-states were substantially smaller than they are today. Competition for land and property was minimal. Egypt was rich in natural resources, more or less self-sustaining, and had little incentive to attack its neighbours. The same was probably true of other advanced states. Early civilisation existed without the necessity for war.

Surprisingly, the absence of warfare was a mixed blessing. On the one hand it allowed prolonged periods of political stability. On the other, there was a tendency towards stagnation. The technology of armaments scarcely developed at all. There is no indication of the discovery of explosives, and projectile weapons seem to have been unknown. When war did come, despite technical advances in other areas, it was fought with flint-tipped bows and arrows.

The tradition preserved at Sais suggests the Egyptians were aware that natural disasters often occurred in prehistoric times. Their trade links must have brought them stories of ruinous earthquakes, volcanic eruptions, great floods and perhaps even rare but destructive meteor strikes. But these calamities affected other people. Egypt itself enjoyed a charmed existence, for the worst of the disasters passed it by.

Until there came a catastrophe of such magnitude that no civilised country escaped.

The close pass of a supernova fragment shifted our planetary axis, changed global weather patterns, triggered a massive meteor bombardment and culminated in a near universal flood that not only destroyed every established civilisation but buried them so deeply that virtually no trace of them remained. This time, Egypt was not spared.

The great North African civilisation that had endured for tens of thousands of years disappeared in a matter of days—a week or two at the most. Homes and palaces, temples, towns and cities, were crushed under the weight of waters, buried under mud, covered by desert sands as the climate changed abruptly. Only a handful of structures survived, some through chance or fortuitous location, some because of their sheer size. Among the latter was the most massive construction the world had ever known, the Great Pyramid at Giza.

A substantial population was reduced to a handful of shocked survivors, fighting for their lives in a newly hostile world.

Although the time-scale of the disaster was short, the aftermath was more prolonged. Arable land was poisoned with salt when the floodwaters receded. Torrential downpours eventually washed the salt away, but the change in climate produced a freezing plunge in world temperatures, heralding a new Ice Age. Farming was impossible. As the game herds of Africa recovered, a decimated humanity had no choice but to revert to a hunter-gatherer lifestyle. It was a lifestyle that was to endure for millennia.

But, while the prevailing conditions forced humanity to return to a primitive existence, the lessons of civilisation were never entirely forgotten. They were preserved by a small grouping of vitally important individuals.

In *The Murder of Tutankhamen*, a readable précis of ancient history, Egyptologist Bob Brier explains the three pillars of the Egyptian state as they were known in historic times—the pharaoh, the military and the priesthood. While all power and authority were theoretically vested in the pharaoh, Brier rightly points out that no king could survive without priestly support. It was even more vital than the support of the army. But why was the priesthood so important?

Brier explains it in simple religious terms: the army needed the support of the gods in their campaigns and donated to the priesthood to obtain divine favour.[65] But this explanation does not stand up to scrutiny. As Brier himself rightly points out, a priest in Ancient Egypt was a far cry from an Anglican vicar today. Pharaoh, as a divinity himself, was the *only* intermediary with his fellow gods. But, divine or not, Pharaoh couldn't be everywhere at once. With hundreds of temples scattered throughout Egypt, somebody had to perform the rituals in his place. This was where the priests came in. They were not necessarily saintly, not even particularly religious. They were simply stand-ins for their king. Those at the head of the hierarchy were rich. Many were corrupt.

But this description is limited, especially when applied to the priesthood of the Old Kingdom. In the early days of dynastic Egypt, a priest was far more than a pharaonic puppet. There is nothing in our modern world that exactly mirrors his function; surprisingly, the closest thing we have is a scientist.

Alongside their purely ceremonial duties, the priests of Egypt functioned as keepers of knowledge. Many, perhaps even most, were astronomers who dedicated their lives to stellar observations and the preservation of celestial records. But they were authorities in other branches of knowledge as well. The priesthood at Sais specialised in history, as we have already noted. Other temple groups studied the secrets of architecture, of engineering and several equally important topics.

If the priesthood of an antediluvian Egypt was based on the same structure, we have a ready-made explanation for the most difficult of the mysteries we have been examining. After the disaster which destroyed the original civilisation, those priests who survived became guardians of the ancient knowledge on which it was founded. Its preservation must have been their prime concern.

In Black Africa today there are still tribes that maintain oral histories stretching back into the mists of time. Even without script, dedicated training enables a select elder or elders to memorise extensive genealogies and incidents which are added to with every succeeding generation. Extrapolating from available evidence, it seems likely that the priesthood of Old Egypt engaged in a similar pursuit, although the possibility of written records cannot be entirely ruled out. (An extraordinarily persistent myth suggests that "a hall of records" is associated with the Sphinx and is still hidden somewhere at Giza.)

Not all the knowledge of the old culture would have been immediately useful, or indeed comprehensible. In a world denuded of its trees, skills like carpentry and shipbuilding were obviously of diminished value. With a decimated population, there might no longer have been sufficient manpower to make use of the great engineering techniques—and little need for monumental stone buildings in any case. Electricity would be irrelevant to a hunter-gatherer existence. In such circumstances, the major effort must have focused on preserving a knowledge of agriculture. This, more than anything else, would lay the foundation for a renewed civilisation.

But like so much else, the implementation of agricultural techniques had to wait for a change in environmental conditions—notably a rise in temperatures and the retreat of the ice. Once this happened, as it eventually did, the descendants of the ancient priesthood taught the secrets to small, select groups along the Nile.

Elsewhere, of course, something similar must have happened involving the initiate survivors of other advanced cultures. Archaeological records show that with the ending of the cold there was an apparently spontaneous development of agriculture in many different centres across the globe. Orthodox scientific opinion insists this was purely coincidental, a theory made even more unlikely by the fact that in almost every case, agriculture tended to develop first on high ground and spread outwards—quite the reverse of what might be expected. But if the teachers of agricultural techniques were heir to ancient memories of a great flood, they might well have considered high ground safer than the more obvious choices.

Following the establishment of agriculture, the hereditary teachers then turned their attention to passing on other skills relevant to the reestablishment of civilisation. In the early stages, these would have been fairly basic—how to make and fire pottery, the use of mud for making bricks and so forth. Since their numbers were limited and consequently spread thinly, one would expect sudden upsurges of unusual technical abilities in several separate areas at once—abilities not yet matched by the overall cultural level of the communities concerned. This is precisely the pattern shown in the archaeology of the Nile Valley.

At this time there is the possibility that some of the teachers embarked on isolated building projects, leading to anomalous dating of certain temples, which seem to have been built neither before the catastrophe nor after the supposed foundation of dynastic Egypt.

Eventually, of course, the separate groupings would tend to coalesce—a development that would naturally have been encouraged, perhaps even led, by the teachers. As the separate elements came together, civilisation re-emerged abruptly along the Nile. It is no coincidence that, from earliest times, it was centred on Heliopolis (now buried beneath modern Cairo) close by the Giza plateau with its imposing remnant of the mother culture, the Great Pyramid.

The engineering and architectural skills preserved from ancient times permitted the early development of imposing works like the extraordinary complex at Saqqara. In all probability these were not up to the standard of buildings from the original culture—for all their best efforts the teachers must have lost more than they preserved—but they were impressive indeed . . . and built to a standard far in advance of what might be expected from a people apparently just emerged from the Stone Age.

For all of its legacy, the new Egyptian civilisation never reached the heights of the old. One problem with inherited knowledge is that it is not always accompanied by complete understanding. Thus there is a tendency for skills to degenerate with time as the new culture moves further and further from the source. The teachers, who worked hard to preserve the ancient knowledge may have become lax when they reached their perceived goal. Perhaps, as has happened with so many native cultures in our own day, the advent of civilisation itself produced a tendency for the young to abandon the old ways. The teachers may have found it as difficult to find initiates willing to study what must have seemed obscure branches of knowledge as Australian Aborigine elders do in their attempts to pass on their ancient cultural values today.

It is possible that some of the knowledge was distorted

as it was passed down the years. Christopher Dunn maintains that the damage evident in the King's Chamber of the Great Pyramid was the result of a massive explosion. Could it be that the new Egyptians overreached themselves in an attempt to restart the ancient power plant?

Although there is evidence of electrical usage in dynastic times, it is nowhere nearly so widespread as it is in our modern era—and as it may have been in prehistoric Egypt. Perhaps the Egyptians abandoned the Great Pyramid as a bad job and concentrated instead on building far smaller pyramid generators that were easier to control. Certainly discoveries like the sealed but empty sarcophagus suggests these structures were used for something other than tombs.

The Ark of the Covenant, which makes a relatively late appearance in this story, may have been a surviving remnant of Old Egypt or an attempt to duplicate an electrical device recalled by the teachers. In any case, the knowledge which built it was either limited or flawed, for the device itself was far too dangerous to be working properly. The likelihood was that it was not even meant to be a weapon—there are descriptions in the Old Testament that suggest it may have been a communications device—but Moses saw its possibilities in warfare and used it successfully to subdue his followers and his neighbours . . . although at some cost.

Psychotronics may have been more successful. Ancient Egypt has always been looked upon as a sort of magical capital of our planet and the mental disciplines required to use psychotronic generators might be more easily preserved—in the form of spiritual or religious exercises—than many other aspects of the old civilisation. Certainly Egypt's reputation for magic endured to a very late stage of its history. The very last native Pharaoh, Nectanebo II, had a fearsome reputation as a sorcerer.

In all this, we can see very clearly why Egyptian priests

stood higher in importance even than Pharaoh. It was they who preserved the ancient knowledge on which the very foundations of their state were built. But, as time went on, the knowledge itself may well have become stylised, ritualised, distorted and misunderstood until the culture it should have fed gradually degenerated. Whatever the cause, a long, slow degeneration is certainly apparent in the history of Ancient Egypt. The greatest engineering, artistic and cultural achievements are clustered in the early centuries of the state. By the time of Nectanebo (third century BC) the country was so weakened that it proved easy prey for a Persian invader. Ptolemaic Egypt, which followed soon after, retained little more than a shadow of its former glory, further diluted by Greek ideas and attitudes.

Egypt itself endured for a few more centuries, but its ancient legacy was spent.

AFTERWORD

IN 1998, I published a book entitled *Martian Genesis* which argued the possibility that human life was seeded on Earth by an extra-terrestrial civilisation that once existed on the planet Mars.[66]

The first chapter of this book dealt with the so-called Face on Mars, a rock formation that showed up among some 60,000 photographs taken by NASA's *Viking* space probes in 1976. Many experts believed the face was artificial, an artefact created by extra-terrestrial intelligence.

Shortly before the book was published, new NASA pictures of the Martian surface showed none of the distinctive human-like features of the early photographs. Some of those who had investigated the Face argued that the latest pictures—taken from a lower orbit—would naturally tend to lose definition when examining a structure more than 2.4 km (1½ miles) long by 1.6 km (1 mile) wide: if you look at a newspaper photograph under a magnifying glass it disintegrates into a series of dots. Others accepted the latest pictures as definitive and decided they had been wrong in concluding that the Face was artificial.

One of the new NASA photographs was included in my book to allow readers to make up their own minds.

The photographic "disappearance" of the Face on Mars had an unfortunate effect. Although only eight of the 216 pages of *Martian Genesis* dealt directly with the Face on Mars, it was enough to persuade some critics that the remaining arguments were beneath their attention.

Despite this, all the other anomalous features at Cydonia Mensae still remain unexplained, as do the multitude of puzzles evident in the prehistory of our own planet. Furthermore, since *Martian Genesis* was first published, new mysteries have come to light. A honeycomb structure in the Martian polar regions has so far defied natural explanation. And Fellow of the Royal Astronomical Society Eric Crew, whose opinions were quoted, in a different context, in the present book, has discovered what he believes to be an accurate model of our solar system on the Martian surface. Other astronomers are increasingly convinced that Mars suffered a massive disaster that would have devastated the entire planet and wiped out any indigenous life. Perhaps even more significantly, biologists have discovered that the human body clock is not, as previously supposed, attuned to Earth's diurnal cycle, but rather to the rotation of Mars.

Clearly, there is still a body of evidence to support the speculation that humanity was seeded on our planet. Should this speculation prove well founded, there may well be another aspect of the secret history of Ancient Egypt yet to explore. Although I was never among the authors who saw a resemblance between the Martian "Face" and the Sphinx at Giza, I *do* believe it possible that the Egyptian myth of "sky gods" ruling their state in deep prehistory may have a literal foundation.

NOTES

1 1999.

2 These are a satellite pyramid and three queens' pyramids and should not be confused with the much larger pyramids at Giza, attributed to the Pharaohs Khafre and Menkaure.

3 *The Giza Power Plant*, Bear & Co, Santa Fe, 1998.

4 Another of the daubs signified "Year 17."

5 Quoted from G. C. Macauley's translation.

6 Ibid.

7 Several other classical authors discuss the Great Pyramid, but they all, without exception, draw on Herodotus or Agatharchides as their source.

8 The other was on Rhodes.

9 *Lost Civilisations of the Stone Age* by Richard Rudgley, Century Books, London, 1998.

10 Quoted from Professor Stecchini's paper "Notes on the Relation of Ancient Measures and the Great Pyramid," published as an appendix to *Secrets of the Great Pyramid* by Peter Tompkins, Allen Lane, London, 1973.

11 Critics have pointed out that the third pyramid does not align as accurately with its specific star as Bauval supposed.

12 Or sometimes from the almost equally important Tropic of Cancer.

13 In *Thoth: Architect of the Universe*, Edfu Books, Dorset, 1998.

14 In *How the Pyramids Were Built*, Element Books, Shaftesbury, 1989.

15 Quoted from *Secrets of the Great Pyramid* by Peter Tompkins, Allen Lane, London, 1973.

16 Some doubt has been cast on this conventional explanation in recent times.

17 This is, of course, the deviation that is measurable today after millennia of weathering and earthquakes. We might reasonably assume the Egyptians did a bit better when the pyramid was new.

18 Eric Crew claims there is scientific evidence of a past (or possibly present) advanced civilisation within our solar system capable of space flight. See http://www.brox1.demon.co.uk and books by Zecharia Sitchin. In private correspondence with the author.

19 In his *Traveller's Key to Ancient Egypt*, Quest Books, Illinois, 1995.

20 In his book *The Giza Power Plant*, Bear & Co, Santa Fe, 1998.

21 In *Keely's Secrets*, TPXS, London, 1888.

22 Quoted in *Free Energy Pioneer: John Worrell Keely* by Theo Paijmans, IllumiNet Press, Lilburn, GA, 1998.

23 When he was unable to repeat this the machine was destroyed at a time of court proceedings against him.

24 Quoted from *Dashed Against the Rock*, a fictionalised account of Keely's career by William Colville, Banner of Light Publishing, New York, 1894.

25 *Martian Genesis*, Piatkus Books, London, 1998.

26 Both captions quoted in full in *In Secret Tibet* by Theodore Illion, Adventures Unlimited Press, Stelle, Illinois, 1991.

27 In *Gods of Eden*, Andrew Collins, Headline, London, 1998.

28 This is common practice in Tibet. The country's famous "singing bowls" are also traditionally made from a mix of different metals—sometimes three, sometimes as many as seven.

29 In *Supernature* published by Hodder & Stoughton, London, 1973.

30 As described in his article "Hi-Tech Pharaohs?" published by the periodical *Amateur Astronomy and Earth Sciences*, December 1995 through February 1996.

31 Which dispensed holy water on the insertion of a coin.

32 A "daughter library" was destroyed by Christians in AD 391.

33 Transcutaneous Electrical Nerve Stimulator.

34 Quoted in *Ancient Inventions* by Peter James and Nick Thorpe, Ballantine Books, New York, 1994.

35 See her contribution to the *Acta of the 2nd International Colloquium on Aegean Prehistory*, Ministry of Culture, Athens, 1972. Modern physics suggests the "lightning seeding" technique would actually work. Interestingly, the masts themselves were the precise shape recommended by Benjamin Franklin millennia later.

36 Published by Piatkus Books, London, 1998.

37 Although it's still done, according to author Graham Hancock, who describes the experience in one of his books.

38 The top 9 m (30 ft) have since disappeared.

39 Flinders Petrie made the same discovery.

40 In much the same way that a standard metre is now held at a controlled temperature in Paris.

41 In *The Giza Power Plant*, Bear & Co, Santa Fe, 1998.

42 *Musical Resonance in the Great Pyramid and the Master Frequency* by Rocky McCollum and Bill Cox, Life Understanding Foundation, Santa Barbara, 1979.

43 Quoted from *Prodigal Genius* by John J. O'Neill, Ives Washburn Inc., New York, 1944.

44 Quoted in *Psychic Discoveries Behind the Iron Curtain* by Sheila Ostrander and Lynn Schroeder, Bantam Books, New York, 1971.

45 Quoted from Stine's fascinating *Mind Machines You Can Build*, Top of the Mountain Publishing, Florida, US, 1997.

46 In *Psychic Discoveries Behind the Iron Curtain* by Sheila Ostrander and Lynn Schroeder. Bantam Books, New York, 1971.

47 *Experimental Investigation of Biologically Induced Energy Transport Anomalies* by Gy Egely, Hungarian Academy of Sciences, Undated.

48 Ibid.

49 The overall dimensions of the largest of them were no greater than 20 cm $\times$ 20 cm $\times$ 20 cm (8 in $\times$ 8 in $\times$ 8 in).

50 Quoted in *Psychic Discoveries Behind the Iron Curtain* by Sheila Ostrander and Lynn Schroeder, Bantam Books, New York, 1971.

51 Ibid.

52 Interested readers can purchase the Energy Wheel from Powell Productions, P.O. Box 2244, Pinellas Park, Florida 33780–2244, USA. For information on current costs access the company's Web site at http://www.ABCInfo.com or email order-dept@abcinfo.com.

53 *Psychic Discoveries Behind the Iron Curtain* by Sheila Ostrander and Lynn Schroeder, Bantam Books, New York, 1971.

54 As, indeed, I did myself using meat that failed to putrefy over several weeks until one of my own cats,

very much alive, put an end to the experiment by eating it.

55 Patent File No. 91304, Republic of Czechoslovakia Office for Patents and Inventions, published August 1959.

56 Including one of my own early books.

57 To their credit, his fellow citizens implemented the reforms as they had promised, despite all their reservations.

58 *Martian Genesis*, Piatkus, London, 1998.

59 In *Forbidden Archaeology*, Bhaktivedanta Institute, San Diego.

60 For a much fuller exposition of this and other subjects covered in the remainder of the present chapter, see my earlier books *Martian Genesis*, Piatkus Books, London, 1998, and *The Atlantis Enigma*, Piatkus, 1999.

61 See Brier's excellent *The Murder of Tutankhamen*, Phoenix Books, London, 1999.

62 Piatkus, London, 1999.

63 Quoted from the Benjamin Jowett translation of Plato's *Timaeus*.

64 See my *The Atlantis Enigma* (Piatkus, London, 1999) for a full exposition of this issue.

65 In *The Murder of Tutankhamen*, Phoenix Books, London, 1999.

66 Piatkus, London.

FURTHER READING

MY interest in Ancient Egypt was originally awakened—more years ago than I care to remember—by my old friend Desmond Leslie. Desmond was, and still is, primarily known for his interest in UFOs, but his best-selling book on the subject (*Flying Saucers Have Landed*, co-authored with George Adamski) introduced me to the mystery of how the pyramids were built long before von Däniken or the myriad of authors writing on the subject nowadays.

Since then, the books I have read on the subject must run into the hundreds. Add to that the books on ancient history generally and the total has probably topped a thousand. My immediate sources for the present work are listed as footnotes in the relevant places, but those—and the other books—listed below are well worth reading in their entirety. (Having said that, some of them should be read with discrimination.)

Amazing and Wonderful Mind Machines You Can Build, G. Harry Stine, Top of the Mountain Publishing (1994)

Ancient Egypt, David P. Silverman (ed.), Piatkus (1997)

Ancient Inventions, Peter James and Nick Thorpe, Ballantine Books (1994)

Ancient Traces, Michael Baigent, Viking (1998)

Atlantis Enigma, The, Herbie Brennan, Piatkus (1999)

Cities of Dreams, Stan Gooch, Aulis Books (1995)

Complete Pyramids, The, Mark Lehner, Thames and Hudson (1997)

Fingerprints of the Gods, Graham Hancock, Heinemann (1995)

Forbidden Archaeology, Michael Cremo and Richard Thompson, Bhaktivedanta Book Publishers (1993)

Free Energy Pioneer: John Worrell Keely, Theo Paijmans, IllumiNet Press (1998)

Giza Power Plant, The, Christopher Dunn, Bear & Co. Publishing (1998)

Gods of Eden, The, Andrew Collins, Headline (1998)

Hamlet's Mill, Giorgio de Santillana and Hertha von Dechend, David R. Godine Publisher (1993)

Heaven's Mirror, Graham Hancock and Santha Faiia, Michael Joseph (1998)

Hermetica, The, Timothy Freke and Peter Gandy, Piatkus (1998)

How the Pyramids were Built, Peter Hodges, Element Books (1989)

In Secret Tibet, Theodore Illion, Adventures Unlimited (1991)

Keys to the Temple, The, David Furlong, Piatkus (1998)

Lost Civilisations of the Stone Age, Richard Rudgley, Century (1998)

Martian Genesis, Herbie Brennan, Piatkus (1998)

Murder of Tutankhamen, The, Bob Brier, Phoenix Books (1999)

Prodigal Genius, John J. O'Neill, Ives Washburn Inc, New York (1944)

Psychic Discoveries, Sheila Ostrander, Lynn Schroeder and Uri Geller, Souvenir Press (1997)

Sacred Geometry Design Sourcebook, Bruce Rawles, Elysian Publishing (1997)

Secrets of the Great Pyramid, Peter Tompkins, Budget Book Service Inc (1997)

Temple of Man, The, R. A. Schwaller de Lubicz, Inner Traditions (1998), 2 vols

Thoth: Architect of the Universe, Ralph Ellis, Edfu Books (1997)

Traveller's Key to Ancient Egypt, The, John Anthony West, Theosophical Publishing House (1996)

INDEX